"Don't bother to look, Honor. I'm right here."

Standing very still in his arms, Honor watched with fascination as Conn lowered his mouth to hers. He was there, all right, filling up every inch of her beautifully designed bedroom with his own brand of strength and presence. All thoughts of a vague wrongness in the atmosphere went out of her head as he took her lips. Conn Landry felt very, very right.

It was not the sort of kiss she normally expected and received the first time she kissed a new date. Landry's mouth did not move on hers with the tentative, questioning approach a man generally used in the beginning.

Instead, he claimed her mouth as though he had a right to it. What should have bothered her was that her body seemed to accept his assumption of that right....

ABOUT THE AUTHOR

Jayne Ann Krentz lives in Seattle, Washington, with her engineer husband, Frank, and a yellow parakeet named Ferd. This prolific author, whose pen names include Stephanie James and Jayne Castle, has written more than twenty-four books. Asserting that she has no fascinating hobbies, Jayne confesses only to enjoying country-western music and sampling a glass of fine wine.

Books by Jayne Ann Krentz

HARLEQUIN INTRIGUE
10—LEGACY

HARLEQUIN TEMPTATION
11—UNEASY ALLIANCE
21—CALL IT DESTINY
34—GHOST OF A CHANCE

LEGACY
JAYNE ANN KRENTZ

Harlequin Books

TORONTO • NEW YORK • LONDON
AMSTERDAM • PARIS • SYDNEY • HAMBURG
STOCKHOLM • ATHENS • TOKYO • MILAN

For Louis Krentz and Charlie Galea,
who know what it's like
to stand in the winner's circle.

Harlequin Intrigue edition published January 1985

ISBN 0-373-22010-3

Chapter One

He hadn't planned to move in on her this quickly, but Honor Mayfield was making it so easy he knew he would be a fool to waste the opening. Spinning a web was a delicate task, and one of the most important aspects of the job was selecting the beginning point. It looked as though Honor was going to provide the perfect beginning herself.

Constantine Landry sat alone in a private box fronting the Santa Anita Racetrack. One booted foot lazily braced against the partition, an expensive set of Japanese-crafted field glasses resting on the empty seat beside him, he could have been any one of a number of the more affluent racing enthusiasts who occupied the row of private boxes.

But his attention wasn't on the results of the second race that were being posted on the lighted board below. Instead, he watched with calculating eyes as a woman with golden-brown hair walked quickly along an aisle in the grandstand behind him. She had a very serious expression on her face and was obviously intent on following a flashily dressed man several yards away from her.

Might as well make it a parade, Landry thought as he

got to his feet with an easy, coordinated movement. The first strand of the web was waiting to be strung, and unless he missed his guess it was going to be a very strong anchor thread. Honor Mayfield, it appeared, was headed for trouble. Keeping her out of it would give him exactly the kind of opening he needed.

Landry was accustomed to waiting and watching for openings. Trained hunters learned those necessary skills quickly or remained singularly unsuccessful. Landry had been very successful in his profession. He had been dealing with two-legged prey a long time. One brightly dressed, unprotected female who had no idea she was being pursued presented no real problem. What was definitely out of the ordinary was this strange restless excitement that was suddenly pervading his bloodstream.

It wasn't the cool intensity of the hunt as he might have expected. It was a deep, thrumming sense of anticipation. And it was all wrong. He knew instinctively that it was not the right sort of emotion for this kind of thing, but he didn't seem to be able to repress it.

The warmth of the Southern California sun beat down on Landry and his quarry with pleasant warmth. Hard to believe it was only January, he thought vaguely. He'd forgotten that on days when the smog factor was low and the California sun was living up to its promise, the towns that sprawled out from the heart of Los Angeles could still remind one of just how beautiful the countryside had once been. The San Gabriel Mountains formed a magnificent backdrop for the picturesque racetrack. If one concentrated on the scenery one could ignore the huge, modern shopping center that, in true California style, stood nearby. Southern Californians never felt entirely comfortable unless they were close to one of the many luxurious enclosed shopping malls.

Landry stalked Honor Mayfield at a discreet distance, questions without clear answers circling in his head as he moved through the crowd. He didn't understand the questions any more than he understood the unexpected sense of anticipation. He knew what he was doing, had planned the contact carefully. So why was he questioning his own motives at this late juncture? Around him people were hurrying to make their bets on the next race, crowding the aisles en route to the windows where cashiers waited patiently to accept what seemed to be an endless river of money.

It was a little difficult keeping Honor in sight without closing in on her. She was only about five feet four inches tall, easily lost amid the crowd. But the watermelon-pink of her shirt helped identify her as she slipped through the crush of bettors. One of the things Conn Landry had learned about her these past few months was that Honor had a passion for brilliantly-hued clothes.

He'd acquired a variety of such small tidbits of information about her and he still couldn't quite explain why he found each little detail so fascinating.

He increased his pace enough to close some of the distance between himself and his quarry as she, in turn, hurried after the man in the avant-garde safari suit. Landry knew whom she was following. His name was Granger and the abundance of rings he wore in addition to his clothes made him an easily recognized figure. Once again Landry wondered why Honor Mayfield was interested in him. Granger was dangerous.

But, then, so was Constantine Landry. And as far as Honor Mayfield was concerned, Landry decided objectively, she had more to fear from him than from Granger. She just didn't know it yet.

There were a lot of things she didn't know yet, and Landry made a decision: He would not tell her everything until he understood exactly why he was experiencing such a strange sense of ambivalence about what he was doing. It was the quarry who should remain uncertain and off-balance, not the hunter. He would approach her as a stranger, he told himself.

Months of hunting came to an end as Landry shortened the distance between himself and Honor.

LEAVING THE GRANDSTANDS BEHIND, Honor experienced a surge of nervous tension that almost broke her resolve. *Face it,* she told herself grimly, *you don't really know what the hell you're doing.* Not knowing, however, didn't solve any problems. She had no choice but to keep pushing blindly along the course she had set for herself.

The crowd thinned out as she followed Granger toward the barns. Grooms soothing high-strung thoroughbreds and maintenance people carrying tools and equipment replaced the betting enthusiasts. Soon she would come up against the impenetrable barrier of the gates that protected the stables. Without a pass she would be unable to get past the uniformed guard. If Granger was going beyond that boundary she would be out of luck.

It was with mixed emotions that she saw him turn off to head toward the parking lot area that was reserved for people whose business was connected directly with racing. Owners, racetrack employees, trainers and similar types were entitled to use the lot toward which Granger was now moving. She knew he hadn't parked there, because she'd seen him come through the front entrance of the track grounds an hour earlier. She suddenly realized that following Granger through a crowded grandstand was one thing. Following him away from the relative safety of the crowd was quite another. Granger moved in a different world, one that existed beyond the legal fringe of racing. People in that world tended to make their own rules.

Honor took a deep, steadying breath and her fingers tightened on the strap of her turquoise-blue shoulder bag. Perhaps she should have hired a professional, she told herself. A private detective, for instance. Someone who knew the people and rules of Granger's world. How did one approach a loan shark, anyway? The idea of dashing up to him and catching hold of the sleeve of his off-white safari suit was rather intimidating. Honor was trying to formulate a list of other possible approaches when a man's hand closed around her upper arm.

"What the—? No! Let go of me!" The words came out in a frightened gasp as she spun around to confront the stranger who was laying claim to her arm. Instantly she pulled herself back under control. Panic wasn't going to get her anywhere. She was still within shouting distance of help.

"Ladies intent on tailing people like Granger should take care not to wear shirts the color of the inside of a ripe watermelon," the man said in a cool, dark, gritty voice that ruffled her already agitated nerves. "It makes you a little too visible, you see."

Honor struggled to keep the raging fear-inspired adrenaline under control. "I beg your pardon," she snapped icily, "but I have no idea what you're talking about. Kindly let go of my arm before I'm forced to scream for help."

The man gave her a curiously twisted smile that didn't have any impact on his gunmetal-gray eyes at all. "You've already got help. I'm it."

She stared up at him, conscious of feeling very vulnerable as she sensed the strength in his grip on her arm. He wasn't quite six feet in height but there was a chilling power in his lean, hard frame that made itself felt on several levels. A bodyguard, she wondered fleetingly. She'd always thought of professional bodyguards as being big and burly, men whose threat lay in their massive, rocklike bodies. But this man made her think of the elegantly lethal qualities found in a stiletto or a coiled whip. Infinitely more dangerous.

"Do you—do you work for Mr. Granger?" she heard herself ask uneasily and then realized how much information she had provided just by admitting to knowing Granger's name.

"No." The strangely bleak smile stayed in place. "I only work for myself."

Which made perfect sense, Honor realized abruptly. Men such as this one did not take orders from slick loan sharks like Granger. But that only made her present situation even more confusing.

"Then I really can't see that we have anything to discuss," she began bravely. "If you'll excuse me, I must be going. I have to take care of some business."

"So do I, lady. So do I."

The grip on her arm tightened just enough to remind her that she couldn't possibly escape it, and then Honor found herself being led back toward the barn area.

"Wait a minute! What do you think you're doing? I don't even know your name."

"Constantine Landry. Call me Conn."

"Mr. Landry, I demand that you release me. I have

something I must do," Honor said with soft urgency. Granger was even now disappearing from view behind a large building. She struggled in Landry's grip and seriously considered yelling for help. There were plenty of people around. Surely this man wouldn't do anything drastic to her in front of so many witnesses.

"If you're talking about your little plan to tail Granger, I'm afraid you're going to have to think of a more pleasant way to spend the afternoon."

"You are working for that bastard!"

He slanted a wry glance down at her as he pulled her toward the guarded stable gate. "I've told you. I don't work for anyone except myself. Not anymore."

"Then why are you interfering with me now? And how do you know who Granger is?" Honor asked grittily.

"A lot of people around here know who Granger is. He's been involved in everything from loan sharking to drug dealing. Not a nice man. I can't help being curious about why a nice lady such as yourself is following him. Believe me, unless you're feeling masochistic, you don't want to go where Granger's going right now."

Honor stared up at Conn Landry's savagely carved profile. "Just where is Granger going?"

"Straight into a police trap. He's been set up. Granger believes he's about to connect with one of his drug couriers. And he is, in a sense. But the courier has been working undercover for the past six months. Today the cops pull the plug. It wasn't an easy trap to set, you know. Granger's big enough to employ others to take his risks for him. But this time he was convinced that the deal was too big to leave in the hands of employees." Landry shook his head ruefully. "Some people just can't learn to delegate when they should."

Honor dug in the high heels of her turquoise leather sandals. "How do you know all this? Who are you, Conn Landry?"

He politely allowed her to drag him to a halt, turning to confront her questioning hazel eyes. "That's simple. I'm the man who's saving your sweet tail from the rather unpleasant surprise awaiting Granger. Just how would you explain your presence to the cops when they closed in on him and found you wriggling in the net, too?"

"I don't understand any of this!"

"That's obvious. And that's why you should have the sense to stay clear. Come along, lady in the watermelon shirt. I want to introduce you to a friend of mine."

Confused and wary, Honor again found herself being led toward the stable yard. At the guarded gate Constantine Landry flashed an owner's pass, and the next thing she knew she was inside the perimeter that protected the expensive animals. Rows of barns, horse trailers and small cottages for the grooms were scattered around the grounds. The pleasant, earthy scent of well-cared-for horses filled the air. In the grandstands all was excitement, disgust, urgency and despair, depending on the outcome of the current race. Here there was a subdued, businesslike bustle of activity.

"Mr. Landry, this is ridiculous. Please let go of my arm!"

"I told you to call me Conn. And I think this is about the safest place for you until Granger's been taken out of commission. From what I could tell you were hell-bent on following him right into trouble."

"Why should you care?" she snapped furiously.

His mouth kicked up briefly at the corner in that odd

little smile that didn't go anywhere. "A good question."

She waited for the answer and when it didn't come, Honor pursued her arguments for freedom. "Look, if you're a police undercover agent or something and I've gotten in your way, I'm sorry. I didn't mean to interfere in any sort of operation designed to take Granger off the streets! Believe me, no one wants him in jail more than I do!"

Landry nodded. "Mind telling me why?"

"I can't see that it's any of your business. You haven't shown me a badge or any identification." Immediately wary, Honor backed off from being pushed into an explanation. "I still don't have any idea of who you really are, do I?"

"The situation is mutual. You haven't introduced yourself, either."

"I don't intend to do so. You seem to know far too much already." There was a certain satisfaction in being able to deny him something, at least, Honor discovered. Constantine Landry was almost frighteningly sure of himself. The rigorously austere planes and angles of his features held no trace of softness or warmth.

"I think," Landry said too quietly, "that it's time you told me who you are."

"Are you asking in an official capacity?" she demanded with a show of bravado that was only skin-deep. With a flash of intuition she sensed that introducing herself would be a small act but a crucial one. It was as though he were asking that she commit herself somehow, demanding that she acknowledge the tenuous acquaintance, insisting that she take a potentially dangerous first step. Oddly enough she could have sworn in that moment that he already knew who she was and that he was only asking to maintain an illusion. She brushed aside the uneasy thought. Of course there was no way he could know her identity.

"I'm asking. Period. No official reasons."

Honor felt the lapping waves of his will and knew that the full force of an ocean of strength lay behind them. They halted in the shade of a long barn and she looked up at him searchingly. Quite suddenly she knew that in the end he would have his answer. She had the feeling he'd gotten answers from people before; he was that kind of man. There was no point resisting the soft command in his voice.

"As I said before, I think you know too much already," she observed quietly. "But for the record, my name is Honor Mayfield."

"Yes." He took her arm again and led her into the barn. There had been satisfaction in the single word.

Just yes. Simple and certain. As if she were merely confirming something he already knew. What was going on here, she wondered.

"Mr. Landry, I've answered your question. Now tell me what your role is in all this. You owe me that much."

"Do I?" He had halted in front of a roomy stall. There was a soft rustling sound from within, and a few seconds later an inquisitive equine head emerged to investigate. "Hello, Legacy. I hope you feel like running today."

"Legacy?" Honor stepped forward, putting out a hand to touch the nose of the horse who watched her with avid interest. "This is Legacy?" For a moment Granger and all the related problems were forgotten as she stared at the beautiful bay colt.

Landry's chilled eyes studied her reaction to the horse. "I own him."

"I see." Honor couldn't think of anything to say. She was looking at a tiny piece of her past and for a moment the impact was unsettling. "I didn't realize," she went on weakly. "That you owned him, I mean. I saw his name on the program. He's running in the fifth, isn't he?"

"That's right."

Honor withdrew her hand and the sleek thorough-bred extended his nose to follow the movement. "He's very beautiful."

"Very."

"He's favored to win today, isn't he?" She couldn't take her eyes off the animal.

"Slightly. This is only his second race and he still has a ways to go to prove himself."

Honor stepped back out of range of the questing mouth that was beginning to nip interestedly at her silk shirt sleeve. "I'm sure he'll do well."

"He comes from good stock," Landry said deliberately.

"One of Stylish Legacy's descendants." Honor didn't realize she'd whispered the words aloud until Landry responded.

"You seem to know something about the line."

She shook her head. "Not very much, really. I don't follow the details of the racing world closely. Once in a while I come to the track when I can find the time. When I was a kid I had the usual female hang-up on horses."

"But you know about Stylish Legacy?"

Honor sighed. There was no harm in admitting the truth. "My father once owned him. He and another man, that is. Is Stylish Legacy still at stud?"

"Yes. He's eighteen years old now. But still producing winners." Landry stroked the warm bay neck, and Legacy nuzzled his chest, inhaling the man's scent through the fabric of the coffee-colored shirt. The horse clearly enjoyed being the center of attention. "So your father once owned Stylish Legacy?"

"It was a long time ago. He and a partner—" Honor broke off quickly. "Look, Mr. Landry, I think this has gone far enough. Please tell me what your connection is with Granger. Is he really walking into a trap out there in the parking lot?"

"Most of us walk into a trap at some point in our lives."

"I am not in the mood for cryptic comments!"

Legacy reacted to the sharp tone of her voice, his sensitive ears flicking in irritation. Landry soothed him.

"Take it easy, boy. She's just a little nervous, that's all."

"I have a right to be nervous," Honor muttered, glancing down the row of stalls. Several curious muzzles were appearing and a half-dozen pairs of interested brown eyes were examining the scene at the far end of the long, shaded barn.

"You'd have a lot more reason to be nervous now if you were out there in the parking lot taking the fall along with Granger," Landry told her.

Honor shifted restlessly. "If what you say is true, then I suppose I should be grateful to you for stopping me."

Landry inclined his head. "Yes, you should be. Feeling grateful, Honor?"

"I'm not sure yet. Basically because I'm not sure how you're involved."

"A bystander. Nothing more. But I'd heard rumors

around the track about what was being planned for Granger today. Racetracks thrive on rumors. When I saw you following the man, I decided to pull you out of the action. Somehow you just didn't look like the type to be up to your neck in loan sharking and drug dealing."

Honor shuddered, utterly repelled. "I'm not."

"But you were following him," Landry pointed out coolly.

"It's a private matter, Mr. Landry," she told him stiffly.

"Will Granger's arrest take care of this private little matter for you?"

"With any luck, yes," she answered fervently.

"Then I think, on the whole, that you really should feel gratful to me, Honor Mayfield."

Her gaze narrowed. "Are you the type to hold that sort of thing over my head?"

He looked at her, gray eyes unreadable and unyielding. "I keep track of what I owe in this life, Honor. And even closer track of what's owed to me."

For a long moment she couldn't drag her gaze free of the invisible bonds Constantine Landry was using to chain her full attention. She had never met a man like this. A part of her was genuinely apprehensive and cautious. But another part of her was deeply aware of him, and that disturbed her even more than the understandable wariness she was experiencing.

"I believe you, Mr. Landry." And she did. Completely. "You aren't a cop, are you?"

"No."

"And you do own Legacy?"

"Oh, yes," Landry told her with great sureness. "I own him." For a moment a genuine expression of emotion flickered in the gray eyes. A mixture of pride and pleasure and enthusiasm.

Scenes from the past flashed briefly through Honor's mind. She remembered a similar expression in the eyes of her father when he had talked about Stylish Legacy. People who owned racehorses were infected with a certain kind of fever, even when they tried to pretend that the horses were purely financial investments or tax shelters. Getting involved in the racing world almost always meant getting involved on an emotional level. It wasn't just a realm of numbers and big financial transactions. It was an arena that involved the emotions. It struck Honor as strange that Constantine Landry should be interested in such a world. He looked like the kind of man who kept the emotional side of his nature under rigid control. In fact, a person could be pardoned for questioning whether or not Conn Landry would even be capable of a strong emotional response, Honor decided dryly.

"You really did just happen to hear about the police's plans for Granger and decided to rescue me when you saw me headed for the ambush?"

"Yes."

"Just because I didn't look like the type to be involved with a man like Granger?" she persisted. Her hand twisted the leather strap of her shoulder bag as she remembered the feeling she'd had that he already knew her name before he asked her to introduce herself.

"I had my reasons. That was one of them."

Honor drew a breath. "Well, then, I *am* grateful to you. To tell you the truth, I was not anxious to confront him, anyway. If the cops have him now that certainly will take a problem off my hands." For the first time since the whole mess had started, Honor permitted herself to give in to a feeling of relief. Overwhelming relief. A tentative smile lightened her eyes.

Landry saw the incipient relaxation and the hint of warmth in her and congratulated himself. The first strand of the web was in place. Honor Mayfield did not yet understand that she would have been better off taking her chances out in the parking lot along with Granger. Explaining herself to the cops probably would have been simpler and safer in the long run than explaining herself to him, Landry decided. But, then, she didn't have any choice.

Come into my parlor, pretty fly.

Actually, he admitted, she wasn't exactly pretty. But there was a compelling quality about her that seemed to fascinate him. The hazel eyes were expressive and serenely intelligent. Here in the shade the subtle golden highlights of her hair were hidden, but the style suited her. It was a smooth, casual curve that just touched her shoulders. A soft mouth and a slightly aggressive nose blended pleasantly enough with the wide, faintly tilted eyes, but taken independently the features would never be labeled beautiful.

Still, Landry realized, he found himself studying Honor's face, searching for whatever it was that intrigued him. Perhaps it was the hint of feminine strength in the way she carried herself. Or perhaps it was the shuttered, cautious warmth he saw in her eyes. She was not a superficial woman. Pride and intelligence and gentleness hovered just beneath the surface. Landry had spent a good many years learning to make accurate judgments of other people. His life had sometimes depended on that ability. Yes, there would be rewards in store for the man who slipped past her barriers.

The rest of her was proving unexpectedly interesting, too. A pair of pleated khaki pants that tapered to the ankles emphasized the curve of a nicely rounded derriere. The watermelon shirt was loose but didn't conceal the fact that her waist was small and so were her pert breasts.

In bed she would be sleek and responsive, Landry decided abruptly. He wasn't certain how he knew that but he was convinced of it. His whole body was convinced of it. The unexpected surge of a very ancient kind of awareness took him vaguely by surprise. It also put a piquant focus on his plans for Honor Mayfield. Once again he was forced to confront the wavering image of the goals that should have been crystal clear in his head. Determinedly he ignored the sense of ambivalence.

"Honor," he murmured, tasting her name aloud.

She looked up at him curiously. "Yes?"

"It's an interesting name."

"My father's choice," she informed him flatly.

"And do you live up to it?"

She didn't care for the direction of the conversation. "Since I'm not playing poker with you, I can't see that it matters."

"Is your father pleased with your efforts?"

"My father is dead, Mr. Landry."

Silence greeted her repressive remark. Landry didn't make the usual "I'm sorry" murmur. He merely accepted the information as if he already knew the answer. She didn't like the way he seemed to anticipate her. It made Honor nervous. She was already uneasy enough as it was today.

On the other hand, she would have been feeling distinctly more anxious right now if Conn Landry hadn't intercepted her en route to the parking lot. Her mouth relaxed into a warm smile.

"What are you thinking, Honor?"

"That I owe you one if you really did save me from getting involved in the setup meant for Granger."

"I agree."

Her smile tilted into a sardonic curve. "A more gallant approach would be to shrug and tell me your assistance was nothing, that I shouldn't feel obligated because of it."

He was silent.

"But you're not going to take the gallant approach, are you?" Quizzically she examined his hard face.

"No. Why should I? I prefer to keep the scales balanced."

He looked slightly puzzled that she should even suggest another way of operating than the one he was using. Honor knew in that moment that the words were a fundamental tenet for him, a doctrine by which he lived. He might be a harsh man in many respects, she decided, but he had his own code. Here in Southern California, where so many people ignored such archaic things as personal codes of behavior in favor of convenience and indulgence, there was something deeply intriguing about a man who lived by his own rules.

"Then you may have to write off this particular debt, Mr. Landry. I don't see how I can repay you," Honor said coolly.

"You can watch Legacy win in the fifth with me," he tossed back smoothly. "I'm using the trainer's box. I'd like you to join me. Especially since you have some connection with his sire."

Relief flared in her as she realized he wasn't going to ask too much after all. "I never actually saw Stylish

Legacy run. My parents were in the process of getting a divorce during those years and there was a lot of... unpleasantness between Mom and Dad. I didn't get to spend a lot of time with my father. It was all a long time ago." Which didn't mean she hadn't been thrilled at the idea of her father's actually owning a racehorse, Honor remembered.

"You'll join me in Humphrey's box?"

"Well, if you insist," she agreed doubtfully, trying to hide her budding excitement.

"Having just saved your neck from the long arm of the law, granting me the favor is the least you can do, isn't it?" Conn said laconically.

"You have a remarkably undiplomatic way of putting things, Conn." Her words were tinged with some of the asperity she was feeling. Damn it, she did owe him some repayment for his fortuitous interference. But she didn't like the way he was using that obligation for his own purposes. Conn Landry, Honor decided, tended to be more than a little ruthless. Some of her initial excitement faded. "I can't see why you'd particularly want my company to watch Legacy run, but—"

"I do. So that settles it."

"Mr. Landry," she began fiercely, only to be interrupted by a new voice. It was a man's voice and it held a deep southern drawl.

She turned to see a large, balding man with a paunch and an easy smile approaching. He was wearing a beige Stetson with what appeared to be a genuine snakeskin band. The rest of the outfit from the western-cut shirt and flared trousers to the hand-tooled cowboy boots harmonized nicely with the hat. He was probably in his sixties, she estimated. The crinkles around his eyes when he smiled made her want to respond in kind.

"Have a heart, ma'am, Conn's only in town for the races. He's all alone and it seems perfectly logical to me that he might want to share Legacy's big race with a pretty little thing like you."

Landry nodded toward the newcomer. "Honor, this is Ethan Bailey. He's got a couple of horses with the same trainer I use, Toby Humphrey. Ethan, meet Honor Mayfield."

"How do you do?" she said politely, extending her hand. Her fingers were immediately crushed in a warm paw.

"Just fine, Miss Honor, just fine. It is Miss, isn't it?" He made a show of examining her ring finger. "Out here in California a man can't always be sure. You folks have a rather interesting approach to life."

"Don't let Ethan put you on," Conn advised dryly. "He may have been born in Texas, but he spends a hell of a lot of time in California."

"Only because Toby Humphrey's the best trainer around and he works here in California." Ethan Bailey sighed. "And I like to be close to my horses as much as possible."

"Just a good old ranch boy at heart," Conn said, but there was an easiness in his tone that told Honor he liked the other man. "You'd never know he made his living wheeling and dealing in West Coast real estate, would you?"

"Now, Landry, old buddy, you know damn well that my calling is every bit as legitimate and inspirational as your own. Some objective folk might say even more so." Ethan Bailey grinned, reaching out to pat Legacy's neck. "He's looking good today, aren't you, Legacy? Going to leave the rest of those clodhoppers behind in the dust."

There was a rustle of movement from the far end of the stable and a small, wiry man who appeared to be somewhere on the far side of sixty-five came striding toward them at a brisk pace. He was accompanied by two young grooms.

"Afternoon, miss." The small man tipped his battered cap politely to Honor as he came to a halt in front of Legacy's stall. "Hello, Conn, Ethan. Time to take Legacy down to the saddling ring." He stepped aside, and so did everyone else as one of the grooms, a young woman, moved forward to take charge of Legacy.

"Toby, I'd like you to meet a friend of Landry's." Ethan Bailey introduced the trainer, whose attention was divided between Legacy and the man who paid him to train the animal.

"He's in good shape, Conn," Humphrey pronounced. "Real good shape."

The horse strode out of the stall with an energy that spoke of his breeding and fitness. Honor found herself entranced by the beautifully built creature. The muscles of Legacy's strong hindquarters moved sleekly beneath a coat that had been burnished by hours of hand grooming. The center of attention now, and well aware of it, he tossed his head and pranced.

"Let's go," Landry said softly. He took Honor's arm and guided her after the small procession formed by the trainer, the grooms and the dancing horse.

"He's so beautiful," Honor breathed, no longer even thinking about getting out of her commitment to watch the horse race. She was getting caught up in the behind-the-scenes excitement and knew it.

"You've got a stake in him, you know," Landry pointed out, watching her changing expression. "A family connection."

"Maybe I'll splurge and put a couple of dollars down on him," Honor decided. She ignored the subtle emphasis he put on the words "family connection."

"We'll go place our bets after we've seen him saddled."

They followed Legacy and his attendants to the stalls near the grandstands where the horses were saddled and the jockeys mounted.

"Who have you got on top of Legacy today?" Ethan Bailey asked conversationally as they watched the postage-stamp-sized saddle put in place.

Landry hooked one booted foot over the bottom rung of the metal barricade and leaned forward on his elbows to watch the prerace activity. "Humphrey picked Milton. Says he'll have enough sense to let Legacy alone when the time comes."

Bailey nodded. "He's putting Milton on Cavalier in the eighth, too. Can't complain about the boy. Did real good by me last time he was on Cavalier."

Honor listened to the racing talk flowing around her and felt her pulse begin to quicken. At least the excitement in her system now wasn't from fear, she thought with a burst of gratitude for the taciturn man beside her. Hoping devoutly that whatever had taken place in the parking lot would result in her never having to worry about Granger again, she allowed herself to be swept up in the unique thrill of being connected, however distantly, to a real, live racehorse once again.

She was barely able to contain herself as they watched Legacy and his competitors led out of the saddling area. Milton, the jockey, was tossed on board and then the restless animals headed toward the tunnel that opened onto the track.

"Come on, Honor. Let's get our bets down. See you

around, Bailey." Landry nodded at the other man as he propelled his willing captive in the direction of the stands.

"He's going to win," Honor declared as she stood in line to place the bet. "I just know it."

"If you're sure of it, why are you only putting a couple of bucks on him?" There was a brief, teasing light in Conn's eyes.

"If you knew me better, you'd realize that's as big a risk as I ever take," she retorted.

"You were taking quite a risk this afternoon by following Granger." The hint of indulgent humor disappeared.

Some of Honor's new bubbling mood evaporated. "That was different." She was saved from explaining just why it was different because her turn came at the window. Hastily she put down her two dollars and accepted the ticket.

Two hundred on his own horse wasn't overly ostentatious, Honor decided a few minutes later as she watched Landry place his own bet at a different window. Of course, the real money for the owner would be in the winning purse and in the prestige. Landry took her arm very firmly once more and led her into the stands.

Seated in the private box Toby Humphrey maintained for the use of his clients, Landry settled back to watch Legacy being edged into the gate. Out of the corner of his eye he could also watch the excitement on Honor's features.

She was caught up in it all now, he thought with satisfaction. She'd had no intention of getting involved with him this afternoon, yet here she was beside him, thoroughly engrossed in the coming race. He knew damn well that she was very grateful for his intervention earlier. He also knew she had been almost as wary of him as she was of Granger. But here she was, right where he wanted her.

It had all worked out very neatly. The first strand of the web was in place. There would be no escape for Honor Mayfield. He had counted on Legacy as a lure and it had worked. He'd assumed she'd have some interest in the horse because of the fact that her father had once owned the sire. Keeping her free of Granger was an added plus and she was bound to be grateful. Conn knew the starting point of the web was firmly attached. From now on he would move more and more surely into her life, taking advantage of every opportunity to get closer to this woman who was a link to the mystery of the past. He wanted her gratitude, her trust, her confidence, and he also wanted her to sense that he was the one in control.

Remaining in control was critical, Conn reminded himself. The last thing he wanted to risk was being tugged into the heart of the web right along with his victim.

Chapter Two

Legacy breezed in three lengths ahead of everything else in the field. Milton, the jockey, sat politely on the horse's back as though he'd just been invited along for the ride. Honor found herself on her feet and shouting along with everyone else. The excitement of horse racing was highly contagious.

"He won! He won! Conn, he did it!"

She thought she saw a brief sign of satisfaction in his expression, and then it changed to an arrogantly aloof interest in the fact. He appeared far more curious about her bubbling reaction to the win.

"Yes, he did."

"You're going to clean up on your bet and so am I. Come on, let's go. We've got to hurry. They'll be taking the photos in the winner's circle." Honor impulsively reached out to grasp his hand and hustle him out of the box.

"What's the rush?" But Conn got slowly to his feet. He sounded slightly perplexed.

"The rush is that they'll take the photo regardless of whether or not the owner is there. And you want to be in the picture, don't you? You can hang it on the wall in your bathroom or something. Didn't you get your picture taken the last time you watched him race?"

"No," he admitted. "I've only watched him race once before, and I'm not all that familiar with the track formalities. I was sitting in the stands and no one sent for me or told me how to get into the picture."

She laughed up at him, finding the trace of genuine disappointment in his voice rather endearing. "No one sends for you. You get into the picture by running. Come on, Conn, let's go!"

Swept up in the thrill of being connected to a winning racehorse, Honor was only vaguely aware of how hard she had to work to get Landry down into the winner's circle where a head-tossing, sweat-soaked Legacy was waiting to have his picture taken.

Everyone in the vicinity, it seemed, except Landry was eager to participate in the little ritual. Conn seemed almost embarrassed by the activity going on around his horse. It occurred to Honor that he wasn't accustomed to being in the limelight. A man of the shadows, she thought fleetingly and wondered vaguely what he'd done during his life. By the time Honor had pushed Conn into position near Legacy's head and the track officials had taken their customary places, a few other totally unrelated faces were already standing near the horse.

At the last moment Landry looked around and saw Honor waiting behind the barrier. Suddenly he held out his hand in a cool, commanding fashion.

"Come here, Honor. You might as well be in this shot, too."

"Oh, no, I had nothing to do with him winning," she protested. But there was more than politeness in his eyes; there was a strangely intense insistence. He wanted her to join him, she realized, and in those hectic moments Honor's instinct was to obey. Besides, how often would she have a chance to be photographed with a winning racehorse, she asked herself cheerfully. She hurried forward to take her place beside him.

It was all over in a moment. The track officials did this sort of thing after every race and had the routine down pat. Four photos of winning horses and their beaming owners had already been taken this afternoon and there were several more to go. The crowd around Legacy broke up quickly as Humphrey took charge and led the horse away toward the stables. Landry still retained his remotely satisfied look, but he didn't completely fool Honor. The deep pleasure in Legacy's win was there. Intuitively, she sensed it.

"A winner has a lot of friends," Honor observed as the strangers who had managed to push their way into the photo drifted off, laughing.

"A fact of life. Losers, on the other hand, fare a little differently," Conn Landry said dryly as he guided Honor back into the stands.

That thought sobered her. "I wonder how many friends Granger will have, now that he's been arrested. If he *was* arrested. What if he's out on bail within a few hours, Conn? Or what if the trap didn't close properly?"

"Since I don't know why you're worried, I can't be very reassuring, can I?"

Honor flushed and firmly changed the subject. "We'd better go collect our winnings."

He hesitated as she made to hurry toward the betting windows. "Honor?"

"What is it, Conn?"

"I think you ought to tell me what's going on."

"Why?" she asked starkly, her mood fading rapidly. The momentary excitement of being carried along with the thrill of the racing world was almost entirely gone.

"Because you owe me an explanation," he said simply.

"You said I only owed you my company while we watched Legacy win."

"That's just a part of what you owe me."

She saw the unreadable chill in his eyes and suppressed a shiver. Around them the crowd ebbed and flowed, ignoring the small confrontation as if it wasn't taking place. Honor felt alone and isolated, forced to deal with a predator on his own terms.

"Perhaps it would have been better if you hadn't interfered earlier," she said quietly.

"But I did interfere, and now it's too late."

"Too late for what, Mr. Landry?"

He smiled bleakly. "You were calling me by my first name a few minutes ago."

"Just tell me what you want from me," she exploded tightly. The turquoise leather strap of her bag was damp with moisture from her palm.

"Dinner tomorrow evening?" he suggested gently.

Her eyes widened. "Dinner!"

"As Ethan told you, I'm only in town to check on Legacy's progress. I don't know anyone else except Ethan and Humphrey and a couple of other people who have horses in Humphrey's stables. Is it so strange that I'd want to have dinner with an attractive woman whose father owned Legacy's sire?"

"I don't know, Conn. Is it strange? There's something about you that confuses me and I think you know it."

"Bailey and Humphrey can vouch for me," he

pointed out calmly. "If you don't trust me, ask them for a reference."

"It's not that exactly—" She broke off, floundering. "It's this other business with Granger. I still don't understand how you knew what was going on this afternoon."

"I told you. Racetrack rumors. They're rampant."

"Apparently they didn't reach Granger's ears in time!"

"Probably because most people around here would just as soon see him removed from the scene. He's lowlife."

"I'll agree with you on that point."

"I'd like to know how you got involved with his sort."

"And if I don't feel like telling you?" she challenged.

"I'd still like to take you out to dinner."

But it wasn't a simple invitation. If it had been, Honor knew she would probably have accepted without much hesitation. There was something about Conn Landry that intrigued and compelled her. But the way he was asking her out to dinner made her wary. His request contained the same sort of insistence and urgency she'd sensed when he'd demanded that she be in the photograph a few minutes ago. On the other hand, she owed him a great deal, probably more than she knew, for his interference earlier in the afternoon. And then there was the fact that Ethan Bailey and Toby Humphrey seemed to like him, for whatever that was worth.

He must have seen the flickering uncertainty in her eyes, because Conn gave her his strangely sardonic smile and pushed her lightly in the direction of the pay windows. "Give me your address and I'll pick you up at seven."

"I don't think—"

"Where's your ticket?" he asked as they reached the window.

"Here." Her fingers moved nervously in her purse, searching for her winning two-dollar ticket. A small plastic envelope fell to the floor during the awkward shuffling. Honor stifled a small sigh as Conn reached down to pick up the business card case and read:

Mayfield Interiors
Designs for Commercial and Residential Space

After noting the title of her business, Landry calmly pocketed one of the cards and then handed the case back to her. "I'll give you a call tomorrow when I find out Granger's status."

Honor shook her head once in silent acceptance of fate. Conn now knew her business address and her phone number. It would be a simple matter for him to get in touch any time he wished. Her last hope of retaining some anonymity and therefore some protection from him evaporated. The disconcerting part of it all was that she wasn't sure but what she was glad the matter had been taken out of her hands.

Half an hour later, after watching a proud Legacy being given his cool-down walk by a groom, Honor finally made her escape from the Santa Anita racetrack. The afternoon had proved a total surprise, she decided as she drove back to Pasadena. On the one hand she had been saved from that tricky business with Granger. But the other side of the coin had revealed a situation that, in its own way, was fraught with just as much risk.

So many questions surrounded Constantine Landry. How would he know Granger's status by tomorrow? Was he really in town just to watch his horse run? What had that vague crack of Ethan Bailey's meant? The one about real estate being a bit more legitimate than Landry's occupation. Perhaps she should have done as Conn had dryly suggested and asked Bailey and the trainer for a reference. No, that would have made her feel ridiculous. Obviously they would say reassuring things about him, or Landry would never have made the suggestion in the first place. Besides, Landry was a good client of Humphrey's. It was unlikely the trainer would have said anything negative, anyway. And as for Bailey, well, the older man had seemed to like Landry.

And then there was the little matter of Landry having saved her from having to deal with Granger.

That alone put her deeply into his debt, Honor decided. There was no way around the issue. When it came to paying her debts, Honor made a point of living up to her name. The family's reputation had been tarnished enough fifteen years ago to last more than a generation. Yes, she would meet Conn Landry for dinner if that's what he thought she owed him.

The phone was ringing as Honor turned the key in the lock of her apartment door. She didn't rush to answer it because she was almost certain she knew who was on the other end. She was right.

"Hello, Adena."

"You're back!" her younger sister exclaimed in frantic tones. Adena rarely spoke in mild or neutral tones. Everything was exaggerated, dramatic, excited or outrageous. Adena fit very well into the Southern California life-style. "What happened? Did you see Granger? Talk to him? Oh, Honor, I've been so scared."

"Yes and no, respectively." Honor tossed her blue bag down on the kitchen counter, aware of the irritation behind the act. She was very fond of Adena but lately the bonds of sisterly affection and family loyalty had been pushed a bit far.

"Yes and no! What on earth does that mean? Did you work something out with the man or not?"

"Calm down, Adena. Things didn't go exactly as planned. But it may all be for the best. You'll be glad to know that Granger is currently in police custody."

There was a stunned silence on the other end. "The police have him?" Adena finally asked in confusion. "But how? When? I don't understand."

"Apparently a trap had been planned for him today," Honor explained steadily and then gave her sister the few details she had.

"But a man like that will be out on bail in a few hours," Adena cried.

Honor said nothing. She was well aware of that possibility.

"And who is this Landry person?"

"Beats me. Owns a beautiful horse, though. A colt sired by Stylish Legacy."

"Stylish Legacy?" There was a questioning note in Adena's voice. "Wasn't that the horse Dad used to own?"

"That's right." Adena had been only eight years old when Nicholas Mayfield had been killed. She remembered the horse only because of some of the mementos that had been left behind. Honor, at thirteen, had been fascinated with the idea of having a horse in the family, even though she had never gotten to watch him run. Stylish Legacy had only been in a handful of races before the two men who owned him had both died in a bloody scandal that had traumatized Honor more than anyone else in the family. Adena had been too young to understand fully what had happened, and Mrs. Mayfield, who had been in the midst of messy divorce proceedings, had been almost relieved to have everything ended.

"Well, I don't see what this has to do with anything. Where does Landry fit into all this?" Adena asked anxiously.

"He kept me out of the trap that had been set for Granger. And when he found out I had some distant connection to his horse, he, uh, invited me to watch the race." "Invited" was something of a euphemism for the command Landry had issued, but Honor didn't feel up to explaining her own wariness of the man.

"And he's going to tell you what happens to Granger?"

"He said he'd find out tomorrow."

"Honor, this is getting messier and messier. Why couldn't you just have paid off Granger and put an end to it all?"

Honor closed her eyes, momentarily seeking patience. "Because by the time I was about to catch up with him, the police were waiting."

"So this Constantine Landry says. What if he was wrong? Or playing some weird game? This doesn't solve anything! I'm in the same mess I was in before. What are we going to do now?"

"Adena, I don't know. I have no way of knowing what was happening out there this afternoon," Honor said flatly. "You'll have to forgive me if I'm not handling this in the proper manner, but I haven't had a whole lot of experience dealing with sharks such as Granger!"

"Meaning I have?"

"You're the one who owes him five thousand dollars, not I!"

Adena broke into tears and, as usual, Honor felt guilty.

"Forget it, Adena," she soothed wearily. "I'll take care of everything. I'm seeing Landry tomorrow and he'll tell me whether or not we still have to worry about Granger."

"Are you sure you can trust this Landry person?" Adena demanded through sobs.

"No." The initial response had been immediate. But then Honor thought about the man with the gunmetal-gray eyes. "Well, maybe," she temporized.

"What kind of an answer is that?"

"The truth is, I just don't know yet. But there's something about him, Adena. I think he might be quite ruthless on occasion but I also have a feeling that he's, well, concerned with keeping the books balanced."

"What books?"

"Never mind. I'll call you tomorrow after I find out more. Goodbye, Adena." Honor put down the phone before her sister could get in another question.

Then she moved deliberately across the living room with its red, black and yellow furnishings on a white carpet and into the red-and-black-tiled kitchen. It had been a rough day in several ways, and she deserved some compensation. Pouring herself a glass of cool Napa Valley Riesling, Honor went back into the living room. She sank down into a black-webbed rocking chair and propped her feet on the red hassock. Silently she toasted the palm tree outside her window.

"Here's to you, Constantine Landry, whoever you are. I'm not sure yet whether I should be thanking you or running as fast as I can in the opposite direction. But one thing's for sure. You aren't going to make my life dull.''

BY THE TIME Conn showed up at her door the following evening, Honor had decided that running really wasn't necessary. In fact, she told herself as she took in the sight of him standing on her doorstep, she was beginning to look forward to the evening.

He wore an immaculately cut gray linen jacket that had a subtle slub weave. Charcoal trousers that ended above hand-sewn calfskin shoes emphasized the coiled strength of his body. The crisply striped shirt and silk tie completed the quiet look of expensive power.

The only factor that bothered Honor was that she couldn't identify the type of power that emanated from Conn Landry. It wasn't, for example, the muted, ritualized power associated with the corporate world. Nor was it the flashy, tacky, heavy-handed power of the Southern California film crowd. It crossed her mind briefly that what she was seeing was the cool arrogance of a professional gangster, but she dismissed the idea at once. Instead, the strength in Landry seemed to be uniquely his own. And she had the sense to know it was, therefore, more dangerous in some ways than the more easily recognized sources of power. It was always simpler to deal with a factor that could be labeled and understood.

But for some reason, although she was warily respectful of the potential danger in him, Honor didn't fear Conn. That knowledge gave her the poise to smile warmly at him.

Landry saw the confidence in her and told himself he was amused. Yet a part of him knew a sense of reluctant admiration. The lady had guts. Having just recently finished with a rather blunt heart-to-heart chat with Granger, he now knew just how much nerve she must have buried beneath that bright, stylish exterior.

She was wearing a yellow-gold chemise that was sashed low on the hips with a crisp, wide band of black. The effect was both rakish and self-confident without being outrageous. The black sandals and the ebony bracelet on her small wrist completed the outfit. Her hair swung in a sleek curtain around her shoulders and as he stood there on the threshold, Landry had an almost overpowering urge to run his fingers through the golden-brown stuff. He wanted to touch her with the familiar intimacy of a lover. She'd look good a little mussed from his touch, he decided.

Once again he realized he should be questioning his own reactions. It was reasonably safe to admit he found himself responding physically to Honor. Conn decided that he understood that part and could deal with it. But it definitely was not on the program to uncover this vein of whimsically indulgent tenderness.

"The desk clerk at my hotel recommended a little restaurant downtown," Landry said as he walked her toward the silver-gray Porsche that waited at the curb. He told her the name. "Know it?"

Honor nodded. "It's an excellent choice." She allowed him to slip her into the front seat and then had to wait impatiently while he circled the front of the car and slid in beside her. "Well?" she invited cheerfully. "When are you going to tell me all the details?"

His promised phone call that afternoon had been brief, disappointingly so, Honor had discovered after she'd replaced the receiver. Landry had only asked for her home address and then said quite calmly that

Granger was no longer a problem. He'd refused to tell her more at that point.

"I'll give you the full story over dinner," Landry promised now as he pulled away from the curb. The quiet, tree-lined streets near the California Institute of Technology campus were relatively empty at this hour, and he made his way through them with an ease that told Honor he didn't need directions.

She wondered briefly how he happened to be so familiar with the Pasadena streets, and then promptly forgot the matter as her mind went back to Granger.

"He really is out of the way, though?"

"He won't bother you or your sister again."

Her head snapped around. "How did you know about my sister's involvement in all this?"

"I'll tell you that over dinner, too." He threw her a sidelong glance. "Relax, Honor. I've taken care of everything."

Some of her breezy confidence faded. "*You've* taken care of everything? I thought it was the police who had handled Granger."

"Whether or not they do doesn't affect you anymore."

"Do you know, Conn Landry, you have a remarkable talent for the cryptic comment?"

"Since my talents are rather limited, I try to perfect the few I have."

"I get the feeling your sense of humor may not be numbered among your few perfected abilities."

"Probably not," he admitted without any show of concern.

"Pity," she said dryly, trying to sound just as cryptic as Conn.

Driving ability was, apparently, one of his limited

number of talents, Honor observed as he parked the Porsche with neat precision in front of the casually elegant little restaurant. When Conn opened her car door and took her arm to escort her across the sidewalk she decided that he had another talent: He had the ability to make her feel safe.

It was an odd sensation on her part, she reflected as she was seated. Honor had never been aware of needing or desiring a man's protection. Whatever protection a man offered his women had disappeared when she was thirteen, and she hadn't depended on any since then.

Containing her curiosity until after she'd obediently ordered her meal of broccoli salad and scallops, Honor waited for an opportune opening. When the Sonoma County Chardonnay arrived at the table after much deliberation between the wine steward and Conn, she decided she had waited long enough. Smiling expectantly she sipped the beautiful white wine and repeated her question.

"Tell me what they did to Granger."

Landry shrugged, reaching for his own glass. "He's out on bail. Eventually he might wind up in jail on a more or less permanent basis, but probably not this time."

Honor's expectant smile disappeared. "You said everything was all right now, that Granger had been dealt with and was no longer a problem. I was afraid of this," she went on morosely. "As long as he's running around loose, I'm going to have to find him."

"You're not going anywhere near that scum. I told you the situation is under control." There was cool command in Conn's gaze again.

"I haven't got much choice," Honor shot back.

"You're right. You don't have much choice. You're going to do as I say in the matter."

"You don't have any conception of what's going on!"

"No?" Broodingly he studied her set face. "I know your sister owed him five thousand dollars because of that loan he gave her to pay off her gambling debts. And I know she didn't have the money. Apparently she went to you for it."

"How do you know all this?" Honor demanded fiercely.

"Some of it I learned from Granger and some of it I figured out for myself," Conn explained easily.

"You've actually talked to Granger today?" She was stunned by the news. "You saw him?"

"He headed for the racetrack as soon as they released him. He's a real racing addict. But, then, you must know that, or you wouldn't have been there yourself yesterday looking for him."

"Adena told me she thought that was the most likely place to find him," Honor admitted slowly. "But I don't understand why you approached him."

"Don't you?"

"Well, no. None of this is any of your business."

"It is now."

"Conn, this is ridiculous. You can't just choose to involve yourself in my personal life!"

He watched her intently for a long moment and then reached across the small table to draw a thumb along the back of her wrist. His hand, Honor realized uneasily, was as strong-looking as the rest of him. Large, square, powerful. At first glance a woman wouldn't guess that those blunt fingers could be so amazingly sensitive. Yet the small pattern he traced on her wrist sent a tremor of awareness through her.

"I've already involved myself in your affairs, Honor. I paid Granger off and told him not to go near your sister again."

Honor's gaze reflected her shock. "You paid him off! You gave him five thousand dollars?"

"That's what your sister owed."

"Yes, but—"

"Honor, it's all over," Conn told her with a surprising twist of gentleness in his voice. "You don't have to deal with Granger. I've already handled him for you."

Confused and alarmed at the implications of having this man take charge of such a personal and dangerous matter, Honor found herself fumbling for words of anger and protest. "You had no right! You should have consulted me. Now I owe you the five thousand dollars. That's assuming you're telling me the truth in the first place. Maybe this is all some sort of scam to take me for another five thousand. How do I know that you're any less dangerous than Granger?"

"You don't."

"Damn you and your cryptic comments!" She tossed her napkin on the table and prepared to get to her feet. The large, square hand that had only moments ago been tantalizing the back of her wrist suddenly closed around it like a manacle.

"Sit down, Honor," Conn ordered quietly.

"Why should I?" she hissed in response.

His mouth lifted in the now familiar faint smile. "Because you owe me five thousand dollars?" he suggested smoothly.

Honor went very still. She couldn't have gotten out of her chair now even if the room were on fire. Her eyes met Conn's unreadable gaze. "My checkbook is at home. Take me back to the apartment and I'll give you your money. The same money I was going to give Granger. I get the feeling it doesn't much matter which of the two of you I pay. You seem to have a lot in common, you and Granger.''

For a split second she was certain she'd gone much too far. The fingers shackling her wrist were now tight bands of steel and the cold of Conn's eyes could only have its source in the farthest reaches of the universe. In that taut instant of time Honor's instinctive wariness of the man made the transition to genuine fear.

And then, quite suddenly, she was free. Landry released her hand and sat back in his chair, reaching for his wineglass. He took a long swallow before he spoke. When he looked at her again, the frightening ice of his eyes had disappeared, leaving only his usual, remote expression. The wry tone of his words dissipated most of the remaining tendrils of alarm that curled through Honor's body. He inclined his head once, very formally.

"Congratulations, lady, you nearly managed to push me over the edge with that last crack. Not many people have the power to do that to me.''

She swallowed awkwardly. "My guess is not many people care to make the attempt.''

"Did I frighten you?''

"I don't know how to take you, Conn,'' she said honestly. "Yes, you frightened me for a moment. After all, I don't know much about you, do I? And now I owe you five thousand dollars.''

"Wouldn't you rather owe it to me than to Granger?''

"I don't know yet. At least I have a fair idea of where Granger fits into the grand scheme of life. He's a loan shark. Once I'd paid him off he would have been out of the way. You're not so easy to classify.''

"I'll take that as a compliment. A minute ago you were pointing out how much I had in common with Granger. Apparently my status isn't really that low in your eyes."

"Why did you do it?" she asked starkly.

He didn't pretend to misunderstand. "Because I didn't want you going near that man," he declared with absolute conviction. "You don't know anything about dealing with people like him. How did your sister get involved?"

Honor sighed, relaxing a little now that Conn seemed under control. "For a while this fall she was dating a man who, among other things, gambled heavily. I guess he made it all look so easy and so much fun. He took her to Vegas and to the races and encouraged her to try her luck. At Santa Anita he introduced her to Granger. I gather he often used Granger as a banker. Granger made the money so readily available that my sister couldn't resist. She wanted to keep up with the high-rolling crowd she was moving with and eventually got run over, instead. She luckily came to her senses and dropped the boyfriend."

"But by that time she was already into Granger for the five thousand?"

"Actually, she only borrowed three thousand," Honor said bluntly. "But the government doesn't regulate interest rates in Granger's world."

"Two thousand dollars in interest on a three-thousand-dollar loan. Yes, Granger is a step ahead of most banks. Well, if it's any consolation, he won't be approaching your sister again, even if she shows up at the track."

Honor considered that. "Because you told him to stay clear?"

"That's right."

"Why is Granger so willing to take orders from you?"

"Maybe I make him nervous the same way I make you nervous," Conn offered laconically as the broccoli salads arrived.

Honor ignored her food. Leaning forward intently she said, "Conn, I will repay you tonight. I have the money."

"It's not necessary."

Honor shook her head violently. "It is most definitely necessary. I will give you the money tonight."

He watched her expressive face for a moment as if trying to make up his mind about something. Then he nodded. "All right. If it will make you feel more comfortable."

"It will!"

He smiled faintly. "Yes, I can see that it will. And I do want you to feel comfortable around me, Honor."

"Do you?" she asked skeptically.

"It's a priority of mine," he assured her calmly.

HONOR HAD TO ADMIT that by the conclusion of the meal, Conn had achieved at least a portion of his goal. Her sense of caution around him was still very much alive, but the compelling attraction he held for her was stronger than ever. There had been no argument over the matter of her giving him the money, so he obviously didn't intend to hold it over her head in any way. His main objective, apparently, had been to protect her from having to face Granger.

Strangely enough his protectiveness left her feeling in some ways more deeply in his debt than she would have felt if she'd simply owed Conn five thousand dollars. It was an odd bit of irony, she reflected as she gave him the key to open her front door.

"Would you like some brandy while I write out the check?" she offered politely as she stepped inside the apartment.

"Thank you. I'd appreciate that," he murmured, prowling through her strikingly decorated living room. "Just tell me where it is. I'll get it."

"In that red lacquered cabinet by the window."

He nodded and paced across the white carpet. He was taking in every detail, Honor thought fleetingly as she went quickly down the hall to her bedroom to get her checkbook. How much could that man read from the design details of her living room? Probably far too much.

It was as she stepped into her Japanese-inspired bedroom that Honor experienced her first sense of something being subtly wrong. For an instant she stood poised in the doorway, frowning as she looked into every corner of the room.

A moment later she shook her head in self-annoyance. Everything was in order. The red-and-black gilt-trimmed drawers of her dressing table were closed, just as they should have been, and her bed was dramatically neat, with its embroidered quilt in place. The room was a visual interpretation of subtle, sophisticated serenity. The only jarring note was the television set, and it was discreetly concealed behind a folding screen.

Honor nibbled on her lower lip for a few seconds, trying to shake off the feeling that there was a new element in the room. Then, half-disgusted with herself she strode over to the closet and yanked open the shoji-screen doors. Inside, her brilliantly colored clothing hung in place above the array of equally bright shoes. Everything was as it should be.

"You're turning into a nervous little old spinster, my girl," she told herself bitingly. Determinedly she bent over the dresser and scrawled out the five-thousand-dollar check. After signing it she straightened, aware that the eerie trickle of uneasiness was still thrumming in her veins.

The only place in the room she hadn't checked was under the bed. Surely she wouldn't give in to the impulse, she chided herself.

"Oh, nuts!" She went to her knees on the white carpet and peered beneath the bed. Conn's blandly interested voice from the doorway sent a jolt through her.

"Well, I'll be damned. I've heard tales of single ladies who reach the point where they start looking under the bed before they go to sleep at night, but I didn't imagine you were one of them."

"I was right earlier this evening when I decided your sense of humor was not among your limited selection of talents, Mr. Landry." Awkward with embarrassment, Honor got to her feet and turned to pick up the check that lay on the dressing table. Aware that her cheeks were stained with a strong shade of pink, she spent an extra moment studying the check so that she wouldn't have to meet his mocking gaze.

But when Honor swung around with a flippant remark ready on her lips she suddenly found herself in Conn's arms. He had crossed the white carpet without making a sound, coming up behind her as stealthily as any predator.

"Conn?"

"There's no need to go looking under your bed, Honor. I'm right here."

Standing very still in his arms, Honor watched with fascination as he lowered his mouth to hers. He was there, all right, filling up every inch of her beautifully designed bedroom with his own brand of strength and presence. All thoughts of a vague wrongness in the atmosphere went out of her head as he took her lips. Conn Landry felt very, very right.

It was not the sort of kiss she normally expected and received the first time she kissed a new date. Landry's mouth did not move on hers with the tentative, questioning approach a man generally used in the beginning.

Instead he took her mouth as though he had been anticipating the action for a long while. The hunger in him was blunt and dangerously near the surface. What should have bothered her was that her body seemed to respond with the same feeling of being suddenly on the verge of discovery and release. It was an exciting, exhilarating sensation.

Her arms came up to wind slowly around his neck as he coaxed apart her lips. She shuddered a little as his tongue swept behind the barrier of her teeth. His response was to tighten his hands on her waist. Conn pulled her into his heat with irresistible pressure, gently forcing her into total awareness of the tautness of his thighs. And all the while he explored her mouth, drinking hungrily from the intimate, moist depths.

Honor's lashes closed slumberously and her body was invaded with a sweet lethargy that was shot through with red threads of anticipation.

"Honor, honey, you taste so good," Conn murmured in a husky growl as he reluctantly freed her mouth. He sampled the hidden skin behind the curve of her hair, his teeth nibbling with exquisite gentleness. "Spicy, sweet and sexy. I knew you'd taste this way."

Reflexively her nails kneaded his shoulders, the coral tips sinking deeply into the gray fabric of his jacket. He groaned and raised his hands slowly along her rib cage until his thumbs rested just beneath the curve of her unconfined breasts.

"Oh, Conn."

"We're going to be good in bed together, you and I," he interrupted with soft satisfaction. He grazed the pad of his thumb across the crest of one breast and felt it flower to life beneath the yellow-gold silk.

His absolute certainty got through the sensual haze that seemed to be clouding her senses. "No," she whispered. "Not bed. Not yet." And, if she had an ounce of genuine intelligence, she added silently, not ever. She should know better than to play with fire at her age.

"I won't rush you," he vowed soothingly as he continued to glide the flat of his thumb across her silk-sheathed nipple.

Questioningly she lifted her head to meet his intent gaze and found herself staring into gray, bottomless seas that swirled with masculine desire. The depths of his hunger startled her even as it called to her.

"I think," she began carefully, "that you'll do things exactly as you want to do them, regardless of whether or not it means rushing me."

"Don't be afraid of me, Honor," he rasped against her ear. "There's no need."

"What's that supposed to mean?" she asked urgently, a strange panic sizzling through her.

"Nothing. Just relax. I want you, but I can wait." He used his strong hands on the nape of her neck, gentling her tense body until she did as he asked and relaxed against him. "I can wait," he repeated half under his breath.

There was something about the way he touched her, the way his hardness felt against her softness that was undermining all her defenses, Honor realized vaguely. The attraction between them was so unexpectedly strong, so out of the ordinary, that she wasn't fully prepared to handle it. Time was the key. She sensed that much.

Apparently Landry did, too. Slowly he eased himself away from her, mouth crooked just a bit at the edge. "I'll give you a little time, Honor." He brushed his mouth lightly across her parted lips. "But I think I'd better get myself out of your bedroom or I won't be able to keep my promise."

Without a word she followed him out into the living room, the check clutched in her hand. He finished his brandy while standing by the window gazing out into the darkness. They spoke little during those few minutes but the atmosphere was heavy with unsatisfied male desire. When at last he turned to leave, Honor thrust the check at him. Conn took it without glancing at it, stuffing it into his jacket pocket.

"Feel better now that you've paid the debt?" he asked softly.

"Yes." But she didn't feel she had paid the debt, Honor decided as she said good-night to him at the door. He had protected her from having to deal with Granger. She didn't have any way to repay that part of the obligation and the knowledge caused a faint tingle of unease.

It wasn't until she had turned out all the lights in the living room and walked slowly back down the hall to the bedroom that the sensation of wrongness returned. Once again she found herself standing in the doorway, trying to understand what it was that bothered her.

This time she finally focused on the cause. The large, folding screen with its delicate Japanese artwork wasn't standing in quite the same place it had been earlier this evening when she had left the house. It didn't quite hide the television behind it.

The designer instincts in her had always insisted on using the screen to hide the brash, high-tech look of the portable TV. The twentieth-century technology had seemed to clash with the elegant serenity of the room.

Curious, Honor walked over to where the screen stood and examined the flattened areas of carpet where the legs of the screen had once pressed it down. She knew she hadn't moved that screen in two weeks. It had been that long since she'd used the television.

It was such a small thing, she told herself nervously. But designers were trained to notice small details in a room. It was often the little things that made the difference between a room with dynamic, personal impact and a simple showplace that had no warmth. The little things could also destroy the image. People in her profession soon learned to recognize odd little details that could produce great effects or ruin beautifully planned projects.

Someone had been in her bedroom that night.

Chapter Three

"She's a nice young lady, Conn," Ethan Bailey said. He was focusing a set of field glasses, watching a fast filly go through her morning workout on the track.

"Your horse or Honor Mayfield?" Landry leaned against the railing, his eyes following Bailey's expensive filly.

"Both, I reckon. But to tell you the truth it was that sweet little Honor I had in mind."

"You trying to tell me something, Ethan?" The odd little smile flickered at the edges of Landry's mouth.

Still gazing through the glasses, Bailey shrugged. "None of my business, of course, but, well, she doesn't seem quite your type, son."

"I agree. It's none of your business and she's probably not my type." But Conn kept his tone easy, not wanting to offend his friend. "On the other hand, I've never been really sure exactly what my type is. And Honor is turning out to be...interesting."

Ethan's brow held a trace of a disapproving frown. "You planning on playing games with Miss Honor?"

"You're certainly concerned about her."

"Like I said, I like her. Back where I come from a man's not supposed to play games with a lady like her."

"She can handle them." Conn relented. "Look, Ethan, don't worry about her. And don't worry about me, either. I know what I'm doing."

"You always seem to be in control of things, I'll grant you that." Ethan grinned abruptly. "Forget I tried to give you the dose of fatherly advice. A man my age sometimes takes a few liberties he's got no right to take. Besides, if you scratch deep enough, you'd probably find out my motivations weren't exactly pure as the new driven snow."

"Meaning you're jealous?"

"You bet," Ethan acknowledged fervently. "The reason a man my age starts offering fatherly advice is precisely because he's a mite envious of a man your age. It's our way of getting even with you young folks. Spiteful. Downright spiteful."

Landry's eyes lightened with fleeting humor. "That showgirl I saw hanging on your arm last month in Vegas didn't seem interested in finding anyone younger than you!"

Ethan sighed grandly and shook his head. "Sad to say, I'm afraid my main attraction for that little gal was my bank account. Unfortunately I doubt that Miss Honor would be similarly impressed."

"You don't think so?" Landry asked thoughtfully.

"Well," Ethan drawled lightly, "I suppose it might be worth a try."

Landry was startled by the sudden, unexpected tension that flashed through him as he pictured Ethan Bailey or anyone else trying to impress Honor Mayfield. He must be crazy, he told himself. Ethan was only teasing him. Deliberately he summoned up a determined casualness. "Hands off, Ethan, old buddy, I saw her first."

"And when do you plan on seeing her next?"

Landry glanced around at the quiet grounds. "This morning. I invited her to come watch the workouts." His eyes narrowed faintly as he glanced at his watch. "She said she'd try to make it."

"Maybe something came up," Ethan said. "The lady's got a business to run, didn't you say? Some kind of decorating work?"

"Interior designs for offices. Homes, too, I think," Conn answered absently, beginning to wonder if Honor might be going to stand him up after all. He'd called her yesterday, the morning after their dinner date, and issued the invitation to join him at the track today. The lure was an attractive one, he'd told himself. He had a hunch she'd enjoy watching the horses working out. She had seemed initially hesitant and then in a little rush of enthusiasm, she'd said she'd try to make it.

He'd been certain she'd show. Everything seemed to be falling into place quite neatly. When he'd accepted the check the other night they'd both known it didn't erase the debt between them. He'd seen the gratitude in her eyes. It had been coupled with caution, but it had been genuine.

She'd been frightened of Granger and he'd assumed the task of dealing with the man on her behalf. In addition, he'd kept her from getting mixed up with the police trap that had been set in the parking lot. A real knight in shining armor, Landry told himself sardonically. Then he wondered why the image bothered him.

There were a lot of things bothering him that shouldn't have been making him uneasy. He didn't understand it. Everything had seemed so simple and straightforward when he'd originally decided to track her down. The decision had been based on an intuitive, gut-level feeling that there were questions to be asked and that the only one left who might have some answers was Honor Mayfield. It wasn't that he thought she would really know what had happened all those years ago, but she was a Mayfield. Through her he might be able to satisfy the uncertainties, the *wrongness*, the sense of injustice that had haunted him so long. But she would run if she found out who he was. In fact, she would probably be wise to run. So he had to ensnare her firmly before he revealed himself.

And now that he'd kissed her, Landry knew the first strands of the web were securely locked in place. The response from her had been unmistakable. His body still remembered it, along with the seething frustration of knowing that the time was not yet right to push her into bed.

Yes, she'd show up this morning, he told himself, aware of a sense of satisfaction. The bonds of gratitude and sexual attraction were in place. The combination was a strong one—with any luck at all, an irresistible one.

"Here she is." Ethan Bailey interrupted Conn's thoughts to wave cheerfully at Honor, who was walking toward them with a Styrofoam cup of coffee in her hand. "Over here, Miss Honor."

Conn turned his head to look at her, aware of a certain possessive pleasure. She looked good this morning, her hair brushed back behind one ear and held with a clip. An indigo-blue chambray shirt was belted over a pair of snug-fitting jeans. Something about the way she moved as she walked toward him sent a flare of anticipation through him. Conn got to his feet.

Honor saw the hunter looking out at her from Conn Landry's eyes as she came up to the railing. It sent a tiny jolt through her, even as she acknowledged the sense of pleasure she felt in his presence. Perhaps she had been right early this morning when she'd told herself it might be better to forgo the invitation. Every time she was with Conn she risked deepening an involvement that she sensed was dangerous. Yet here she was, unable to stay away.

"I was beginning to think you might not make it," Conn said quietly after the greetings had been exchanged. His gaze moved over her, seeming to take in every detail.

"I wasn't sure myself." She smiled politely and sipped her coffee, refusing to elaborate. "Is that one of your horses, Ethan?"

"Yes, ma'am," Bailey declared proudly as he set a stopwatch to time the filly. "Paid a handsome sum for that little lady. Expect great things from her."

"Ethan expects great things from all his horses," Conn remarked.

"I want more than tax shelters, I want winners," Ethan said firmly. "All the tax sheltering in the world ain't as satisfying as one good win."

"How long have you owned racehorses?" Honor asked curiously.

"Oh, years. More than I care to count. Gets in a man's blood."

"Is it in your blood, Conn?" she asked, looking directly at him.

"I don't know yet. Legacy is the first horse I've owned," he told her flatly. The gray eyes were very cool as he returned her questioning glance. "A lot of things besides racing can get in a man's blood."

Honor felt a prickle of alarm. "Such as?" she challenged with false lightness.

"A woman."

"Or hot coffee," Ethan Bailey inserted suddenly, as if sensing the new tension in the air. "That cup of java sure looks good, Honor."

"I got it at a concession stand. They've opened one to serve people who are attending the workout session this morning. If I'd known you didn't have any I would have picked up an extra couple of cups." She felt oddly grateful to the older man for having dispelled the momentary uneasiness caused by Conn's words.

"What say we get ourselves some, Conn?" Ethan suggested promptly.

Landry got to his feet. "I'll get the coffee." He turned and paced toward the concession stand.

Honor watched him, conscious of the smooth coordination of his stride. He was wearing jeans today and an open-throated khaki shirt that suited the hunter she had seen in his eyes a few moments earlier. Honor shifted restlessly and took another sip of her coffee.

For the hundredth time since he had left her the night before last, she told herself she would be wise to ease out of the relationship that was developing between herself and Conn Landry. And for the hundredth time she decided she'd wait just a little longer before making a firm decision in the matter.

"He's an interesting man, Honor." Ethan spoke quite gently as he picked up the field glasses and focused them on his filly.

"Have you known him long, Ethan?" She wasn't quite sure how to ask all the questions she wanted answered about Conn.

"Just since he bought Legacy. He's new to the racing world."

It seemed to Honor that Ethan was about to say more

and then changed his mind. She felt an overpowering urge to push a little further. "Do you know what, uh, kind of business he's in?"

Ethan lifted one shoulder indifferently. "Well, I believe he's made a few substantial investments."

"In what?"

Ethan lowered the field glasses and gave her a vaguely troubled look. "Business investments. You know, a bit of this and a bit of that."

"Where are these investments?" she tried to ask casually, deeply aware of the older man's hesitation.

Ethan cleared his throat. "I think he mentioned Tahoe at one point." Then his face brightened. "Lots of lovely land up around Lake Tahoe."

"Lots of lovely gambling casinos, too," Honor noted dryly. "Is Conn involved in gambling, Ethan?"

"Don't you think you should be asking Landry these questions, Honor?" the older man asked with obvious unease. It was clear he was feeling awkward.

She felt a wave of embarrassment. "You're probably right. Sorry. It's just that he's a difficult man to get to know. Doesn't talk about himself much."

"There's usually a good reason why a man doesn't want to talk about himself," Ethan said very soberly. "Sometimes it's best to respect that privacy."

Honor considered her next comment but went ahead and made it anyway. "He did me a big favor yesterday, Ethan."

"Handling Granger for you? Yeah, he said something about that. Everyone knows Granger's bad news." There was a meaningful pause. "But a lady probably ought to be careful about taking favors from Conn Landry."

She went still, aware of more than just a subtle hint

of warning in Ethan Bailey's words. Impulsively she put out a hand and touched his arm. "Ethan, please. Is there something I should know about Conn?"

Bailey exhaled deeply. "Honor, I like Conn Landry. I like him a lot. But the plain truth is, I'm not sure he's the sort of man a woman such as yourself should be getting mixed up with, if you take my meaning."

"I'm not sure that I do," she said quietly.

"Oh, hell, listen to me," Ethan growled with what sounded like forced humor, "I've been sounding like someone's Dutch uncle all morning. I surely didn't mean to go and make you nervous. You're a big girl. Last thing you need is advice from an old goat like me."

Honor smiled warmly at him, knowing he wanted to be off the hook. "You're hardly an old goat, Ethan Bailey."

He slanted her a quick glance. "Are you kidding? I'm old enough to be your father. Or Landry's father, come to that."

"Don't you know that owning horses makes you fascinating to most females?" She chuckled as she spotted Conn on his way back with the coffee. "Women love horses."

"Is that a fact?"

"Is what a fact?" Landry asked as he handed Ethan a cup.

"Honor, here, was just telling me that women love horses, and that men like me who own them are *fascinating*." He seemed vastly pleased with the word.

"Let's not forget I own one, too," Conn said blandly, his gaze raking Honor's features. "Does that mean I'm in the fascinating category?"

Honor was saved from having to answer because at

that moment Bailey's beautiful filly came thundering past. Immediately all attention went to the horse. Morning workouts were, after all, a serious business.

An hour later, when Honor finally decided she ought to be getting back to work, Conn walked her to her red Fiat. It was the first time they'd been alone that morning. As they halted beside the car, he turned her to face him, his strong hands settling on her waist.

"Did you miss me the other night after I left?"

It was difficult to lie to a man with eyes the color of gunmetal, Honor discovered. She compromised. "Actually, I had other things on my mind," she informed him flippantly.

"Another man?"

She didn't like the way he said that. "Not quite. A little matter of a folding screen that wasn't where it should have been."

He frowned. "What are you talking about?"

Honor sighed. "Remember when you came into my bedroom and found me checking under the bed?"

"I remember."

"Well, I was doing that because I had a funny feeling that something wasn't quite right. I know it sounds ridiculous, but a designer develops an unconscious eye for the details of a room. And I know my own place so well that when the least little item isn't in the right location, I'm aware of it."

"A screen wasn't in the right place?"

"I use it to hide my television set," she explained, feeling vaguely silly. "It had been moved a few inches. Figuring out why and when kept me busy for a while."

He tilted his head to one side, studying her. "And what kind of answers did you come up with?"

"The most logical one is that my younger sister visited the apartment while we were out that evening. She has a set of keys, and she's been known to make raids on my wardrobe."

"Had she visited your place?" Conn persisted.

Honor shook her head, remembering the phone call she had made the next morning to Adena. "She said she hadn't, but to tell you the truth she was so busy singing your praises for having handled Granger that I'm not sure she was paying much attention to my question! You've got a real fan in Adena."

He ignored that last comment. "So what about the screen?"

"Well, another possibility is that the apartment manager let herself in for some reason or another. Unfortunately she went out of town yesterday morning and won't be back until tomorrow. I won't be able to ask her until then. And then there's the last possible reason."

"Which is?"

Honor smiled humorously. "That my so-called trained designer eye isn't quite as good as I assumed. All in all, the whole incident doesn't amount to much."

"Nothing was missing?"

"Nothing."

"Then it wasn't a robbery attempt."

"Fortunately I was saved that bit of melodrama," Honor said feelingly. "One of my friends got hit six months ago. The thieves cleaned out everything except the carpet. Don't look so concerned, Conn. Obviously there's some perfectly logical explanation for the screen having been shifted a few inches. I've stopped worrying about it."

"But it kept you from thinking about me that night," he murmured, rubbing the edge of his thumb along the line of her jaw.

No, it hadn't kept her from thinking about him but Honor decided it was best to let his assumption stand. Instinct warned her that it would be risky to let Conn know just how much he filled her mind. What was it Ethan had said? *I'm not sure he's the sort of man a woman such as yourself should be getting mixed up with.* She wasn't at all sure, either.

"Will six o'clock be okay for dinner tonight?" Conn asked softly, his thumb caressing her chin now.

Almost violently aware of the small, intimate touch, Honor reminded herself of her own uncertainties regarding this man. The way he asked told her he had no doubts at all but that she'd be free for him tonight. His confidence scared her.

"I'm sorry, Conn, but I have a business engagement tonight."

The gray eyes chilled. "A date?"

"You could call it that." She owed him no explanations, she assured herself.

His thumb stopped its gentle stroking and she felt his fingers as he lightly touched her throat. "Cancel it, Honor."

She swallowed, a frisson of fear flickering through her. "I can't do that. I have a business to run, Conn. Don't you know anything about the pressures of business?"

"I know about business pressures. I also know something about nervous fillies. Relax, Honor. Cancel your other engagement and come to dinner with me." His voice was rough and persuasive, a lover's voice.

Honor reacted to it, hovered on the brink of surrender and then retreated barely in time. "No, no, I can't do that, Conn. I'm sorry but I really do have to be going. Thank you for inviting me to the workouts this morning. I enjoyed them. How much longer will you be in town?'' She made the question casual, subtly emphasizing the short-term nature of their association.

He watched her slide quickly into the front seat of the Fiat, closing the door as if it were a locked gate behind which she would be safe.

''It all depends.''

Honor frowned up at him, eyes narrowed against the sun. ''Depends on what?'' she asked as she turned the key in the ignition.

''On some business matters I'm handling.''

''I thought you were only here to see Legacy run.''

''I'm taking the opportunity of tying up a few loose ends,'' he said coolly.

She hated it when he was so damn cryptic. ''Well, I certainly wouldn't want to keep you from attending to business.'' Honor put the car in gear and drove off without glancing back.

SHE HAD BEEN UNDECIDED about whether to attend the private party being held to celebrate the opening of a new restaurant that evening. The interior had been designed by a friend, however, and Honor knew Susan Mallory would appreciate having her show up. A finished project gave a designer the same sense of pleasure and satisfaction as a finished painting gave an artist. By the very nature of the business, neither could retain possession of the creations. There was only a limited period of time for the creator to enjoy it and show it off.

Honor didn't try to kid herself as she dressed for the event. She had made the decision to attend based almost entirely on an instinctive desire to put some distance between herself and Conn Landry.

Ethan Bailey's awkward but well-meant warnings

had only served to crystallize her own uncertainties concerning Conn. He was getting too close, too fast.

Honor checked the sweep of the magenta-colored blouson dress she had chosen to wear and then brushed her hair back into a neat twist at the nape of her neck. It was difficult to get excited about the evening ahead. All she could think of was how much anticipation she would be feeling now if she were waiting for Conn Landry to collect her.

The festivities were in full swing by the time Honor arrived. She drifted through the crowd of fellow designers, reporters, friends of the proud new owner and local restaurateurs, idly searching for Susan. En route she helped herself to the unlimited quantities of exotic cheeses that had been set out. When the crush of people maneuvered her close to the bar, she ended up with a plastic cup of a low-budget Italian wine that helped wash down the cheese. She wondered what Conn was doing at that moment.

"Honor! You made it! I'm so glad. Tell me, what do you think?" Susan Mallory, attired in the latest of oddly layered Japanese fashions, pushed through the crowd toward her. In one hand she held a plastic glass of wine and with the other she waved at the art deco interiors she had designed.

Honor smiled at her attractive dark-haired friend. "It's wonderful, Susan. Absolutely wonderful. It's just too bad that it's not customary to put up a little plaque saying who designed the space."

"I know." Susan sighed theatrically. "No one ever thinks to credit the designer." She brightened. "But I have gotten some good referrals out of it."

"Good. How are the wedding plans going?" Honor helped herself to a chunk of imported Camembert.

"Perfectly," Susan enthused. "As a matter of fact I

was going to call you next week and ask if the beach cottage was going to be available.''

"Second week in June?'' Honor tried to reconstruct the rental schedule in her head. "I think so. The agent said he'd booked it for the month of August, but part of June was still free. What made you decide to honeymoon in Ventura? Isn't that a bit ordinary? I thought you were going to Hawaii or Puerto Vallarta?''

"Everyone goes to Hawaii,'' Susan informed her blithely. "And those who don't, go to Puerto Vallarta. Richard and I discussed the matter the other night, and when I told him that you owned a charming, secluded place right on the beach just up the coast, we decided to ask if it was available. Going to use the house yourself this year?''

"I rarely use it,'' Honor said quietly, thinking of the beach cottage that had been her only inheritance from her father, other than a small trust fund that had helped see her through college. "Once in a while during the winter when it's not being rented out I spend a weekend there, but that's about it.''

"I don't see why you don't use it more often. I love the marvelous country retreat look you achieved with all that lovely rustic furniture and those horse-racing photos scattered on the walls. I had a great time there last summer.''

Honor thought of the pictures of Stylish Legacy that had belonged to her father and that she had left in place at the cottage, along with a variety of other racing mementos and paraphernalia. It was difficult to explain that she had always found visits to the cottage vaguely depressing. Memories of that traumatic year when she was thirteen seemed to be waiting for her there. It was easier to give a more rational explanation for her failure to use the beach house.

"I'd lose the rental tax advantages if I spent too much time there," she said easily.

"Oh, of course," Susan said. Being a Californian, she understood the implications of tax-advantaged investments immediately. People in California worried a lot about such investments. "Does your sister use it?"

"Rarely. My mother used to go there occasionally before she remarried and moved back east. Basically I'm just hanging on to the place for the appreciation and for tax purposes. And if it's free that second week in June, you're welcome to use it."

"Great, I'll tell Richard. Come along, I want to introduce you to my client."

"The gentleman in the mauve suit?"

"That's him."

By ten o'clock Honor decided she'd had enough cheese to supply her calcium needs for a month. She was tired of the party and tired of the endless cocktail chatter. It was time to leave. It was with a feeling of relief that she headed out into the parking lot to find her Fiat.

She didn't notice the headlights in her rearview mirror until she was only a few blocks from her apartment. Honor didn't know when it occurred to her that the same pair of headlights seemed to have been behind her for quite some distance, but when the thought finally did strike home she felt her palms grow damp on the steering wheel.

It was not unheard of for a lone woman driver to find herself being followed, forced off the road and assaulted. Honor had read that one technique for dealing with the situation was to drive to the nearest police station. On no account were you supposed to lead the trailing car to your home.

But she was only a block away from the apartment house now and she couldn't be absolutely certain she was being followed.

The headlights edged in closer behind her as she turned onto her quiet street. If she was being followed the vehicle could probably close in so quickly that it would slip through the automatic gate of the apartment garage when she opened it to let herself inside. Honor could easily find herself trapped inside the locked garage with whoever was driving the other car.

Then, again, it could be her imagination at work. The same vivid imagination that had insisted on believing someone had moved the screen in her room the other night.

Honor considered her options and decided to drive on past her apartment. She would circle the block and see if the other car followed. If it did, then she would lose no time racing back out onto a more crowded thoroughfare and heading toward the nearest police station.

The other vehicle was suddenly very close behind her, its headlights on high beam so that she could see nothing in the mirror except a blinding glare. She was about to accelerate past the apartment complex when her own lights picked out the silver-gray Porsche parked at the curb. There was a dark figure in the driver's seat.

Quite suddenly Conn Landry's presence seemed the most reassuring sight she'd seen in a long time. Without pausing to think, Honor pulled in to the curb behind him, aware that the car behind her was slowing, too.

Switching off the ignition she was out of the Fiat and running toward the Porsche before the tailing vehicle could edge in to the curb.

She saw the door of the Porsche swing open and then Landry was in front of her. In that moment his quiet power offered precisely the comfort and safety she wanted. Honor threw herself into his arms.

"Honor? What the hell—?"

The angry roar of a pickup truck motor cut off his startled demands. A second later the black truck accelerated past and disappeared around the corner.

Honor glanced up briefly to get a quick look at the vehicle but she made no effort to pull free of the iron-hard embrace in which she was wrapped.

"I think...I think that truck was following me," she managed as relief surged through her. "It had been behind me for blocks. I've heard of weirdos who do that, you know, follow a woman home and then attack her. I was going to drive on past when I saw your car. Oh, Conn, I've never been so glad to see anyone before in my life! What on earth are you doing here, anyway?"

"Guess," he growled succinctly. When she looked up at him with puzzled eyes, he sighed and loosened his grip on her long enough to close his car door. "I was waiting for you, naturally. Why else would I be sitting out here in front of your apartment building at this hour of the night?"

Honor's racing pulse slowed to a more normal level as the full implications of his presence hit her. "I'll assume that last crack is a rhetorical question." She pulled free of his encircling arm, smoothing her dress. "Don't get me wrong, Conn, I really was glad to see you, but I think it would be interesting to know exactly what you thought you were going to accomplish sitting out here in the first place."

"Let's go inside and I'll explain it all in great detail,"

he murmured, taking her arm. "But first of all tell me about that truck."

"I honestly don't know any more than I just told you. A California crazy who gets his kicks following single women, I suppose. I should report him to the cops."

"Report what? That truck didn't even have a license plate on it."

"Well, he's gone now, thank heavens."

Conn propelled her lightly through the gate and up one flight of stairs to her apartment. It was as he took her key to open her front door that Honor realized she still didn't know what he was doing here.

"Conn, about this business of you waiting for me," she began with what she hoped was a suitably imperious air, "I'd like to know just what you thought you were going to accomplish."

He slanted her an unreadable glance as he stepped around her and headed for the red lacquered cabinet that contained the brandy.

"Priority number one was to see who would be bringing you home." He poured a shot of brandy into a glass. Then he raised the glass in a faint salute. "Priority number two was to make sure you didn't take him upstairs."

Honor heard the quiet arrogance in his words and swallowed uneasily. "As you can see, I'm really not into truck drivers." She decided to go on the offensive. "Did it occur to you that I might object to your making yourself right at home with my brandy?"

He stalked toward her with cool, masculine grace. "It seems to me that offering me a drink is the least you could do under the circumstances."

"What circumstances?" she flared.

"I've been around when you needed me lately, haven't I?"

She licked her lower lip. "No one asked you to be around, Conn."

"But you've been grateful, nevertheless, haven't you?" He took a large swallow of the brandy and regarded her with his gunmetal eyes. "How was your *business* engagement, Honor? Have a good time?"

"Reasonably so," she said, mustering her composure. "Until that truck picked me up on the way home."

He nodded, taking another sip of brandy. Conn was wearing the jeans and the khaki shirt he'd had on earlier that day, Honor realized vaguely. The dark clothing combined with his somber, dangerous mood made him a formidable force in her living room.

"I think it's time for a little honesty from you, Honor Mayfield," he told her consideringly.

"What, exactly, do you want me to be honest about?"

"The reason you wouldn't have dinner with me tonight will do for a start."

"I told you, I had a business engagement."

"A very convenient one."

"Are you accusing me of something, Conn?"

"Yes. Avoiding me. And I'd like to know why."

Honor tried to move around him and found he was somehow blocking her path. She lifted her chin with cool hauteur. "Because there's too much I don't know about you. You frighten me a little, Conn, and I think you realize it."

The gray eyes flickered. "Yes."

"Then why put me through the third degree about this evening?" she challenged tightly. "Unless you really want to scare me for some reason."

She had the oddest feeling that he was forced to stop and think about the answer to that question. There was a tension in the room that wasn't doing much to dry her already damp palms. This evening was turning into a full-scale disaster.

"You have a point, Honor," Conn said finally. "I don't have any right to dictate how you spend your nights, do I?"

"No," she got out in a thin whisper.

"The problem is that I'd like that right," he continued.

"Conn, please..."

"I'd like you to know that I'll be there when things turn nasty the way they did with Granger and the way they did tonight when that truck followed you. I'd like you to trust me, Honor. I want you to know you don't have to get nervous and make up excuses for not seeing me."

His words poured over her in a rough, sensual cascade that caught at Honor's senses. But they weren't simply smooth lover's lies. There was an underlying urgency in them that forced her to accept their sincerity. In that moment she wasn't even sure Conn himself realized the intensity with which he was speaking.

Honor watched him as he moved toward her, aware of the swirl of male hunger in his gaze. She remembered the reassuring feeling of his arms going around her earlier out on the street and realized she wanted to know that sensation again.

"Conn, there's so much we don't know about each other," she tried with a touch of desperation.

He set down the brandy glass and touched the base of her throat with a remarkably sensitive fingertip. The desire in his eyes was an endless gray sea.

"I agree. There is much we don't know about each other. But I think tonight would be a good time to discover some basic truths."

Whatever her answer would have been, it was swallowed up in the depths of his kiss.

Chapter Four

It came as a shock to Conn to discover that he didn't want her to be afraid of him, that, instead, he wanted her to trust him. It was a further surprise to find out just how protective he now felt toward her. The image of himself wearing a suit of polished armor should have made him laugh but it didn't. He was beginning to experience a possessiveness that should have made him uneasy.

When he'd found himself sitting in the car out in front of her apartment, waiting to see who would bring her home, Conn had finally acknowledged that he had a problem, one he hadn't counted on having to handle.

He'd planned on being the one who spun the web; he hadn't anticipated the danger of getting tangled up in the delicate, sticky strands himself. He would never remain objective enough to sort out the truth if he lost control of himself and the situation.

Now, tonight, it seemed very important that he regain control over events and in the process satisfy this dangerous desire that was threatening to undermine his original goals.

Yes, Conn told himself as he felt the trembling response on Honor's lips, that's what he was doing tonight. He was simply regaining control.

Her mouth was soft and warm. He wanted to crush it beneath his own, just as he wanted to crush her body into the embroidered quilt on her bed. The uncertainty in her was turning rapidly into passion. He was holding a woman who wanted him, even if she wasn't sure she ought to want him. Sensing her desire, his own soared.

"It's all right, sweetheart," he breathed as he freed her mouth to taste the warm sweetness at her throat. "Just let go. Just let it happen. I'll be right there with you and I'll take care of everything."

"Conn," she whispered shakily, "I wanted time. I'm not sure of anything right now."

He wrapped his fingers lightly around the nape of her neck and used his thumbs to lift her chin so that she had to meet his eyes. Her gaze was half-drugged with a combination of desire and wariness.

"I'm the man who's there when you need him, re-member?" he reminded her softly. "And you need me tonight. We need each other. I don't make a habit of sitting in front of a woman's apartment waiting to see who will bring her home. I was there for nearly two hours, trying to imagine how I would handle the other guy."

"What... what would you have done if I'd been with someone else?"

He groaned and pulled her fiercely against him. "Don't ask. Finding out you'd been followed by some punk in a pickup truck was even more of a shock, though. I don't like your living alone. It's dangerous."

"Yes, I know." She made the comment into his dark shirt, and Conn knew she meant it to cover him as well as stray hoodlums in black trucks.

"Don't be afraid of me, Honor."

He didn't know how to counter her caution with

words, but Conn did know that he needed to touch her more intimately. The scent of her was tantalizing, beckoning, full of womanly promise.

"I couldn't resist you tonight even if I wanted to try. And the last thing I want to do is try," he grated. He slid his palms down her back to the rounded curve of her hips. She murmured something into his shirt as he pulled her lower body against his own. Conn knew from the way she tensed and then softened that she was now fully aware of his arousal.

"Conn, we should talk..." Her voice trailed off beneath his mouth.

"In the morning," he promised when he released her lips. "We'll talk in the morning. We'll settle everything in the morning."

"Will we?" Her eyes were questioning, luminous pools in which a man could get lost.

"Please trust me tonight, Honor." Was that he pleading for a woman's trust, Conn wondered vaguely. Tomorrow when he was more rational he would probably be shocked at the husky words. But tonight he longed only for an affirmative response.

"Can I trust you, Conn Landry?"

He moved abruptly, lifting her up into his arms. "Yes, you can trust me!" The vow was ground out with a force that amazed him. She seemed to accept the rough promise. Her arms wound around his neck and surrender flickered through her body, making her even warmer and gentler than he had imagined.

Conn left the lights off in her bedroom as he carried her through the door. The pale glow from the hall provided all the illumination he needed. Standing her carefully on her feet he fumbled for the fastenings of her bright-magenta dress. When she leaned against him, her head nestled on his shoulder, he wondered what the hell had happened to his normally coordinated hands. His fingers never trembled like this.

It seemed to take forever before the silky garment obligingly gave way and fell into a frothy heap around her feet.

"Honor," he murmured wonderingly, drawing his hands lightly around her shoulders and down to the curve of her breasts. He touched the lacy edge of her bra, sliding one finger underneath to find the peaking tip of her nipple. "Honor, I want you so much."

She said his name into his shoulder, her nails sinking into the fabric of his shirt. "You make it impossible for me to even think tonight. Why is it like this with you, Conn?"

With a small, impatient gesture he unsnapped the front hook of her bra. His palms slipped over her breasts. "I don't know," he heard himself say with unexpected honesty. "I could ask you the same question. Why do I feel like this with you? I never meant—"

"Never meant what?" She raised her head to look up at him through her lashes.

"Never mind. Don't think about anything other than tonight, sweetheart. Heaven knows you're all I can think about at the moment." He framed her face with his hands and kissed her druggingly, glorying in the vibrant response he received. "Take off my shirt. Let me feel your hands on my body," he ordered thickly.

She obeyed willingly, her fingers shaking faintly as she struggled with the buttons of his shirt. But in a moment she had it off and then she tugged awkwardly with the buckle of his leather belt.

Trying not to hurry, but knowing he could barely

contain his need, Conn finished undressing her. He slid his hands down the length of her, dragging off the satiny underpants and the gossamer panty hose. When she pushed at his snug-fitting jeans, he stepped back and tugged at them himself.

A moment later his jockey shorts fell to his feet and he heard Honor's sharp intake of breath as she saw the evidence of his rising desire.

"I told you I wanted you, sweetheart. Did you doubt me?" he said in a husky voice, aware that he needed some sign of her acceptance of him as a lover. Why it mattered he couldn't have said. He only knew that he wanted her to affirm her desire for him. He wanted her to need him as much as he needed her. "Are you still afraid of me?"

She shook her head, stepping close so that she could feel his excitement pressing hungrily against the smooth skin of her stomach. She cupped him gently with her hands and Conn thought he would lose all control.

"I want you, Conn." There was a mesmerizing sincerity in her throaty voice. "I don't completely understand all of my feelings tonight, but I know I want you."

"Honor, I'll make it good for you, I swear it."

Her mouth curved gently in an age-old smile of feminine promise and provocation. "What if I'm the one who doesn't make it good for you?"

"Little cat," he muttered, determined to kiss the sensual teasing out of her. "You couldn't be anything but perfect for me." He lowered his head and parted her lips with his mouth, forcing his tongue deep inside. Then he shaped her buttocks in his hands, letting his fingers graze tantalizingly over her flesh. When he heard her gasp of anticipation he stroked around to the front of her body and touched her intimately between her thighs.

Honor moaned, and his own pulse beat heavily as he felt the dampening heat of her. When she seemed to lose her balance and collapse lightly against him, Conn knew a primitive sense of masculine satisfaction. Leaning down he yanked back the quilt on her bed and then he lifted Honor and settled her gently into the depths of the bedclothes.

She fell back sensuously, her hair fanning out on the pillow, hazel eyes gleaming up at him through her lashes. "Have you hypnotized me, Conn Landry? It's either that or I must be slightly out of my head tonight."

He felt the fire in his veins as he stood staring down at her. If he'd experienced a feeling of possessiveness earlier it was nothing compared to this inferno leaping through him now.

"I'm glad you're feeling disoriented," he muttered as he came down beside her in a heavy rush. "This is just the way I want you, warm and welcoming and all mine. I don't want you to be able to think straight. Not tonight."

He buried his mouth against the base of her throat, stroking his palm down her stomach to the treasures below. She whispered his name in aching desire and he felt the readiness in her. When she arched her hips against him in silent demand he told himself he'd make her wait a little longer. He wanted her so hot and passionate that she would not be able to imagine living the rest of the night without having him inside her. It was, after all, exactly the way he himself was feeling.

"Tell me about it, Honor, honey. Tell me how much

you want me." He made the demands in a husky tone in between stringing kisses across her breasts.

"So much, Conn, I want you so very much. I've never felt like this." She lifted her hips again, grasping his shoulders to urge him to her.

He pushed one knee between her legs and felt her open immediately for him. The invitation jerked a rough cry of passion from him and he knew he couldn't wait any longer. Conn settled himself between her thighs, aware of her fiery need teasing him.

"Take me inside, sweetheart. I have to be inside you or I'll go crazy!" He moved his hand down to touch the folds of exquisitely sensitive feminine flesh, assuring himself once again that she was ready. She murmured in passionate response.

"Please, Conn. Please, *now!*"

He couldn't hold back any longer. Catching her shoulders, he thrust deeply, embedding himself in her pulsating, clinging warmth. He felt the shudder go through her as her body adjusted to the masculine invasion. Instantly he stopped.

"Honor?"

She didn't open her eyes but her legs moved slowly to wrap his lean hips. He felt her nails in his back and the small pain sent another ripple of excitement through him.

"Love me, Conn. Please make love to me."

"Honor, I couldn't do anything else!" He began to move within her, feeling her body growing increasingly tense around him.

"Conn, *Conn!*"

He sensed the uncertainty in the breathless way she called his name and dimly realized she wasn't quite sure of what was happening to her body.

"Let go, sweetheart," he rasped against her breast. "Just let go. I'll catch you."

She cried out as the heightening tension suddenly unleashed itself in one shattering conclusion. Conn lifted his head to cover her mouth, drinking the passionate sounds she made far back in her throat, and then he felt his body arching heavily as it sought its own release.

For long, timeless seconds he rode the storm with the woman in his arms, holding on to her more tightly than he'd ever held on to anything or anyone in his life.

Honor came slowly out of the hazy world into which she had drifted. She was aware of Conn's heavy frame sprawled along hers, felt the weight of his thigh chaining her leg. She was still wrapped securely in his arms, and the knowledge filled her with deep pleasure. Languidly she toyed with the silver-shot blackness of his hair, studying the dark lashes that were the only hint of softness in his face. Then he opened his eyes.

Like a cat, he was fully alert instantly, no hint of sleepiness or sensual lethargy in his gaze. But there was a strong element of satisfaction there, Honor realized—sure, arrogant, masculine satisfaction. She found it somewhat amusing until he spoke.

"No more nights like tonight," he said bluntly.

"No? You didn't enjoy tonight?" she teased lightly, knowing he couldn't possibly be referring to what had just happened between them.

Conn shook his head once, impatiently, and then lifted himself off her body with obvious reluctance. "I meant no more nights where I sit in front of your apartment and wait to see who's bringing you home." He cradled her possessively in the crook of his arm. The musky scent of him filled her nostrils as she burrowed willingly against his shoulder.

"How many more nights will there be to worry about, Conn? Soon you'll be going back to Tahoe and you won't be terribly interested in how I spend my evenings."

The wave of unhappiness that washed over her as she listened to her own words occupied her for several seconds. Then she noticed in astonishment that Conn had gone dangerously still.

"Who told you about Tahoe?" he asked, his voice low and harsh.

Honor stirred uneasily. "Ethan said something about your having business interests there." She turned her head to meet his eyes.

"That's all I have there. I don't make my home in Tahoe," he said in clipped tones. "I just own some real estate there."

"I see." Honor wasn't certain what to say next. Clearly he didn't want to talk about Tahoe or where he actually did live. And she didn't want to spoil the magic intimacy of the moment. There would be time enough in the morning for discovering all the facts that mattered. "It's all right, Conn. I didn't mean to pry. And you don't owe me any promises or commitments. I understand that."

The information didn't seem to please him. "The hell I don't," he growled, twisting to pin her gently back against the pillow. "Honor, you and I are bound together now. Don't you understand that? You just gave yourself to me."

"Do you realize what you're saying, Conn?" she asked carefully, afraid to let herself hope for too much from him.

"I know exactly what I'm saying," he told her even-ly. "I couldn't walk away from what we've started. And I won't let you walk, either."

She smiled tremulously. "Do I look as though I'm trying to get away?"

"You tried to avoid me this evening," he pointed out gruffly. He sounded as if the fact had hurt him in some fashion.

Her fingers moved in delicate patterns on his broad shoulders. Unintimidated by the harsh lines of his face, she looked up at him with the soft eyes of a woman who knows she's falling in love.

"That was earlier. This is now," she explained as if it were obvious.

"You're not frightened of me any longer?"

"I don't think I was ever really scared, just wary," she said dismissingly.

"And you're not still wary?" he pressed.

"Should I be?" she countered lightly, not under-standing why he was so insistent.

"No," he rasped, lowering his mouth once more to hers. "There's no need any longer."

A part of her wanted to ask what that meant, but he was already restoking the fires it seemed only he could ignite. Honor felt the throbbing intensity in him and had no wish to resist.

The commitment between them was new and un-tried, fragile and unexplored, but it had been estab-lished. Conn was right. Neither of them could walk away from it now.

Hours later Honor came slowly awake, aware that the man beside her was not asleep. She snuggled against his side.

"Conn? Is something wrong? Can't you sleep?"

"I'm just doing some thinking, honey."

"What about?"

"About that pickup truck that followed you home tonight. Among other things." The last three words were tacked on in an almost inaudible tone.

"What about the truck?" she pressed, yawning.

"I don't like the fact that somebody tried to get at you tonight."

She frowned slightly in the darkness. "You don't suppose there's a chance Granger sent someone after me?"

Conn shook his head once. "No, he'd have no reason to go after you. It would be your sister he'd try to terrorize and she—" He broke off as Honor suddenly sat bolt upright.

"My sister! Conn, what if he's going to do something to Adena?"

Conn reached up to pull her down. "Relax. As I was about to say, she's paid her debt. Granger wouldn't go after her now."

"You sound awfully sure of that."

"I am sure."

For some reason Honor believed him. The quiet strength in his words spoke volumes. She relaxed. "Then the incident tonight was just another crazy Southern California event."

"Unless you add it to that business of your screen being moved the other night," he said thoughtfully.

Honor was silent for a moment. "I'm sure that was just a mistake on my part."

"Positive?"

Lying there in the darkness with Conn's easy, masculine strength to cling to, it was easy to be positive. Honor nibbled invitingly at his lower lip.

"Positive."

Honor awoke early the next morning with the feeling that her whole life had changed overnight. When she turned her head to gaze down on Conn's magnificently sprawled form, she knew the intuition was right. Even if he walked out on her today her life would never be quite the same because she would never be able to put him completely out of her head.

His body was lean and tan against the tangled white sheets. The intriguing darkness of his hair on the pillow made Honor want to reach out and run her fingers through it as she had last night.

Weren't harsh-faced men supposed to appear more relaxed and even gentler in sleep, she wondered idly as she studied the grim planes and angles of his face. If that was true, Conn didn't fit the mold. His strength and determination were too much a part of him to disappear temporarily while he slept. In the fresh light of a sunny morning he still looked like the kind of man only a fool would want for an enemy, the kind of man a woman would not risk pushing too far.

The realization sent a wave of restlessness through her that drove Honor out of bed. Barefoot, she padded into the black-and-white-tiled bath. The full-length mirror threw her nude image back at her, revealing a mussed halo of golden-brown hair and eyes that reflected a deep, feminine wonder.

Conn had made love to her last night in the most satisfying way possible. He had not played sophisticated games, trying to dazzle her with technique and style. Instead he had lost himself in her, at the same time possessing her completely.

Admittedly her experience was limited, but Honor

instinctively knew that the kind of passion she had experienced last night could not be a common thing.

Stepping into the shower, she let her pleasantly sore body soak beneath the hot spray. Every time she moved today she was going to be reminded of Conn's elemental style of lovemaking, she thought wryly.

She heard the bathroom door open and close. A moment later Conn appeared on the other side of the glass shower door, smiling lazily. One thing had changed about him, Honor realized suddenly. The smile was a full-fledged one this morning, not that strange, grim twist of his mouth with which she had become so familiar. That knowledge pleased her deeply.

He opened the shower and stepped inside, reaching for her. "Mmmm," he murmured through a long, luxurious kiss, "you taste good in the morning."

"Considering the amount of goat cheese I sampled last night, that's saying something." She grinned, winding her arms around his neck.

"I consider it a part of the earthy side of your nature." He slicked his hands down her wet body to her hips, squeezing gently.

"I'm a Southern Californian. I'm not supposed to have an earthy side to my nature. I'm supposed to be all gloss and cutting-edge glitter," she complained.

"Then you're a failure as a Southern Californian. But I knew that the moment I met you."

She tilted her head. "You did?"

To her surprise he gave her a sober, intent look. "The last thing you are is superficial, Honor. Even if your apartment does resemble a picture in a design magazine. I knew when I realized why you were going to confront Granger that you had guts. And your enthusiasm for Legacy's big win the other day was genuine, even though you only had two dollars on him. Last night you gave yourself completely to me. No games. I could list a lot of other reasons why I know you aren't the kind who flits along on the surface of life."

"But?" she prompted, a little shaken by his blunt observations and determined to lighten the atmosphere a little.

"But all my glowing compliments would probably go to your head and spoil the basic sweetness of your nature." He chuckled, slapping her affectionately on the rear and turning to pick up the soap.

"Beast. I was just getting to like the compliments. I'd rather hear them than listen to you yelling at me for daring to have another engagement last night."

"I didn't yell at you." He stuck his head under the full force of the water, eyes closed. "I simply explained a few facts of life."

She went still as she listened to the possessiveness in his voice. "Conn?"

"Hmmm?"

"It works both ways, you know."

He pulled his head out from under the shower and opened his eyes. He looked down at her searchingly. "Both ways?"

"I won't be involved in a one-sided relationship," she said with quiet insistence. "I have to know that you'll live by the same rules you're imposing on me."

"You think I won't?" There was soft challenge in the words.

Honor studied him for a moment longer, thinking over what she knew of this man. It wasn't all that much in some respects. Yet a part of her longed to trust him implicitly. "I think you will." She finally smiled tremulously. Hadn't she sensed from the start that he was a man who lived by a code? He kept the scales balanced.

Conn moved, wrapping her close against his warm, wet chest. "Does that mean you trust me, finally?"

Her fingers splayed through the damp, curling hair that covered him in a sexy pelt. "Yes."

"Thank you, Honor. I'm glad," he said simply.

So am I, she thought, *because I'm in love with you.*

An hour later Honor was slicing papaya and sprinkling it with lime while Conn made coffee. The doorbell chimed just as she was putting the fresh fruit on the table. Wiping her hands on a red kitchen towel, Honor went to answer it.

"Adena!" she exclaimed. "What are you doing here?"

"Just dropped by on my way to work to see if I could borrow that great chunky leather belt you bought the other day. Hey, is that an extra slice of papaya? Great, I didn't have time for breakfast this morning."

With her usual impulsive approach to everything, Adena whipped around the edge of the door and came to a halt, staring at Conn. Conn stared back, politely examining the flashy little gamine in front of him.

Adena's bright blond hair was cut in an eye-catching wedge that framed her outrageously made-up hazel eyes. While Honor's tastes in clothing were stylish, her sister's were definitely trendy. A less charitable observer might have termed them outrageous. This morning Adena was wearing knee-high cavalry boots, tight-fitting red pants and a huge, boxy, loosely woven cropped top. She carried it off with her usual enthusiastic panache.

"Good grief," Adena said in obvious astonishment, "who are you? Honor *never* has men stay for breakfast."

"I insisted, I'm afraid. You're Adena?"

"That's right." Adena swung around with a grin. "Where did you dig him up, Honor? He's much more interesting than those designer types you usually hang out with. Good grief! This one's not even wearing mauve!"

"This is Constantine Landry," Honor said very firmly. She could feel the faint flush on her cheeks as her inquisitive sister began to pry for information. "I believe I mentioned him," she continued sardonically.

"Landry! The guy who handled Granger for me. Of course." Adena almost pounced on a somewhat startled Conn. "You're an absolute jewel, you know." She kissed him noisily before he realized what was happening and then she released him to leap for the coffeepot. "Can't tell you how much I appreciate your help. Took a terrible load off my mind. Granger gives me the creeps. And if I was worried, that's nothing to what poor Honor felt!" Adena shivered theatrically as she helped herself to coffee.

"Then I trust you will stay away from him and others like him in the future. I don't expect to have to handle that kind of situation again, and if I find out you've tried to coerce Honor into doing it for you, I will be very displeased," Conn said flatly as he picked up the coffeepot and set it down on the table.

Honor heard the cold, lecturing tone and saw that Adena had heard it, too. Her volatile sister was not accustomed to having men lecture her.

"Hey, what's with the big brother attitude?" Adena demanded, plunking herself down at the table. "It's too early in the morning for that sort of thing. Any more papaya, Honor?"

"There's another one in the refrigerator, if you want to cut it."

"Too much work. I'll share yours." Adena leaned forward to scoop out a sizable chunk of the deliciously colored fruit.

Stifling a sigh of resignation, Honor quickly began to eat the rest of the papaya, knowing that if she didn't she would lose most of it to Adena.

"I'm not your brother, big or otherwise," Conn pointed out grimly. "My only interest is in your sister. I will therefore hold you responsible for anything you do that gets her into a difficult situation. Do I make myself clear?"

"Conn, there's no need to come down on her like a ton of bricks," Honor said a bit stiffly as she saw the uncomprehending expression on Adena's face. "It was all a mistake and Adena knows it. She won't be getting into that kind of trouble again, will you, Adena?"

"Golly, I feel as if I'm sitting in the middle of a scene from 'Father Knows Best.' Doesn't it strike either of you that it's too nice a morning for lectures?" Adena complained.

"What kind of a morning was it the day you first started borrowing from Granger?" Conn calmly ate his papaya, oblivious of Honor's frowning glance.

"I get the point," Adena said disgustedly, shooting to her feet with lively grace. "If you'll excuse me I think I'll be on my way. Something about the atmosphere around here is depressing. How about that belt, Honor? Okay if I take it?"

"Help yourself," Honor agreed, as she nearly always did. "Oh, and Adena...?"

"What?" Adena was halfway down the hall.

"Are you sure you weren't in here the other evening?"

"Positive. I went with Gary to see that new slasher

movie I told you about." She disappeared into the bedroom and reappeared a moment later carrying the prized belt. "My goodness, you two certainly did something energetic on that bed. Well, see you guys later." She was gone before either Conn or Honor could respond.

For a moment after the whirlwind left, silence hung over the table. Then Conn said very thoughtfully, "I can see that she's been something of a handful for you. Your mother...?"

"My mother remarried a few years ago and moved to the East Coast. Adena wanted to stay out here with me. There are times when I'm afraid I may not have handled her all that well, but she's basically a good person."

"Perhaps," Conn suggested carefully, "she needed a firmer hand while she was growing up."

"She was only eight when Dad was killed." Honor tried to put a lot of finality into the sentence.

"How old were you?"

"Thirteen. Conn, I don't really like to talk about the past," she explained quietly.

He stared at her for a moment. "You can't pretend it doesn't exist."

"I don't pretend it doesn't exist," she said coolly. "I just prefer not to discuss it. The circumstances surrounding my father's death were, well, traumatic for all of us. It nearly devastated me. Thirteen-year-olds tend to take things very seriously, I'm afraid."

"What happened, Honor?"

She looked at him over the rim of her coffee cup. "Why do you want to know?"

"Because I want to know everything about you."

Honor closed her eyes. "Believe me, you don't want to know about that aspect of my life."

"Yes, I do," he countered in a soft but steely voice. "And I won't stop asking until I get all the answers."

She slammed her cup down into the saucer, growing annoyed with his insistence. "All right, I'll tell you. I'm the daughter of a man who was killed, along with his partner, while running an illegal shipment of guns into the Middle East. Does that answer your question? It was tacky, embarrassing and traumatic. The papers had a field day with it. They called my father a traitor and a criminal. The general implication was that in the end he got what he deserved."

"Along with his partner," Conn said slowly.

"If you want my opinion," Honor said bitterly, "I've always thought that the real criminal probably was his partner. I'll bet my father caught him with the shipment and his good buddy pulled a gun. In the end they both died. My father was apparently armed, too." Honor swallowed some of her childhood anger. "They were supposed to be respectable oil executives." She sighed.

Conn's eyes narrowed and the fingers around the handle of his coffee cup tightened as he regarded her tense face. "You've always assumed that your father's partner was the guilty one?"

"No one will ever know. The authorities said they were both in on the gunrunning." Honor shook her head, striving to return to normal. "And I guess it no longer really matters, does it? It was all a long time ago."

"Some people aren't satisfied until they've tied up all the loose ends," Conn Landry said so softly that Honor wasn't certain she'd heard him.

Her head came up quickly as she scanned his face with her growing knowledge of him. "You're one of those people, aren't you?" she hazarded. "The kind who ties up loose ends. You like things balanced."

"Yes."

Honor absorbed the loaded sound of the single affirmative word. It had all the impact of a poised knife. Constantine Landry was being honest, straightforward and utterly truthful, she decided. He wasn't telling her anything she hadn't already guessed, but by reinforcing the knowledge he reinforced the sensation she had of danger hovering like an aura around him.

Memories of the night tangled in her mind with the trickle of unease Conn seemed to generate in her. Adena had been right in saying this man was unlike the other men in Honor's world. Honor reflected for a moment on the wisdom of terminating the relationship and knew in her heart of hearts that she would not be able to do it. Not yet. Conn had claimed there was a bond between them now and a part of Honor recognized it. There was a hunger in her to follow the dangerous path that might lead past Conn Landry's emotional barriers. For a few minutes last night she had been allowed through the gates. She wanted more opportunities to discover the man behind the seemingly impervious walls of cool control.

Honor made a decision in the warm light of a new day. She would take the risks inherent in becoming involved with Constantine Landry. She had no real choice.

Chapter Five

It couldn't be love, Honor told herself at least fifteen times several days later on a Friday as she worked on some space-planning arrangements in her office. She'd only known the man for approximately two weeks, and if she were truthful with herself she actually knew very little about him.

But Conn was making a habit of staying for breakfast, and she realized she wanted him at her table tomorrow morning, too.

Idly she pushed around the little cutouts that represented various sizes and shapes of office furniture, but it was hard to keep her mind on the floor plan in front of her. All she could think about was the fragile new relationship she had begun with Constantine Landry.

It shouldn't be love, not so soon and not when there were so many unanswered questions, but she was very much afraid that it was. She'd never felt so vulnerable before in her life. Only love left a woman of twenty-eight feeling so precariously poised on the brink. Why was she fighting it, she wondered.

But she knew the answer. Conn Landry didn't fit any mental image or preconceptions she'd had about the man to whom she would one day give herself so completely. His background was still exceedingly vague, for example. He'd alluded briefly to various investments and mentioned that he'd spent a great deal of time overseas until two years ago. Something to do with being a go-between for corporations. Whatever that meant. And he'd told her he lived in the San Francisco area.

Honor sighed and reached for another cutout of a table that could be used for large meetings. It was oval and would be far more interesting in the office space she was designing than the square one she'd been trying. She could see it now in rich gray slate on a black steel pedestal. It would give an impression of solid reliability to the clients of the securities brokerage house for which she was doing the design.

When you got right down to it, Honor told herself, what she knew about Conn revolved around impressions of him as a man rather than knowledge of the realities of his life. As a man he appealed to her senses on every level. She knew it was far more than a physical attraction. It had been from the first, even when she'd been so wary of him.

Some of her initial caution still existed, she had to admit, but she had shoved it far to the back of her thoughts. Instead she now focused on ways of gently penetrating the emotionally controlled exterior that surrounded Conn. So far her only real success in that area seemed to take place in bed. Honor grimaced ruefully. She didn't like the idea that the only way she could really reach him was with sex.

Honor glanced up from her desk as the front door opened. Ethan Bailey smiled genially as he stepped inside the sleekly furnished room. He glanced around with interest.

"This is right nice," he observed, touching the finely-grained beige leather of a chrome-and-leather chair. "Is that real marble?" He indicated her desk top.

"Absolutely." She smiled, motioning him to one of the chrome-and-leather chairs. "Nothing like a sheet of black marble to impress potential clients. What can I do for you, Ethan? Don't tell me you need some design work!"

He chuckled, lounging back comfortably in the chair. His hand-tooled boots were revealed as he extended his legs and steepled his fingers. "To tell you the truth, I hadn't thought much about it until now." He glanced around at some of the photos on the walls. "Looks to me like you know your business. I like that one there."

Honor followed the direction of his glance. "Ah, my one shot at the Southwestern look. I can see why that would appeal to you." She smiled at him. "What on earth made you decide to stop by and see me, Ethan? I would think you'd be out at Santa Anita."

"Already watched the morning workouts," he said easily. "Conn was there, too."

She nodded composedly. "Yes, he said he wanted to discuss Legacy's future with Toby Humphrey."

"Well," Ethan said as if he weren't quite certain how to continue. "He did. He also talked a bit about Legacy's past."

Honor's gaze was quizzical. "Is something wrong, Ethan?" she finally asked gently.

The older man shifted uncomfortably. "To tell you the truth, I don't rightly know. But I've been around a long time, Miss Mayfield. Maybe too long. A man can get cynical in his sunset years."

"You're hardly in your sunset years. I don't think you'll be the type to ever hit them." Honor grinned.

He returned her smile but there was a measure of seriousness in his normally cheerful eyes. "Honor, I wonder if I could speak quite frankly."

"Of course."

"What I'm going to say is probably none of my business. But I feel obliged to say it, anyway. You're such a nice young lady. And seeing you off and on with Conn at the track I've come to think of you as a friend."

A trickle of warning went down Honor's spine. "What's wrong, Ethan? Why are you here?"

He sighed, glancing up at the photo of the Southwestern-style office. "Your last name is Mayfield."

She blinked in astonishment. "Well, yes."

"Conn said this morning that your father had once owned Legacy's sire, an animal called Stylish Legacy."

"That's right."

Ethan closed his eyes briefly and when he opened them his gaze was very level. "Your father's full name would have been Nick Mayfield?"

The warning sensation was stronger now. "Did you know him, Ethan?"

The older man shook his head. "I've been in racing a long time, Honor. It's kind of a small world. When I heard your last name was Mayfield, I just brushed the whole thing off as a coincidence. After all, it's been a long time..."

"It's been fifteen years since my father died, if that's what you're trying to say."

Ethan cleared his throat. "Not exactly. That is, I remember the newspapers really played it up big."

"Yes." The residual anger of a helpless thirteen-year-old girl still simmered. "Everyone seems rather interested in ancient history these days. Did you know my father?"

"Not well. But I was certainly aware of the horse he owned. Stylish Legacy was the most promising colt on the West Coast fifteen years ago. Since he was sold to that syndicate he's lived up to that promise. Legacy cost Conn a fair-sized fortune."

"Ethan, I still don't understand what you're trying to say."

"I'm making a mess of this," he grumbled. "Honor, this is real tough on me. Lord knows I don't want to get involved in anything personal between you and Conn, but I don't want to see you hurt, either. Conn, well, he can take care of himself, but you're just a little thing and you don't know what's going on behind the scenes. I didn't know myself, or rather, I didn't want to admit I knew until this morning when Conn mentioned that your father was the Mayfield that had owned Stylish Legacy."

"Please get to the point, Ethan," Honor said tensely. "It's obvious you're trying to tell me something."

He inhaled deeply. "Honor, you probably know your dad had a partner."

"I'm aware of it."

"The man the newspapers said was with him in that nasty business in the Middle East," Ethan went on doggedly. "Do you remember that man's name?"

"Vaguely. I think it began with an S. Stone or Stanton or something. Why?" Honor realized she was tapping the tip of a pencil against her floor plans and leaving small black marks. Annoyed, she forced her hand to remain still.

"His name was Stoner. Richard Stoner," Ethan said flatly.

"So? I'm afraid I don't understand where all this is leading."

"All right. I don't know how else to give this to you except straight. Landry is Conn's middle name. He's used it for years because he was working overseas for a lot of fancy corporations that might have been nervous about dealing with Richard Stoner's son."

The pencil in Honor's hand snapped in two. Blindly she stared down at the broken halves. Slowly she raised her head to meet Ethan's unhappy expression. "Conn Landry is the son of my father's partner?" she whispered uncomprehendingly. "But why didn't he tell me?"

Ethan leaned forward anxiously. "Honor, you were only a kid when your father and Stoner killed each other during that quarrel. Conn was twenty-three, just out of college and starting his first job with the oil company for which his dad and your father had worked. Leastways, that's what I recall. The scandal hit him pretty hard, I gather. It's not something he talks about, but I heard rumors around the track when the story hit the papers. Racing people talk. Too much sometimes."

"Racetrack rumors," Honor echoed huskily.

"They said—" Ethan halted abruptly, as if searching for the right words and then tried again. "They said Conn was convinced your father had betrayed his. People said he swore vengeance on your family fifteen years ago."

"Vengeance!" A man who liked to tie up loose ends. A man who kept the books balanced. The words went through her head in staccato fashion.

"It's the kind of thing an angry, hurt twenty-three-year-old man would say," Ethan pointed out gently.

"The kind of thing a twenty-three-year-old Conn Landry would say, I suppose," Honor said bleakly.

Ethan was silent for a moment before continuing.

"Fifteen years have gone by. I expect most everyone's forgotten now. I hadn't thought of the story in ages. When Landry bought Legacy and his horse and mine wound up in Humphrey's training stables, somebody remembered that Richard Stoner had had a son who used the name Landry. I kept my questions to myself. Didn't seem like any of my business, after all. Not until you showed up in the picture."

"I see." Honor's eyes narrowed. "And then you started wondering?"

He nodded forlornly. "It was the coincidence of the whole thing that worried me. It didn't seem strange that Conn might have returned to the States after several years and decided to buy a colt sired by the stallion his father had once owned. But when he picked you up at Santa Anita the other day, I started remembering all those stories about how he'd vowed to make your family pay for what your father did to his."

"My father didn't do anything to Richard Stoner! Certainly he didn't betray him," Honor hissed, the old anger welling higher within her. "I always thought there was a damn good chance that Stoner was the one who was smuggling weapons and that my father had the bad luck to discover him doing it."

Ethan held up his hands in a placating gesture. "Please, Honor. I don't know anything more about that end of things than anyone else who was reading the papers at the time. From what little I knew of your father personally, I have to say he always seemed a decent man. He never spent much time around the track, so I really didn't get too well acquainted, but I was under the impression that folks respected him."

"Really?" There was a scathing tone in her voice as Honor remembered the humiliation that her mother had been forced to endure as so-called friends turned their backs on her after the scandal hit the papers. The fact that her mother had been filing for divorce hadn't lessened the humiliation Mrs. Mayfield had to handle. And nothing could have mitigated the pain Honor had gone through.

"I knew I shouldn't have come here today," Ethan growled in embarrassment. "But I just couldn't stand by and not tell you who Landry really was. You have to make your own decision about the man, but I thought you ought to know that his interest in you might be based on something besides...besides..."

"I think you're trying to tell me that he might have some motivation other than love at first sight," Honor observed coolly.

Ethan stared at her for a moment. "I tried to tell you that the other day. Men like Conn Landry don't know much about love, Honor. But that was just an old man trying to pass along a little advice to a young woman who was in danger of getting swept off her feet. I knew then that you weren't his usual kind of date. But I also figured you were old enough to make your own judgments. This morning, though, when Landry mentioned your father as having been the Mayfield who owned Stylish Legacy, I got rather worried."

"Why would Conn bring up the subject?"

Ethan shrugged. "I don't know. He doesn't realize I know who he is. I suppose he didn't think I'd make any connection. Or maybe he wouldn't care if I did."

"You've never told him you're aware he's Richard Stoner's son?" she asked in amazement.

Ethan's mouth firmed. "You have to understand how it is in the racing world, Honor," he said gently. "For the most part a man's past is his own business. As long as he's honorable in his dealings, sees to it that his horses are well cared for, tips his jockeys properly when they win, no one really questions his past. At least they wouldn't do so to his face. People around the track might gossip about it, but that's as far as it goes. A fellow owner wouldn't dream of confronting another owner and demanding explanations. Our only association is through racing. I don't generally pry into matters that don't concern me.''

Poor Ethan, Honor thought distractedly. He was very upset at having taken on the responsibility of warning her. She could see he was already regretting his involvement.

Her own mood was precarious, she realized. In all honesty, Honor wasn't sure how she felt as she absorbed the implications of the news of Landry's identity.

But it explained so many things, she thought grimly. Looking back over the past several days she began to see the pattern of his actions, and it was almost frightening. He had kept her from getting involved in the trap meant for Granger. Then he'd handled the business of Adena's debts to the man so that Honor wouldn't have to deal with him. It was after that that Honor had begun to experience the odd sensation of being in Conn Landry's debt. Conn had done nothing to ease that sensation.

Then there had been that incident the other night when his presence had scared off the punk in the pickup truck. Following that, Conn had made fiercely passionate love to her, placing bonds on her that chained her senses.

Honor was appalled, seeing herself as a small female animal that had been neatly driven into a strange sort of trap. What was Conn Landry Stoner planning on doing next, she wondered in frozen pain. What was the point of the trap?

"I suppose I ought to thank you for telling me all this," she managed distantly.

"Not hardly!" Ethan exploded in self-disgust. "If I were you'd I'd kick me out of this office. I probably had no business coming to see you about all this. But I swear, Honor, I just didn't know quite what to do. If you'd been anyone else except the daughter of the man Conn blamed for betraying his father, I wouldn't have opened my mouth any more than I did the other morning when you started asking questions about his, uh, investments. I figured I'd overstepped myself then. Now I've really put a foot in it, haven't I?"

"I know you meant well, Ethan."

"Meant well! Hell, Landry's a friend of mine. I felt torn apart, not knowing which way my duty lay. Heaven knows what he'll say when he finds out I'm the one who told you who he really is." Ethan sighed.

"He couldn't have expected to keep it a secret forever," she pointed out.

"That's true," Ethan agreed. "But what if I've got this all botched up? What if it's all perfectly innocent? A genuine coincidence? He meets you by accident at Santa Anita, takes to you and decides to keep his identity quiet because he knows you might be nervous about seeing him if you know who he really is."

"Do you believe that, Ethan?" she asked soberly.

"I might. If it weren't for one thing," Ethan admitted slowly.

She frowned. "What's that?"

"That business about Granger being about to walk into a police trap the other day?"

"What about it?"

"Well, I got to thinking about it. I hadn't heard any rumors about that ambush. So I checked with some folks I know. Granger wasn't arrested that day, Honor. Best anyone can figure out, he didn't walk into a police setup. He wasn't set free on bail, either. Just been running around loose as usual."

TWO HOURS AFTER Ethan Bailey had left her office, Honor finally accepted the fact that she wasn't going to get any productive work done that day. She locked her door and walked out onto the busy thoroughfare that fronted the building in which her office was located. It was another of the days for which Southern California was famous: temperatures in the mid-seventies and reasonably clear of smog. A good day to go the beach, she thought. The water would still be uncomfortably cold for anyone except surfers, but it would be pleasant to take off her shoes and walk in the sand.

This wasn't the first time since Ethan had left that she had thought of the beach and of the cottage her father had bequeathed to her. She rarely used the house, as she had told her friend the other evening at the party. But quite suddenly she had begun to see it as a place to which she could escape. Honor had a strong need to lick some very raw wounds and she wanted to do so in private.

How did one confront the Conn Landrys of this world and demand explanations, she asked herself as she sat down at a table in an outdoor café. The menu wouldn't come into focus long enough for her to concentrate on the special of the day, so she ordered her usual avocado-and-sprouts sandwich. When it arrived she barely tasted it.

Her fingers trembled as she sat beneath the huge umbrella that shaded her table and tried to picture Conn's face. Such a harshly carved face, with eyes that reminded her of the color of a lethal weapon.

Dangerous. She had known from the beginning that he was dangerous. He had told her he was a man who kept the score even. But she'd had no way of knowing then that he had a score to settle with her family.

Honor didn't finish the sandwich. She paid for it and walked to the parking lot where her Fiat waited. Slowly she drove home, her mind in a turmoil. By the time Ethan Bailey had left she was feeling sorry for the older man. It was obvious he had been in a terrible quandary about whether to come to her with his information. Now he was no doubt consumed with guilt for having warned her about a man he considered a friend.

Looking back, Honor was sickened by the easy way she had allowed Conn Landry to get close to her. What a fool she had been to fall in love with a man who was driven by some twisted notion of revenge.

Assuming, of course, that revenge really did lie behind his actions, Honor reminded herself without a great deal of hope. She knew the odds were against it all being some horrendous coincidence, and there was that business of Conn's having lied about Granger. But what if there was some viable explanation for everything, she asked herself over and over again as she parked her car in front of her apartment.

The only thing she could do was confront Conn and ask him. She had to know the truth and she had to hear it from him. Nothing else was going to kill the love that had begun to grow within her.

It was impossible to concentrate on anything that afternoon as she waited for Conn. He had said that morning that he would be at her door at six this evening. As the day dragged on Honor realized how much she was beginning to cling to the hope that he would have explanations for everything.

It was ridiculous to allow herself that hope. She was setting herself up for a fall. But there was no real alternative. Nothing would convince her completely that she had been manipulated for some bizarre reason of revenge until she heard the damning words from Conn himself. The catch, of course, was that in all probability he would simply lie to her.

"Surely I'll know if he's lying. We've become so close in the past few days," she said half under her breath as she paced the white carpet. Another illusion. What made her think she would know if he was telling her the truth, she thought. After all, if everything had been a lie until now and she had believed it, there was no reason things would be any different tonight.

Close. That was another illusion. The only true closeness they had achieved had been in bed, and for all she knew, that feeling had been entirely one-sided. There was no reason to believe their mutual passion had been more than a good toss in the hay from his point of view.

Pausing by the window, Honor stared sightlessly out at the palm tree and wondered what kind of revenge Conn Landry Stoner would go after from a woman. She wasn't wealthy. She wasn't married, so there was no relationship for him to spoil with insinuations or threats. She had inherited nothing from the partnership formed by their respective fathers, so there was nothing of value to demand from her, at least nothing she knew of except that beach cottage up the coast. As far as Honor knew, it had belonged only to her father It had never been a part of the partnership. Stylish Legacy, the most valuable remainder of that business arrangement, had long since been sold and the profits evenly split between Nick Mayfield's widow and whoever had inherited Richard Stoner's estate.

But there was no denying that some way, somehow, Conn would want to even the score. She had to accept the fact that he seemed to have chosen her as the one who would pay for that betrayal fifteen years in the past.

The old resentment washed through her. As a young girl who had loved her father, she would never have been willing to believe that he had betrayed his friend. The evidence of that bloody night was fated to be forever vague and uncertain. The killings had taken place in a far-off land, and those who had been in charge of the investigation had been more concerned with dealing with the embarrassment the incident had caused a huge oil corporation than with getting at the truth. The main goal of the company for which Richard Stoner and Nick Mayfield worked had been to hush up the whole mess. Both men had been working for the company until just prior to the discovery of the gunrunning. Stoner and Mayfield had formed their own firm, but still had ties and contacts in the larger corporation they had just left. The huge conglomerate had its image to consider.

By rights, Honor told herself violently, she had as much reason to want revenge as Constantine Landry Stoner. She ought to be thinking of a way to turn the tables.

But all she could think of this afternoon was how she had fallen in love with a man who apparently wanted only vengeance.

Honor was in a pair of old jeans and an emerald-green dolman-sleeved top when she went to answer the door at six o'clock. She had pulled her hair back into a stict knot at the nape of her neck. It must have been obvious immediately that she was not dressed for an evening out. Conn took one look at her unsmiling face and stepped inside.

"I take it we're staying in this evening?" he said coolly as he shrugged out of his impeccably tailored dark linen jacket.

"I think we need to talk, Conn." Honor was remotely pleased that her voice was calm. She watched him toss the jacket over a chair and marveled at his easy familiarity with her apartment. He hadn't hesitated to move right in on her private space, she realized.

He slanted her an assessing glance and sank easily into a chair. "Something wrong, Honor?"

She drew in a deep breath and walked back to the window to stare into the darkness. "That's what I want to ask you, Conn."

"You're the one who's being cryptic now."

She heard the hard-edged caution in him and wondered at it. He knew enough about her to realize that matters were serious, she thought bleakly.

"You never bothered to mention that your last name was Stoner," she said quietly.

There was a second of dead silence behind her. Honor was almost afraid to move.

"Stoner never has been my last name."

Startled, the wild hope leaping up within her in spite of her efforts to quell it, Honor spun around. "You're not Richard Stoner's son?"

"I'm his son."

Hope died. "I see."

"In all the ways that count, Richard Stoner was my father. I was twelve years old when my mother married him. My biological father was killed when I was a baby, but she never wanted me to deny his existence. Stoner agreed with her, so there was never a formal adoption. But I grew up thinking Richard Stoner was the kind of man I wanted to become."

Honor stared at the granite-hard expression on the face of the man she loved and knew there was no more reason to hope. Some perverse element in her nature insisted on spelling it all out, however, and she found herself asking the next question.

"You knew who I was before you met me?"

He leaned his head back in the chair, watching her through narrowed eyes. "You've been busy today."

"Just answer the question," she pleaded.

"I knew. I've known for several months."

She closed her eyes briefly and turned back to the window, her hands clasped tightly in front of her. "Other than making me feel like a fool, what did you plan to accomplish, Conn?" she asked steadily.

He came up out of the chair without making a sound. Honor didn't know he was so close until he spoke from only inches behind her. "The flat truth is that I didn't really know what I wanted from you in the beginning. I only knew there was something to be settled between my family and yours."

"You wanted revenge. You believe my father betrayed yours," she whispered starkly.

"The official investigation of what happened that night concluded there had been a quarrel between partners, that Nick Mayfield had planned to kill my father and finalize the sale of the guns himself. Something went wrong. Richard Stoner had managed to get off a couple of shots before he died and neither man came out of it alive. Personally, I think my father discovered yours was using his cover as a respected executive to smuggle those arms shipments and confronted him."

"And in the ensuing fight, they killed each other," Honor finished distantly.

"Something like that."

"Either way, you're convinced my father was guilty of betraying yours."

"I've had no reason to think otherwise for fifteen years," Conn said levelly. "I knew Richard Stoner well. He wouldn't have been involved in anything like gun-running."

"My God," she breathed. "Fifteen years. Fifteen years of plotting your revenge. It must have eaten away your soul."

She sensed a slight movement, and then his fingers touched her shoulder. Honor froze.

"It wasn't like that, Honor. If it had been, I would have done something drastic long ago. Are you willing to listen to me tonight?"

"I don't have much choice."

"No," he agreed grimly, "you don't. You're the one who brought up the subject."

She wished he would take his hand off her shoulder. His touch made her want to turn around, bury her face against his chest and cry out all the anger and pain. "How long would it have been before you bothered to bring up the real reason you've been sleeping in my bed, Conn?"

His fingers tightened dangerously, and she sensed the tension in him. "Listen to me, Honor, and listen well. This isn't going to be easy to explain. I've had a hard time comprehending it myself."

"It seems quite simple to me."

"That's because you don't know what the hell it's all about! I haven't been hidden away in some dark hole plotting vengeance for the past fifteen years, for heaven's sake. I've been working overseas, just as I explained to you. It was a good job, a high-paying position. I was busy and I was always on the move. What's more, I was very good at what I did."

"You never got around to explaining just what a go-between does, Conn," she pointed out dryly.

He bit off an exclamation of impatience. "I was a sort of troubleshooter. I got sent in when a company was having problems on a foreign job site."

"What sort of problems?" she pressed dismally. "Don't tell me you handled labor disputes."

"No," he said, gritting his teeth, "my specialty was security problems. Honor, my former job hasn't got anything to do with this. I only mentioned it because I was trying to show you that I haven't been exactly brooding for the past fifteen years."

"But you haven't exactly forgotten the night our fathers shot each other, either, have you?" she flung back.

"Neither have you."

She inclined her head once in aloof acknowledgment of that truth. "No, neither have I."

He applied pressure to her shoulder, turning her easily under his strong hand. She found herself forced to face the full intensity of those gunmetal eyes. The implacable hardness in him was almost overpowering.

"Honor, I'm a man who believes in tying up loose ends. I've told you that."

"Yes."

"When I decided to resign from my job and return to the States two years ago, a part of me started thinking about the unfinished business between my family and yours. I remembered my father's interest in horse racing, too, and something made me decide to find out what had happened to Stylish Legacy. Discovering what had happened to the horse seemed like a place to begin the search for the truth about what had happened between our fathers that night. The next thing I knew I was buying one of the colts. It seemed the right thing to do. Perhaps I absorbed some of Richard Stoner's fascination with thoroughbreds. Or maybe I find the horse a link to the past. Buying Legacy was a mistake in some ways, though."

"Because every time you looked at him you thought of his sire and of our fathers' partnership," Honor guessed unhappily.

"Honor, I have a thing about betrayal. Perhaps I've seen too much of it in my line of work. Perhaps it all stems from the way my stepfather died. I don't know. Maybe it's just built into me. Whatever the reason, once I'd bought Legacy, my need to settle the past became more and more important. I told myself I would at least find out what had happened to Nick Mayfield's kids. It wasn't hard to track you down. Once I had located you, I decided to keep going. Something kept pushing me."

"A need for revenge." She met his eyes with a level gaze of her own, refusing to flinch from the grimness in him.

"All right," Conn replied, "maybe that's what it was. Call it what you want. But I think it was something else. I had this feeling, you see, that if I found out what

Nick Mayfield's eldest daughter was really like I might learn something about what Mayfield himself was like. I might be able to decide once and for all if he was the kind of man who would have killed his partner in cold blood. I'd be able to put the past to rest. And once I'd bought Legacy, I couldn't seem to stop the search for the truth. One thing led to another. For the past three months I've known where you lived, where you worked, whom you dated and that you occasionally went to the track."

"You had me followed!" She was appalled.

"Only for a week. Long enough to find out the critical details. Then I took over the job myself. It's the sort of thing I've been trained to do." His mouth tightened.

"You must hate me very much, Conn Landry," she whispered.

"No, damn it, I don't hate you! That's what I'm trying to explain," he snapped furiously. "After I bought Legacy I had to keep going. Don't you understand? One thing led to another. After I had discovered the whereabouts of Mayfield's elder daughter I had to find out what she was like."

"Why?" she cried. "Because of some criminal theory out of the Middle Ages that states the tendency toward betrayal runs in a family?"

"Maybe I just wanted to see if she'd turned out like her father. I don't know exactly why I had to track you down and meet you. You were another link, like Legacy. I only knew that it was important."

"Because there was unfinished business to settle," she finished savagely. "Why the trap, Conn?"

"What trap?" But she saw the wariness shimmer in his gaze.

"Come on, there's no need to pretend. From the

first moment I met you, you've been boxing me into some kind of cage. There was that incident with Granger, for example.''

There was rough-edged steel in his response. "You want the truth? I'll tell you. In the beginning I wanted to make certain that when I made contact, I would be the one in control. The best way to manage that, I decided, would be by spinning a web around you. I wanted you in my debt at first and later—" He stopped suddenly.

Honor already knew what he'd been going to say. "And later you decided that seducing me would add to your sense of control. You're a very thorough man, Conn.''

"It's the reason I was successful at my job while I worked overseas. And it's the reason I've been successful in my investments during the past two years. Being thorough is part of the way I do things, Honor.''

"I still don't understand what you want from me," she said stonily, all hope dead within her now. "You seduced me. Believe me, that's about all I have to give. There's a little money, I suppose—"

"I don't want your money, damn it!''

"My father left me a beach cottage up the coast," Honor went on doggedly, her gaze never wavering. "It's worth something. You've met Adena. You must realize there's not much to be had from her. She's still just a kid in a lot of ways. I imagine you could successfully seduce her, too, if you put your mind to it, but that seems a bit tacky, doesn't it?''

"Will you shut up? You're not even trying to understand!''

"What exactly am I failing to comprehend?''

He released her, removing his hand so quickly she

wondered if he'd been afraid of losing control and actually hurting her. It was so hard to imagine Conn losing control in any situation. Stepping around her he reached inside the red lacquered liquor cabinet and found a bottle of Scotch. Honor watched as he splashed some of the amber liquor into a glass. He swirled the liquid once and then took a swallow.

"It's hard to explain what I've been feeling for the past couple of months, let alone the past few days. I only know that my feelings toward you were, well, ambivalent. You were the elder daughter of the man who had betrayed my father. Something in me has always wanted to put to rest what happened between our parents fifteen years ago. There was nothing I could do at the time. I was a twenty-three-year-old kid, and none of the honchos in the corporation would give me any real help in finding out exactly what had happened that night. I had to piece it all together for myself between what I knew of Richard Stoner and what the newspapers told me. It's never felt right, never felt finished." He ran his fingers restlessly through his hair.

"Did seducing me somehow put an end to it for you?" Honor asked coldly.

Conn looked at her. "Seducing you changed everything."

She caught her breath. "Is this the part where you tell me you've fallen madly in love? That since meeting me you've given up all notion of revenge? That the past doesn't matter any longer?"

The gunmetal-gray eyes were colder than the landscape of the moon. "Look, Honor, I'm trying to be completely honest with you."

"That's a change."

"You little—" He took a step forward and halted

abruptly, visibly restraining himself. The poised-to-spring tension in him now was very evident. "Honor, I don't know much about love. It's an undefined, vague concept that usually doesn't sustain itself for long from what I've seen. And I won't tell you that I've completely forgotten what happened between Richard Stoner and Nick Mayfield fifteen years ago. But something very basic has changed in this equation and that's the way I feel toward you. My feelings about you are no longer in the least ambivalent. I want you. And I have some first-hand evidence that you want me. I'm prepared to start over on that basis."

"Start over!" She couldn't believe what she was hearing. "Are you out of your mind?"

His face was a set mask. "I've been asking myself that question for the past few days. No, I'm not out of my mind. At least I don't think so," he added wryly. "There are bonds between us, Honor, and I suspect you realize that as much as I do. There are ties, factors that link us. Factors that brought us together and that we can't shake off very easily. Whatever the initial cause and effect was, the result exists. You and I are together now."

"I would never have guessed you were a believer in fate!" she stormed.

He shrugged. "Maybe I've spent too much of my life in parts of the world where people believe in things such as fate and destiny."

"Well, I'm from Southern California," Honor flung back fiercely, "and here we shape our own future. I was a fool to get involved with you, Conn Landry, but I can assure you I'm not going to stay involved. Please get out of my apartment. Now!"

He set down the half-finished glass of Scotch. "You know it isn't going to end this simply."

"Get out."

"I'll be back. We'll talk this over when you've calmed down. There is too much between us." His mouth lifted in the faint cynical smile. "Murder and betrayal fifteen years ago between our fathers, passion and *obligation* between you and me. Don't forget that last bit, honey. You owe me. We're all tangled up together in this now."

He turned and walked out the door before Honor could find an answer.

Chapter Six

He would give her twenty-four hours, Conn decided. Hell, whom was he kidding? He needed the time just as much as she did. Conn piloted the Porsche to his hotel, parked the car in the lot and stalked inside to the English-pub-style bar. It wasn't until he ordered the Scotch that he realized just how much of his tightly controlled sense of frustration and anger must be visible. The bartender acted as though he were serving a shark who had casually wandered into the comfortable lounge. From across the room Conn recognized a couple of men who had horses at Santa Anita. They were staying at the same hotel, but neither of them made any move to invite Conn to join them. His dark mood must have been evident even from this distance.

Landry downed a long swallow of the Scotch after it was placed gingerly in front of him and then sat glowering at his reflection in the back-bar mirror. A grim-faced man with eyes that were sheets of frozen metal stared back.

Twenty-four hours. That should be long enough, he thought. She was shaken and upset right now, but twenty-four hours hence she would have calmed down enough to listen to reason. With any luck he would have calmed down a little himself.

He hadn't expected it to happen this way, hadn't thought she would learn the truth on her own. He'd intended to give her the facts carefully so that she wouldn't be alarmed. He would have told her eventually, when he judged the time was right and when he'd sorted it all out in his own mind.

That was the most complicated part, he realized. Sorting it all out in his own head was taking some work. Faced with having to put his strange initial ambivalence toward Honor into words, he'd fumbled badly and he knew it. He hadn't done a good job at all of soothing her fears or of explaining something he barely understood himself. If only he'd had some time to prepare.

But his feelings toward Honor had been crystallizing slowly and in fragments. He hadn't yet put them together into a complete whole that could be comprehended. It was as if he'd started fitting together the various glittering shards of a broken mirror. Some things were clear already. Conn realized. He knew beyond a shadow of a doubt that he wanted her. He'd accepted his need to protect her. And he no longer struggled to ignore the strange possessiveness he felt.

But other images in the mirror were still jagged and out of focus. He wasn't sure of Honor's feelings, for example, other than a certainty that he could make her respond magnificently in bed. When he'd told her that seducing her had changed everything, he hadn't been lying. It had. What she might not have realized was that matters hadn't been fundamentally changed just for him. They had altered just as completely for her.

At least, Conn admitted in a flash of clearheaded honesty, he wanted very badly to think they had changed for her. The possibility that the lovemaking hadn't been as intense and meaningful for Honor as it had been for him created a sick dread in the pit of his stomach. He drank some more Scotch to mask it.

There were other fragments of certainty, he assured himself. He sensed a basic integrity in her that he hadn't expected to find in Nick Mayfield's daughter. When she was with him he had a feeling of rightness that he couldn't explain. He liked the expressiveness of her hazel eyes and he liked the way she had run to him the other night when the guy in the pickup truck had frightened her. He'd liked the feeling of playing hero and protector, Conn decided. He appreciated the courage it had taken for her to try to deal with Granger on behalf of her sister. So many things about her seemed to draw him.

For those reasons and a thousand more he had told himself that he needed time while he reevaluated the situation. But something had happened today to steal that factor from him. How the hell had she found out that he was Richard Stoner's son? For the record, he'd have to clear that up the next time he saw her. Race-track gossip, probably.

His mouth thinning dangerously, Conn ordered another Scotch and considered the lonely dinner that lay ahead. Maybe he'd just stay here until it was time to go upstairs and face an even lonelier bed. Plenty of nutrition in good Scotch.

SEVERAL BLOCKS AWAY from the hotel, Honor locked the door of her apartment and picked up the red leather suitcase at her feet. She'd left a message for Adena on her sister's answering machine. Adena could handle anything that came up that affected the apartment.

Honor carried the bag down to the garage and stuffed it into the Fiat's trunk. Then she slipped into the driver's seat and shoved the key into the ignition. It was going to be a long drive, but she would have plenty of time to think en route.

She was so wrapped up in her churning thoughts that she didn't notice the black pickup behind her until she was on the on-ramp of the freeway. When a casual glance in her rearview mirror picked it up, Honor's stomach twisted into a sudden knot of fear.

You can't be sure it's the same truck, she told herself. But she couldn't see any license plate, and Conn had mentioned the other night that the black pickup that had followed her home hadn't had plates. It was dark now, however, and she couldn't be certain of the image in her rearview mirror.

The tension in her doubled as she considered the possibility that she'd been singled out by a genuine lunatic. Perhaps some crazy had decided to follow her around terrorizing her. She could try driving to a police station to see what happened, Honor thought as her knuckles went white on the wheel.

Just as she was deciding which off-ramp might take her to a station, however, the truck dropped back several car lengths. Two other vehicles filled the space between herself and the pickup, and Honor began to relax. Perhaps it had been just a coincidence or her imagination. The potential perils of freeway driving claimed her attention for the next several miles as the lanes became crowded. The freeways around Los Angeles were packed at this hour on Friday evenings. She lost sight of the pickup completely and told herself it had been nothing to worry about. There were a heck of a lot of pickups on the roads these days.

The temporary nervousness quelled, Honor's mind went back to the festering emotions that had driven her into leaving town. The pain of discovering that Conn Landry had lied to her wasn't diminishing. If anything, it was far stronger now that she'd had his deception confirmed from his own lips. There was no denying that she'd been secretly hoping there would be some logical explanation for everything.

And, of course, there had been a logical explanation, she thought bitterly. What Ethan Bailey had told her was the truth. Explanations couldn't get much more logical than that.

She'd fallen in love with Richard Stoner's son. She had been so very stupid. Landry had manipulated her from the moment they had met. No, he'd begun setting her up long before that. He'd admitted he'd been stalking her for months.

She was being pursued by a dangerous man, all right, but not the one in the pickup truck. Her nemesis drove a Porsche and harbored a taste for revenge that was more than old-fashioned; it was primitive. Her only choice was to escape the vicinity while she tried to deal with the traumatic turn of events.

Honor fled up Highway 101 as if she were being chased by demons.

CONN HAD GOOD REASON to remember his decision to drink his dinner the previous evening when the phone in his hotel room rang shrilly at seven-thirty the next morning. The simple act of trying to answer it kick-started a throbbing headache that had apparently been waiting in the wings.

"Hell," he groaned as he fumbled for the receiver. "I didn't leave a wake-up call," he grumbled before the person on the other end could greet him.

"Conn? Is that you, Landry?"

Conn sprawled back against the headboard, one hand on his throbbing temple. His stomach was definitely unsteady, he realized. "Who is this? Ethan? What the hell are you doing calling me in the middle of the night?"

"Sorry to wake you. I'm at Santa Anita. Came to watch the morning workouts." There was a pause.

"I plan to skip them this morning," Conn muttered, closing his eyes and inhaling carefully. "I've got some other things on my mind." He thought he could handle the stomach. It was his head that would be the death of him.

"Yeah. Listen, Conn, I'm not calling about that. There's something else. Something strange. I think you ought to get out here."

"Give me one good reason."

"It has to do with Legacy," Ethan said levelly.

Conn opened his eyes and immediately regretted the violent exercise. "Legacy? What's wrong with him? Is he okay?"

"Well, yes, but—"

"Where's Humphrey?" Conn sat up in bed, ignoring his head with a fierce act of willpower. "If there's anything wrong, get Humphrey to look at the horse. I'll be out there as soon as I can."

"Legacy's all right, Conn. But this has something to do with him, and frankly, I'd rather not talk about it. This is a public phone."

Through the pain in his temples, Conn heard the man's concern. "Okay, okay. I'll be right out. You're sure the horse is all right, though?"

"He's fine, Conn," Ethan said wearily.

Landry slammed down the receiver and swung his feet to the carpeted floor. It took guts just to get out of bed, but he made it to the bathroom. Unzipping the shaving kit, he found a bottle of aspirin and gulped down a few tablets. Then he turned on the shower and stood under the spray for several minutes brooding about how long it had been since he'd gotten drunk because of a woman. He couldn't even remember if he'd ever deliberately set out to get stoned because of a female. A first for Honor.

He'd have to tell her just what she'd done to him. He'd put it on the list of grievances he planned to present to her when the twenty-four hours were up.

His head had settled down a bit by the time he located the Porsche in the hotel parking lot and started out to Santa Anita, but Conn was still moving with a bit of care as he walked through the track parking lot toward the barns.

Ethan Bailey met him just outside the guard gate. One glance at the older man's face and Conn knew there was a truly major headache waiting. Bailey's normally laid-back, easygoing manner was nonexistent this morning.

"You'd better tell me the worst and get it over with," Conn said, sighing.

"Let's go out to my car," Ethan suggested gently. He didn't wait to see if Conn would follow, but started toward the parking lot.

"What the hell are you being so mysterious about this morning? I'm really not up to this sort of thing today. If something terrible has happened to Legacy, just tell me." Conn paced beside his friend, his unsettled temper bubbling just below the surface. He felt angry at the whole world this morning. The past, the present, Honor Mayfield, Scotch, the whole world. And now Bailey was playing games.

No, that was unfair. Bailey was very concerned. He wasn't playing games. In fact, in the couple of years he'd known the man he'd never seen Ethan Bailey this upset.

"You look worse than you did the time that real estate deal in Orange County went sour," Conn grumbled.

"That was business. This is personal," Ethan told him in a troubled tone. He paused beside his big white Mercedes and turned to look at Landry. "Maybe too personal. Maybe I handled this all wrong." He wrenched open the door and reached inside to pull out a bundle wrapped in burlap. "you can tell me where to get off if I screwed this up, Conn. But I wanted you to see this before I did anything too dramatic."

"What is it?" Frowning, Conn glanced down at the harmless-looking bundle.

"I found these inside Legacy's stall this morning. I went past it while he was out having his morning gallop and I just happened to glance inside." Slowly Ethan unwound the burlap and revealed two green apples.

Conn stared at the fruit in mild surprise. "A couple of apples. So? One of the grooms probably brought them in for him."

Ethan shook his head. "You know how strict Humphrey is about the horses' diet. None of his grooms would dare bring in anything special for Legacy or any of the others. Humphrey's got all his animals on scientifically formulated feed. Conn, someone brought these in for Legacy and put them in his feed while he was out getting his morning workout. Look at this." Ethan turned over one of the apples, revealing that it had been cored.

The carefully honed instincts of several years spent

in the security business finally emerged. Conn reached for one of the apples and examined the hole in the base of it. Without a word he moved his hand to the pocket of his blue denim work shirt and removed a small star-shaped metal object.

Ethan's brows came together in a thick shaggy line. "What the heck's that widget?"

"Something I picked up a few years back," Conn explained absently as he used one of the sharp points of the star to neatly slice the apple in two. "Kind of a good-luck piece, I guess you could say."

"Didn't know you were the superstitious sort," Ethan observed.

Conn cleaned the star on his jeans and dropped it back into his pocket, his attention completely on separating the two halves of the apple. "A man picks up some odd habits when he works in some of the places I've worked. Well, what do you know?" he concluded in a whisper as the large capsule hidden in the apple was revealed.

Ethan stared at the powder-filled capsule. "I was afraid there wasn't going to be any really good explanation for those apples being in Legacy's stall."

Landry lifted chilled eyes to meet the other man's dismal stare. "I wonder if Granger decided he didn't like being told to lay off Adena Mayfield."

Ethan looked back at him steadily. "Conn, Granger's from the bottom of the barrel, but he's sort of old-fashioned."

"Spell it out, Ethan."

"From all accounts he's what the women's movement would call a genuine, dyed-in-the wool male chauvinist pig. He doesn't hire females."

Conn went very still. "What the devil are you talking about, Bailey?"

Ethan made a visible effort to steel himself to deliver the rest of his news. "When I found those apples this morning, I casually asked the guard if there'd been a lot of strangers coming into the stable area. He said no."

"Granger could have bribed someone who works here," Conn interrupted irritably.

"That was my next thought." Ethan heaved a sigh and glanced at the wall of mountains in the distance. "But the guard went on to say there had been one person through the gate on a visitor's pass. A woman. A lady with light-brown hair who wore a pair of yellow pants and a blue Windbreaker. She didn't stay long."

Conn didn't move for a timeless instant, images of Honor's bright-brown hair and vivid wardrobe flashing into his aching head. Honor, who saw herself as a woman who had been used, the victim of a man who had tracked her down out of revenge. Honor, the daughter of a man who had once betrayed and killed his best friend.

Like father, like daughter? "No," he whispered under his breath.

"You all right, Conn?" Ethan squinted at him worriedly.

"I'll live." Maybe. He suddenly wasn't sure. There was a strange, painful tightness in him, a nausea that had nothing to do with his hangover.

"Do we go to the track authorities with these apples?"

Conn forced himself to deal with one thing at a time, although his mind was racing in a hundred meaningless directions. "No." Damn it, why couldn't he think straight?

"I don't know," Ethan said uneasily, "maybe we ought to get the contents of that capsule analyzed before you make any decisions. After all, we don't know for sure just what's in there."

"How many reasons can you think of for stuffing a capsule inside an apple and feeding it to a hundred-thousand-dollar racehorse?" Conn asked sardonically as he rewrapped the apples. He was amazed at how much effort the small task required until he looked down at his hands and realized they were shaking.

"I can't rightly think of any good reasons. Unless Toby Humphrey was trying to trick Legacy into taking some medication?" he added hopefully.

"I had a long talk with Toby yesterday about Legacy's health and future. The horse isn't on any medication." Conn spoke flatly, without any emotion. "Whatever's in this capsule was meant to poison Legacy."

"The authorities—"

"No!" The denial was much too harsh, too loud. He brought himself under control with savage willpower. If he wasn't very careful his voice would soon be shaking as badly as his fingers. "I'll handle this on my own." Conn held the wrapped apples in one hand and looked at his friend. "You knew I'd want to deal with this myself, didn't you? That's why you called me first instead of the track authorities."

Ethan nodded gloomily. "When the guard said something about a woman, well, I..." He didn't finish the sentence.

"You knew who the description fit."

"Conn, this is just about the most goddamned miserable mess I've ever seen. What did you do to that little lady to make her want to do something like this?"

Conn glanced down at the bundle in his hand. "Made her mad, I guess." He turned and started toward his Porsche. "But that's nothing compared to what she just did to me."

That was the truth, he added silently, as he flung himself into the Porsche and tossed the burlap bundle onto the floor of the car. He probably shouldn't even be behind the wheel of a car right now. If he had any sense he would go somewhere and calm down before confronting Honor.

Then, again, if he had any intelligence he wouldn't be in this situation. Everything he'd learned about human nature during all those years working security for multinationals around the world seemed to have evaporated around Honor Mayfield. What the hell had happened to his normal, realistic approach to people, he wondered.

He ought to have expected something like this, Conn thought in disgust, glancing at the incriminating bundle. She was the daughter of a man who had betrayed and killed his best friend. Did that sort of inclination run in the blood? There were places in the world where people believed it did. Even if the instinct wasn't hereditary, there were other factors he should have taken into account last night, such as the fact that he hardly qualified as her best friend.

Honor had been infuriated yesterday when she'd learned the truth. He knew she was capable of passion. It stood to reason that such a fundamental capacity would affect other areas of her life in addition to her responses in bed.

Reason. He couldn't seem to reason clearly at all this morning and not just because of the effects of his hangover. It took Conn almost the entire distance of the drive from Santa Anita Racetrack to Honor's apartment house to acknowledge that his own passions were running dangerously close to being out of control. Between the throbbing ache in his head and the twisting pain in his gut he was incapable of calming himself.

It was the pain he didn't fully understand. It should have been the cold, hard tension of fury. Instead it was something else, something he wouldn't have guessed himself capable of feeling anymore. He *hurt*, not just physically but on a primitive emotional level that hadn't been touched since the day they'd told him Richard Stoner had been murdered.

As he slammed the Porsche to a halt at the curb in front of the apartment complex the simmering caldron of his emotions threatened to explode. He was actually having to fight for self-control, and the knowledge only served to increase the level of explosive tension. He'd never had this kind of problem. He was always the one in command of himself and any given situation. Such talents had been a necessary skill in his job and he had come by those abilities naturally. For years he'd taken his chilled, controlled, efficiently ruthless approach to life for granted. The fact that this particular woman had pushed him beyond those boundaries was almost stunning in its impact.

Conn took the stairs to the second floor, loping up them two at a time, and came to a halt in front of Honor's front door. There he drew a couple of deep breaths in a useless bid to pick up the leash on his anger. Then he pounded brutally on the door.

It took several minutes of pounding and the frowning inquiries of a couple of Honor's neighbors to convince Conn that his quarry had fled.

"Look, mister," a man damp with sweat he'd worked

up jogging said, "I just came up through the garage. Her car isn't down there. Take my word for it. She's gone for the weekend." Wiping the perspiration off his forehead, the jogger dug out the key to his own apartment.

"Do you know where?"

The knife blade buried in Conn's tone brought the man's head up just as he unlocked the door. "Sorry," he said crisply. "I don't." Rather hurriedly he stepped inside and slammed the door behind him. Conn heard the bolt being shot home.

Terrifying Honor's neighbors wasn't going to achieve much. Time to track down Adena. He had the younger woman's address in that pile of information he'd garnered during the past few months. Driving back to the hotel and digging through the data took time and chewed at his insides, but it was the only approach. He was about to walk out of the room with the piece of paper in his hand when he remembered the aspirin. He could use a few more. His head was not improving at all. At least his stomach was staying under control. Pausing to gulp a couple more tablets, Conn wasted no more time. Ten minutes later he was pounding on Adena Mayfield's door. This time he got an answer.

"Good heavens, what do you want? It's only eight-thirty and it's Saturday. If you're here to give me another lecture about Granger, kindly skip it. I have an excellent memory." Adena glared at her visitor, clutching at the red-and-purple kimono-style bathrobe she'd apparently slung on to answer the door. Her stylish haircut had not yet been blow-dried into its proper wedge shape and her blond hair was in a tangle. Without her normal outrageous makeup she looked much younger, Conn realized.

"I'm looking for your sister," he spat out.

"Honor?" Adena blinked vaguely. "How should I know where she is? You're the one who's been spending so much time with her lately. You've probably got a better idea of her whereabouts than I do."

"She's not at her apartment." It was taking a savage effort to keep his voice even remotely level.

"Don't blame me if you've managed to misplace her," Adena grumbled. "Hey, what is this?" she added in a gasp as Conn suddenly pushed open the door and stalked into the entry hall. "Look, she's not here, if that's what you're thinking." Something about his mood finally hit her still-sleepy brain. "What's wrong, Conn? Is Honor okay?"

"I have to find her."

"Why?" There was a sudden, wary concern in her voice.

Conn heard the change in her tone and forced himself to contain his fury. If he alarmed Adena too much it would be tough to get information out of her. "We argued last night. She's apparently left town. I'm trying to locate her."

"Ah," Adena said, her face clearing. "You want to do a little groveling, is that it?"

Conn stared at her. "I hadn't thought of it quite that way."

"Well, don't worry. Honor is a very forgiving, tolerant soul. Heaven knows she's put up with a lot from me during the past few years. Let me see if she left any messages for me on the machine. She usually tells me when she's leaving town." Stifling a yawn, Adena padded into the kitchen and switched on the telephone-answering machine.

Conn listened to two calls from young men begging

Adena to go to the same punk rock concert and a call from a young woman wanting to know if Adena cared to go to the mall to check out the latest fashion scene before Honor's tense voice was heard. Unconsciously Conn's hand clenched so tightly the knuckles went white.

"Adena? This is Honor. I'm going out of town for a couple of days. Thought I'd get some use out of Dad's cottage before the season starts. I'll call you when I decide to return. Please don't tell..." There was a pause before Honor's voice continued. "I'd appreciate it if you wouldn't let anyone know where I am. I need some time alone."

"Uh-oh." Adena grinned wryly as she switched off the machine. "Looks like I should have vetted that call before letting you listen, hmmm? Then again, I expect Honor's ready to hear your abject and humble apologies. Are you going to the cottage?"

"I'll need directions."

"Sure." Quickly Adena rattled them off and then she eyed her visitor keenly. "What did you and Honor fight about?"

"It's a private matter," Conn said stiffly, heading for the door.

"Oh. Well, as I said, I'm sure Honor will take you back," Adena assured him cheerfully. "I've never seen her this way about a man before. Of course, I've never seen her with a man like you, either. You're not her standard fare."

Conn halted halfway through the door. "Because I don't own a pair of designer loafers and wear mauve ties?"

"Somehow," Adena said dryly, "I think there's more to it than that. Goodbye, Conn. Don't forget to practice your groveling technique while you're driving. I think it needs work."

Conn left before he gave in to the impulse to explain to Adena that groveling wasn't exactly what he planned to do when he finally tracked down Honor.

He made one more stop at the hotel to pick up his shaving kit and a couple of other items and then climbed back into the Porsche. An hour out on the freeway he still couldn't detect any change in his unstable mood. Maybe he should have had something to eat. Taking all that aspirin on an empty stomach probably wasn't such a bright idea. On the other hand, the thought of eating didn't do much for his seething temper, either. He only had to glance at the burlap bundle on the floor of the car to rekindle the simmering pain and its accompanying rage.

Betrayal shouldn't hurt this much, he decided. It was, after all, just another fact of life. Why was it that a woman's act of betrayal could slice a man to the bone? The image was apt. He felt as though he were, indeed, bleeding.

WHEN SHE ARRIVED at the cottage late the previous evening, Honor had experienced the sense of unease and distant, unhappy resentment that she always felt when she opened the door of the beachfront house. The feelings had lessened with time. They weren't nearly as strong as they had once been, but they had remained forceful enough through the years to keep her visits to a minimum.

Saturday morning she rose after a restless night's sleep and prepared a breakfast of dry cereal and coffee. As she ate she glanced around the walls, absently noting the framed photos of Stylish Legacy in various winners' circles. Honor rarely studied the pictures closely. It hurt to see the face of her father smiling back at the world as if the future looked good to him.

There were other mementos of her father's interest in racing scattered about the room. A bridle hung on the wall beside a small racing saddle that had been left over after the sale of Stylish Legacy. In one corner stood an old wood-and-iron chest containing various racing memorabilia. One of Stylish Legacy's blankets was folded on top. Locked in a drawer in the bedroom were copies of the *Daily Racing Form* from fifteen years ago, containing glowing accounts of the promising colt. There were also some copies of the horse's pedigree and other papers that had once held meaning to her father. Honor kept those locked away, too.

Perhaps she'd made a mistake coming here after all, Honor thought. The cottage depressed her. But she had been running the way a wounded animal runs, and this was where she instinctively headed. It was either this or check into some anonymous motel. Somehow that alternative seemed even more depressing. Maybe a walk on the beach this morning would lighten her mood.

Honor changed into a pair of jeans and some tennis shoes and pulled a heavy peach-colored velour top out of the suitcase. It was turning chilly. By the evening the coastal fog would no doubt be rolling in and blanketing this stretch of beach. The promising warmth in Pasadena did not extend this far north today.

The empty sandy beach didn't prove as therapeutic as she had hoped. It stretched for a distance of a couple of hundred yards before terminating in a rocky outcropping. At the foot of the rocks the water foamed dangerously, driven by a current that made swimming unsafe. It helped to walk, and the crisp wind from the sea was invigorating, but nothing eased Honor's pain. She found herself going over and over the sequence of events surrounding her relationship with Conn Landry, looking for the point at which she should have seen what he was doing to her. It appalled her to realize that she had been so incredibly vulnerable.

It was even more appalling trying to deal with the turbulent mix of emotions that shook her to the center of her being. She had fallen in love with the man. *In love!* Remembering all her initial wariness of Conn, Honor wondered how she could have been so stupid.

Giving up on the walking therapy after forty minutes or so, Honor turned reluctantly back toward the house. It really was turning cold, and the fog would be arriving earlier than she had originally anticipated. She could feel it in the air.

Her father's cottage stood isolated and alone on the bluff overlooking the beach. There were a couple of other cottages nearby but they were both empty at this time of year. The region had remained undeveloped because it was just a little too far from Santa Barbara to become chic. Someday, Honor had told herself, when development caught up with this area of the coast, her inheritance would be a gold mine. She had used that rationalization whenever logic had dictated that she sell the cottage.

The truth was that a part of her never wanted to sell. Although the place depressed her and made her strangely uneasy, she couldn't bring herself to get rid of it. It was as if too many questions remained unanswered about the past, questions that should have been settled fifteen years ago. Honor had been unable to settle the questions or let go of the things in the cottage that raised those questions in the first place.

She was pondering the vagaries of her own nature when she heard the roar of the Porsche engine as the sleek black-and-silver vehicle pulled into the cottage driveway. Honor halted abruptly, all her swirling emotions threatening to consume her.

Conn Landry had come after her.

In stunned silence she watched as he thrust open the car door and strode to the cottage. She was several feet away, standing in the shadow of the house, but she could see the implacable expression on his harsh face. Honor let him raise his hand to pound on the door before she stepped around the corner, her head high, hands shoved into the pockets of her velour top. The breeze caught her hair, whipping it around her shoulders.

"Hello, Conn. Still looking for your revenge? I should think you'd have had your fill by now. Even if you haven't, it's all you're going to get."

He spun around to face her, his lithe, strong body dangerously balanced. The cold gray eyes raked her with a simmering emotion she couldn't name. It couldn't possibly be pain, she thought.

"Lady, you could teach me a few things about revenge," he retorted softly. "You surprised me, do you know that? I would never have guessed you'd try to get at me through the horse. God only knows why, but I would have staked my life on the belief that you weren't the type."

Honor felt a jolt of fear. "What are you talking about?"

"Your little scheme to poison Legacy."

"Are you out of your mind?" she gasped out.

He inclined his head once, in brutal mockery. "That possibility exists. I've been asking myself the same question for the past couple of hours. I must have been crazy to think you were a different breed from your father.''

''Don't bring my father into this!'' she flared furiously.

''Why not? It all started with him. But it's going to end here, Honor Mayfield. I swear, it's going to end here, between you and me.''

''Don't touch me,'' she breathed, truly frightened now. At the same time her own fury wouldn't allow her to turn and run, as all her instincts dictated.

''I've got to,'' he told her roughly as he came toward her. ''I have to find a way to get you out of my system. You've pushed me over some edge I haven't come close to since the night they told me Richard Stoner had been killed. That was the last time I felt this wild, Honor. But fifteen years ago there was no one who could be made to pay for what had happened. This time it's different. This time I've got my hands on you.''

Chapter Seven

Honor turned and ran, not because she had some misconception that she might actually be faster than Conn or that he wouldn't come after her. She ran because one glimpse of the rage in his normally remote gray eyes convinced her she was dealing one hundred percent with the avenging, predatory side of his nature. And when you were the potential victim in a situation like that, you ran.

She fled around the corner of the house, heading for the beach simply because there was nowhere else to go. She knew he was right behind her even though the sound of his movement was inaudible above the slap of the surf and the rising rush of the sea breeze. Honor also knew that fleeing was hopeless. She had yearned to get past the barriers of Conn's self-control but she had never dreamed of doing it this way.

He didn't call out to her or order her to stop. Conn simply bore down on her with the silent intensity of a large hunting cat intent on bringing a gazelle to the ground. Running across the sand was like running through snow. It dragged at her feet, making Honor think of those odd nightmares in which the sleeper found herself being pursued but was unable to escape.

She sucked in the cold air, her heart pounding from exertion and fear, and as she reached the water's edge Honor felt Conn's hand on her waist.

"No!" she shrieked, spinning around to strike at him in desperation. "Let me go, damn you!"

"Did you think you could run from me? There's no place on this planet you could hide." He pulled her against the hard length of his body, trying to control her struggles.

But as far as Honor was concerned at that moment, she was fighting for her life. She lashed at him with her nails, kicked at him with her feet, twisted relentlessly in his grasp and tried to use her teeth on his arm.

"You little—" Conn's words were muffled as Honor's constant struggling threw both victim and pursuer off balance. They landed in a sprawl on the cold, wet packed sand. "I'll teach you to betray me," Conn rasped, throwing his thigh heavily across her legs to still their thrashing movement.

"I didn't betray you!" The words were torn from her as she pushed uselessly at his descending weight. "I don't know what you're talking about, but you can't do this to me. You have no right to hurt me!"

"I haven't even begun to hurt you. After the way you've hurt me—"

He broke off abruptly, but not before Honor had heard the startling rawness in his voice. She wondered at it, trying to make that evidence of pain mesh with the rage she was certain was governing his actions. Breathlessly she pushed at him.

He pinned her relentlessly to the damp sand, using his weight to crush her beneath him until her struggles finally stilled. For a long moment Conn stared down into her blazing eyes. He held her wrists above her head as he lay on top of her.

"You bastard." The anger and fear were still warring within her. There was no time to analyze the flash of emotional agony she thought she'd detected in his gaze. She had her own pain to deal with. Honor felt Conn's strength overwhelming her, leaving her physically helpless.

"You've got a hell of a nerve calling *me* names."

Her head moved on the sand. "I never even knew you, did I? I never had a chance. You lied to me about yourself from the beginning."

His face was a harsh composition of hard lines and flaring eyes. As she stared up at him Honor was vaguely aware of the twin red marks that coursed down the side of his cheek. She was vaguely shocked at the wound she had inflicted. He would carry the sign of her struggle for a few days, she knew. Yet other than holding her helpless, Conn hadn't physically hurt her.

"I wasn't the one who lied," he gasped. "You lied to me every time I took you to bed. All that softness and warmth, it was all an illusion, wasn't it? I had begun to think you were different."

"Different from what?" she flung back, stricken that he could believe she had somehow faked her reaction in bed.

"Different from other women. And different from your father!"

"Leave my father out of this!"

"I can't. What he did is at the middle of this whole damn thing. I should have realized that. Should have known that his daughter wasn't likely to be any different. She's just as capable of betrayal."

"I haven't betrayed you!"

"Then why hide? Tell me why you ran, Honor."

"I'm not hiding. I just wanted to get out of the vicinity of the man who had been using me for his own warped notions of revenge. Is that so strange? Damn you, Conn Landry, who gave you the right to inflict your warped sense of justice on me? And who says I have to let you do it?"

"I wasn't inflicting any punishment on you," he exploded. "I hadn't done a thing except take you to bed, come in handy when you were being followed by a punk in a pickup, and rescue your sister from the mess she was in with Granger, remember? I never hurt you! I never wanted to hurt you!"

"You tracked me down just so you could 'tie up loose ends,'" she hissed. "You wanted to settle old scores. You admitted it! Taking me to bed was part of your twisted idea of getting even. And now you have the nerve to accuse me of betraying you!"

"You tried to poison Legacy!"

She gasped in amazement and then her eyes slitted in fury. "Never. I would never hurt your horse. Or any other horse, for that matter!"

"It was the only way you could get back at me after I told you I hadn't simply been swept off my feet by you, wasn't it? After you found out that I had other reasons for meeting you than because I'd fallen in love at first sight or some such idiocy, your feminine ego was enraged, wasn't it?"

"I was upset that you didn't feel the same way toward me as I felt toward you! Yes, I was angry. I had a right!"

"You were the one who wanted to punish someone, Honor. You wanted to get back at me and you chose Legacy as the means to do it."

"That's not true," she cried, appalled. "Do you really believe I would do such a thing? Is that how little trust you have in me, Landry? I admit we haven't spent a lot of time together and I'll also admit that you told me lies for most of that time, but everything I said or did was real. I meant everything. *Everything!*"

"Then why did you try to feed those apples to Legacy this morning?" he almost shouted.

Honor stilled as she heard the agonized plea for an explanation in his words. If she was feeling torn apart, Conn was also in shreds. "I've been here at the cottage since late last night. I haven't gone near Legacy." The cold from the sand seemed to be seeping into her. She was chilled emotionally and physically. The only warmth in the world right now was the heat from Conn's hard frame.

"You were seen at the stables this morning. A bright pair of yellow pants and light-brown hair. The only visitor through at that hour. It had to be you."

"If you believe that, then why don't you go ahead and finish whatever it is you're going to do to me? What are you planning to do, Conn? Strangle me? Beat me? Call the cops? Make up your mind. I'm getting cold out here on the sand."

"Damn you!"

For an instant she thought he really was going to strangle her. The frustrated fury in his eyes was terrifying. But before Honor's instinctive scream could leave her lips her mouth was crushed ruthlessly beneath his.

It was not a kiss of either passion or gentleness. There was nothing but naked despair and masculine outrage involved. Conn tore through her mouth, annihilating resistance as he went until she stopped fighting altogether and went passive beneath him. There were no other options for her, Honor thought. It was the despair she sensed in him that made it impossible for her to struggle. Some fundamental part of her wanted to offer comfort and warmth, even though she was putting herself at risk.

It seemed forever before some of the emotion began to drain out of the marauding assault. When Conn finally raised his head, Honor risked lifting her lashes just far enough to examine his features. Her mouth felt bruised and her body felt as if it were trapped under a granite boulder but she knew that Conn wasn't going to strangle her. That realization went deep, and she could not have said just why she was so certain. But the relief she felt was in her eyes.

"Don't get the impression that it's all over, Honor," Conn snarled softly. "It's hardly begun." He rolled off her, uncoiling to his feet and reaching down to pull her roughly up beside him. Without a word he started back toward the cottage, his hand locked around her wrist.

Honor stumbled along behind him, confused and still frightened. She pushed her sandy hair out of her face as the wind caught it. "What now, Conn? How are you going to take your revenge?" she challenged.

"I haven't decided." He slanted her a cold sidelong glance. "Believe me, when I do, you'll be the first to know."

"You think I'm going to be dumb enough to hang around and wait for your bizarre brain to come up with something suitably satisfying for you?"

"You're going to hang around, all right. You're not going anywhere, Honor. Not until I've had my fill of you. I'm going to work you out of my system and then I'm going to get as far away from you as possible."

She heard the ruthless promise in his words and

shivered violently. The cold within her worked deeper into her body. "Not a chance, Conn. I'm no masochist."

"You don't have any choice. You owe me, lady. More than you can ever repay. Somehow I'm going to collect. I swear it. I won't let you rip me to pieces and then walk away!"

He shoved open the door of the unlocked cottage, tugging Honor in behind him. Then he kicked the door shut and released his victim. His gray eyes raked her. "Go take a hot shower and change your clothes. You're a mess."

Honor didn't argue. She fled to the single bedroom and locked herself inside. On the other side of the door she took several deep breaths, fighting to get herself back under control. So many emotions roiled within her—anger, shock, pain and a sense of loss. Unsteadily she began to undress. Conn was right. She needed that hot shower and dry clothing. She had never felt so cold in her life.

When she emerged from the shower sometime later and tugged on a fresh pair of jeans and a bulky knit sweater, Honor felt more in command of herself. She stood in front of the mirror blow-drying her hair and wondered why she didn't look as bruised and battered as she felt. Only her eyes reflected the pain she had suffered. But even as she stared at her reflection Honor saw the courage return to her gaze.

The man she had been stupid enough to love was dangerous, but he was back in control of himself. She finished pulling a brush through her hair, clipping the soft tendrils at the nape of her neck. Then she turned and walked out of the bedroom with a determination to hold her own with the man who waited for her.

Conn was in the kitchen, running water into the coffeepot. For a moment Honor stood in the doorway watching him in taut silence. He didn't look up, but she knew he was aware of her presence. The set of his face was as grim as ever and there was a tension in him that communicated itself across the room.

"By all means, feel free to make yourself at home," Honor muttered.

He ignored the small piece of sarcasm, concentrating on the task of getting the coffee going as if it took all his attention. "Sit down, Honor. We have to talk."

"About what? Your mind is apparently made up, and I don't recall your asking for any input from me." She sank wearily into one of the white wicker chairs at the table. "I've been tried and convicted, haven't I?"

"The evidence is pretty conclusive. And then there's motive." He threw himself into a chair across from her, regarding her with a deep, brooding expression. "We both know you think you had a motive, don't we?"

Her hand curved into a fist. "I had a motive, all right. I was the one who felt betrayed. But I'll tell you this, Landry. If I had set out to get even I wouldn't have used poor Legacy to achieve my ends. I'd have gone after you directly. I wouldn't have involved an innocent animal." She shook her head in despairing wonder. "You must think I'm as low and filthy as...as that loan shark, Granger."

Conn shifted restlessly. "No. I think you were furious. A woman scorned. Isn't that how you saw yourself? They say a woman who feels that way is capable of just about anything. True?"

"It doesn't matter." She stared at him. "It just doesn't matter."

Conn was about to say something else and then thought better of it, apparently. He got to his feet and stalked across the kitchen to pour the coffee. With his back to her he stood for a moment staring out the window, watching the sea. Slowly he sipped the piping-hot black brew.

"Maybe it does matter," he finally growled. "You're a passionate woman. In a moment of rage and hurt you might have lost your head and—"

"I didn't do anything to your horse, so don't bother searching for excuses for me to use. I can't imagine why you'd want to find reasons, anyway."

"Believe me, I'm asking myself the same question. I'm going to get you out of my system and then I'm going to leave."

Honor felt the renewed tension but she didn't move. "Why should you need to get me out of your system? How could you possibly let a woman you think so little of get so close?"

"I was a fool." He didn't turn around.

"Well, that makes two of us, doesn't it?"

"Yes."

Honor blinked back the tears, refusing to give in to them. "At least we aren't trying to shoot each other the way our fathers did when things went wrong in their business relationship. Although I wasn't altogether certain just what you had planned out there on the beach. I suppose it's lucky for me you don't pack a gun, isn't it?"

He swung around with controlled violence. "This isn't a joke."

"Do I look as though I'm joking? Conn, this is the end of it and you know it. Unless you're going to physically hurt me, you might as well leave. You hate me, and the sooner I'm out of your sight, the better," she whispered.

He slammed down the coffee cup. "I'm not leaving. Not yet. I told you yesterday that I want you and I'm going to have you. On my terms."

"I thought I made it clear that I'm not a masochist. I won't play victim for you, Conn, not anymore." She got slowly to her feet, one hand on the edge of the table for support. Her gaze was unwavering.

"And I thought I'd made it clear you don't have any choice." He started forward with a cool, measured stride.

Honor stepped back. He wasn't enraged this time, but she knew she was in just as much danger. She edged backward until she was in the main room of the cottage, standing beside an end table that held a lamp. "I won't let you do this to me, Conn."

"From what I remember about the way you respond in my arms, you want me as much as I want you!"

"Damn you! I went to bed with you because I fell in love with you!" For an instant she regretted letting the truth emerge, but a moment later her pride surfaced. What did it matter if he knew she had gone so far as to fall in love? He already despised her.

Conn halted, his eyes blazing. "Love? You expect me to believe that? After what you've done?"

"Believe what you like," she replied steadily. "It's the truth, I only went to bed with you because I cared. Because I was in love."

"Prove it," he taunted coolly.

Her eyes narrowed. "What are you talking about? There's no way I can prove a thing like that. How should I prove my love? Go out and throw myself off a cliff into the ocean? I doubt that you'd believe me even if I did. I don't think you know how to trust anyone, Conn Landry. That's probably why you're so hot to settle old scores and collect all outstanding debts. Life is safer that way, isn't it? You don't have to worry about taking a risk."

"Skip the psychoanalysis. If you loved me a couple of days ago, you must still love me now, right? By all accounts true love isn't an emotion that dies easily."

"How would you know?" she flung back tightly. "You don't even believe in it!"

He came another step forward. "So why don't you try to convince me?" Conn taunted.

"How?" She eyed him with renewed wariness, uncertain of his mood now.

"Tonight when we go to bed you can give yourself to me without any arguments or recriminations. Just the way you did last week. Let me have all that warmth and sweet passion as if they were for real! Maybe you can convince me that it was unrequited love that made you try to poison Legacy!"

"Prove my love for you by going to bed with you? Conn, you're supposed to stop using that line the day you graduate from high school!"

"I take it you're not still in love?" he mocked cruelly. "A somewhat short-lived emotion, wasn't it?"

"It didn't die a natural death. You murdered it."

"Then it wasn't a very sturdy emotion, either, was it?"

"Stop goading me," Honor hissed. She reached out and scooped up the small brass table lamp. Her hands were trembling.

Conn glared at her. "Put that down, Honor."

"Not until you get away from me."

"You really think you'd use that on my skull?"

"Anyone who would deliberately try to poison a horse would be capable of cracking a man like you over the head," she warned half-hysterically.

For some reason that halted him in his tracks. He stood staring at her in stunned amazement. "Are you saying you did put those apples in Legacy's feed?"

"I don't know anything about any apples. But I do know I'm not going to let you touch me as long as you hate and distrust me so much," Honor vowed. Her grip on the lamp base tightened.

The passionate fury that sparked between them seemed to flicker and then, very slowly, it began to fade. Conn didn't move for a long moment and then he asked softly, "Is my trust so important?"

"It's the most I could have hoped for from you, isn't it? You don't know the meaning of love." Honor heard the raw truth in her own words as she slowly lowered the lamp.

Conn hesitated. Then quite coolly he stepped forward and removed the lamp from her unresisting fingers. "You'd come to me without any guarantees of love?"

"I haven't had any guarantees for the past week, have I?" She stood very straight, hazel eyes brilliant. "But I was under the illusion that there was at least some mutual trust and respect between us."

"And that's enough for you?" he pressed deliberately.

"I was fool enough to think so," she admitted, knowing deep down that she had been banking on the wealth of her own love for him to fill in the gaps.

"If I said I believed you, was willing to accept the possibility that it wasn't you who put the apples in Legacy's feed, would you let the situation between us go back to the way it was before...before yesterday?"

Honor caught her breath at the implications of what he was saying. He was going to back her into a corner from which there would be no escape except into his arms. It took her a moment to comprehend why he was doing it. Then the truth hit her in a cold shower of realization.

"That's the only way you'll feel safe with me, isn't it? The only way you'll be able to handle an affair with me now. I'm to tell you that I love you and give myself to you without any reservations. In turn you'll tell me you believe I might not have been the one to poison your horse."

"It sounds like a fair split to me." He shrugged carelessly. "Both of us take a risk."

"What risk are you taking?" she demanded tightly.

"That I might wake up one morning to find you've tried to crush my skull with a handy object such as that lamp," he said dryly.

"And in turn I get to love a man who doesn't know how to love me and who might still be using me to satisfy his need for revenge. That's a hell of a bargain, Landry. You must have been playing in some rough leagues for the past few years to learn that kind of wheeling and dealing," she told him scathingly.

He ignored that. "As I said, we both take a few risks. Does this famous love of yours give you enough guts to make the deal?"

He was walking on ice he couldn't measure, Honor realized sadly. Conn Landry was terrified of having it crack beneath him and finding himself in water that was way over his head. He wanted her, perhaps so much so that he was even willing to believe she might not have tried to poison his horse. But he was afraid to risk loving her.

The other side of the coin showed her wanting him. But she wasn't nearly so adept at bargaining with emotions. The only way she could give herself to him was if she simultaneously took the risk of loving him.

"A few minutes ago there wasn't any doubt at all in your mind but that I was the one who had tried to poison Legacy. Why are you willing to consider other possibilities now, Conn?"

He looked at her, silent for a long moment. Then he said softly, "You're wrong, you know. During the past few years I have learned how to take a few risks. I don't like them. I do my best to minimize them whenever I can, and I prefer to plan matters so that there are as few chances as possible. But that doesn't mean I don't know how to take them. What about you, Honor? Can you take them?"

Honor drew a long breath and then she sank wearily into the chair beside the end table. She clasped her hands in her lap, not looking at him. "I might. For the right man. But you're not that man, are you, Conn? The right man for me would never have believed me capable of trying to avenge myself by poisoning a horse. The right man for me wouldn't have threatened violence. The right man would have trusted me when the chips were down."

She sensed his restless movement, but he didn't try to touch her.

"The chips are down," he bit out huskily. "And I'm willing to... to consider your side of the story. I could almost believe that even if you did it, you might have thought you had a reason."

The awkward, uncertain way he said it infuriated Honor. Her head snapped toward him. "Oh, golly gee, thanks. You don't know how terrific that makes me feel. Your generosity of spirit overwhelms me, Landry.''

He glowered at her, shoving a hand through his tousled hair. "You don't know what I've been through last night and this morning. I woke up with a hangover that would have constituted a reasonable excuse for turning myself in to a hospital emergency room. Then I get a phone call telling me to come down to the track, where I'm shown some very convincing evidence that the woman I've been sleeping with has tried to take some revenge by poisoning my horse. I haven't had a thing to eat since yesterday and I can't think of anything except the fact that the woman I'd decided was different from her father has probably made a fool of me. She tells me she loves me in one breath and then turns around and deliberately taunts me when I give a little ground and admit I'm willing to look at her side of the matter. Is it any wonder I'm not feeling extremely charitable?''

"What about me? I've been through the wringer myself. I discover that the man I've fallen in love with has only been playing some kind of strange game with me. I come to the beach for a little peace and quiet and find out he's followed me, intending to punish me for a crime I didn't commit. He succeeds in terrifying me and then announces he's willing to make a deal. I'm going to be allowed to go to bed with him a few more times so that he can work me out of his system. In exchange, he's willing to concede I might not have tried to injure his horse. No guarantees, no nonsense about falling in love, no promises for tomorrow. Heck of a deal you're offering, Landry.''

He moved then, reaching down to haul her abruptly to her feet. "Believe me," he muttered, his face very close to hers, his eyes ablaze with a strange light, "it's better than the deals I usually offer." Conn's arms locked around her as he brought his mouth down on hers.

But this time the kiss was different. Honor sensed the change at once and knew that this time she didn't have to fight back. She relaxed faintly, letting his frustrated, demanding need wash over her in waves.

She shouldn't have had even a vestige of concern for his emotional state. It was her own she ought to have been worrying about. But she was a woman in love, and in spite of what she had told him earlier, nothing could alter that. Her palms stroked slowly down his back in a gentling fashion.

"Honor," Conn growled softly. "Honor, don't fight me. I want you the way you've been since our first night together. Warm and sweet and welcoming."

She wondered vaguely if he'd even realized what he'd just said and decided that he probably didn't. Not entirely. Regardless of what had happened between them, she was coming to understand this complicated man. He needed love whether he knew it or not. And a part of him was trying to reach out and take it even though another aspect of his nature was warning him that she was capable of betrayal. The conflict within him was almost palpable.

Slowly she pulled free of his embrace and he let her go reluctantly.

"Honor?"

"You said you hadn't eaten since yesterday," she murmured, starting back toward the kitchen without meeting his eyes. "It's almost lunchtime."

He hesitated and then followed her. "Are you going to feed me?" Conn asked with deliberate mockery.

"I'm going to feed myself. I can make an extra sandwich for you, if you'd like." Honor opened the refrigerator door.

"Yes," he said so quietly she wasn't sure she heard him. "I'd like." He sat down at the kitchen table, watching her intently as she went about the business of slicing bread for sandwiches. He didn't say a word as she finished slathering the chutney-and-cream-cheese mixture on the bread and set a plate down in front of him. When she sat down on the other side of the table, Conn finally spoke again. "You were right about one thing."

"What's that?"

"At least we're not at each other's throats the way our fathers ended up all those years ago." He picked up a sandwich half and took a large, healthy bite.

"Could have fooled me," Honor said bluntly. "I could have sworn you were at my throat."

Conn's gaze narrowed as he munched his sandwich. "You don't know me all that well, Honor. If I'd really gone for your throat..." He let the sentence die, turning back to his food with a vengeance as though he didn't want to finish his words.

Honor swallowed and stared at him for a long moment. "Yes, I know. If you'd really gone for my throat you'd have torn it out by now. What's been holding you back, Conn?" For the first time she allowed herself to think about the full ramifications of his behavior. Intuitively she knew she was right. If Conn Landry had been intent on tearing her apart, he'd have done it by now. Men like Landry didn't compromise.

Yet Conn was willing to compromise with her.

He looked at her, considering. "Beats me," he finally said, shrugging.

Honor sighed. "I like a man who knows his own mind."

"I'll admit that right now I'm not entirely sure of myself or of you. I don't like the feeling, but I'm stuck with it."

"You prefer everything cut and dried, don't you?"

"I prefer everything clear and comprehensible," he drawled. "There are a lot of things going on between us that aren't either clear or comprehensible. They make me"—he hesitated and then concluded—"uneasy."

"Did you really have a hangover this morning?" Honor asked suddenly.

His glance was mildly savage. "I went to bed very drunk last night."

"Because of what had happened between us?" she pressed.

"I was annoyed. Irritated. Disgusted. Impatient. I decided to medicate my emotions with an old-fashioned remedy. What the hell's so amusing about that?"

Honor's faint flicker of humor disappeared at once. Indeed, she wasn't even sure from where it had sprung. "Nothing. I guess it's just, well, *interesting* to think of you deliberately getting drunk because of a quarrel with a woman. Somehow it doesn't sound like something you'd do."

"You're such an expert on what I'm likely to do in any given situation?" he challenged roughly.

"I'm learning fast," she shot back. "Do you want another sandwich?"

He chewed for a moment before answering, his gaze reflective. Then he nodded briskly. "Yes, please. I think I'm going to live."

"Poor Landry," Honor said with surprisingly gentle mockery. "You really have had a hard day, haven't you?'' She got to her feet and went over to the counter to construct another cream-cheese-and-chutney sandwich. Then she poured some more coffee.

Carrying both over to the table, Honor sat down again and silently asked herself the question she couldn't decide how to ask aloud. *What now?*

"This cabin belonged to your father?" Conn asked after a moment, glancing around at the rustic interior.

Honor had the distinct impression he was searching for a topic that, while it might not be completely neutral, because nothing was neutral between them right now, was at least less emotional.

"Yes." Compelled to further his efforts at nonlethal communication, Honor sought for something else to add. "He used to bring Adena and me and Mother here whenever possible. I don't use it much anymore. Generally I keep it rented out, but this time of year it's often empty."

"That's Stylish Legacy?" Conn nodded toward one of the winner's circle photos. A framed clipping cut out of a fifteen-year-old issue of the *Daily Racing Form* hung beside it.

"Yes." Again Honor struggled for neutral words. "All the photos are of Stylish Legacy."

Conn finished his sandwich and picked up his coffee cup. Then he got to his feet and wandered over to the nearest photograph. The picture showed the stallion, head high, jockey still perched on his back, posing for the camera with the usual assortment of people crowded around. Nearly twenty people had squeezed into the photo, most of whom were total strangers who had dashed in front of the photographer just for fun.

Richard Stoner and Nick Mayfield stood nearest the groom, who held Stylish Legacy's head. Conn studied the fifteen-year-old photo of his father and his father's best friend for a silent moment and then he turned away.

"You've kept all your father's records and mementos of Stylish Legacy?" he asked, wandering out into the living room to glance at some more of the pictures.

"I couldn't bring myself to throw them away, but I didn't want them in my apartment, either. Too many memories," Honor confessed.

"Too many unanswered questions, you mean." Conn fingered the small racing saddle.

"Perhaps."

"They look very pleased with themselves, don't they?" Conn stopped again in front of another winner's circle photo.

"Dad and Richard Stoner? Yes, they do," Honor agreed, getting up to go stand in the kitchen doorway. She watched Conn as he studied the picture. "Proud and excited by the win."

"They trusted each other at that point."

"Yes." She waited, uncertain what to say next. "They were partners and they owned a winner."

"Apparently that wasn't enough to hold the partnership together." Conn swung around, pinning her with his eyes. "I wonder what it takes."

"To hold a partnership together?"

"To hold two people together. A man and a woman, for instance," he said deliberately.

"I don't know," Honor retorted carefully. "I suppose it depends on the particular man and woman involved."

"There would have to be trust," Conn suggested too quietly.

"At a minimum." She decided to ask the question she hadn't dared ask earlier. "What now, Conn?"

He set down his coffee cup and looked at her. "A walk on the beach?"

"I've already been for a walk on the beach."

"I could use the fresh air."

It was an overture, Honor realized. Tentative, cautious, uncertain, but an overture nonetheless. "All right."

Chapter Eight

Honor lay alone in bed that night and wondered for the hundredth time what was going through Conn Landry's head. He was out there in the living room, supposedly sleeping on the couch. He'd accepted the arrangement without a murmur of protest, as if he couldn't have cared less where he slept. She had been very calm, very deliberate, about fetching pillows and a quilt from the closet and setting them out on the sofa. He'd simply watched her, sitting by the fire, his head back against the cushion of the chair.

She'd been deeply aware of his intent stare all evening, aware of dark, unspoken questions hovering in his mind, aware of the tightly restrained desire in him. All of Honor's feminine instincts warned her that the smoldering caldron of emotions tormenting Conn tonight constituted real danger for her. But a part of her was resonating in response to the mixture of sensations emanating from him.

Honor turned on her side, twisting restlessly amid the sheets and blankets. She hadn't slept at all since going to bed an hour and a half earlier. Dinner had been a quiet affair. Neither Conn nor Honor seemed able to make casual conversation under the tense circumstances. Honor had considered various ways of telling Conn that he couldn't stay the night, but all the phrases of rejection had died on her lips.

It wasn't just that she was afraid he wouldn't leave; it was that, deep down, she didn't want him to leave. A tentative truce had been established out there on the beach that afternoon. She wanted time to pursue it, time to rebuild some basis for trust.

She was a fool to want to reestablish something that had never really existed in the first place, Honor told herself again and again as she lay listening to the insistent pulse of the sea. There was nothing to be salvaged between herself and Conn. He had been using her from the beginning to work out a warped notion of revenge, and now that someone had menaced his extremely valuable racehorse he would probably never trust Honor, even if she could somehow prove her innocence.

And how could she prove her innocence? Someone had apparently seen a visitor at the barns who looked like her. Given the shaky situation between herself and Conn, that was more than enough to damn her in his eyes. Furthermore, he was convinced she'd had a motive.

He'd arrived at the cottage in a fury, full of threats and retaliation. But somehow none of those promises of menace had really materialized. There had been moments of genuine danger; Honor was well aware of them, but Conn hadn't actually carried any of them to the ultimate conclusion. He hadn't hurt her, and tonight he was sleeping on her sofa, not forcing his way into her bed.

Honor tried to think logically, to analyze Conn Landry's actions since his arrival at the cottage. There was no doubt in her mind that he was coiled like a whip, poised to strike. But this evening he seemed uncertain of his target, even though she had been within range all day. She wondered what was holding him back.

Perhaps the part of him that seemed to need her was stronger than the side of him that couldn't trust her. The need in him would involve much more than physical desire, Honor realized. A man like Conn Landry would not be at the mercy of his hormones. He was too self-contained, too controlled. If he was in a turmoil because of a woman it was because he wanted or needed something from her more than physical satisfaction. By the same token, Honor decided, it would be difficult for him to accept that he needed more from a relationship. It would force him to acknowledge a certain vulnerability and that would be hard on Landry.

It was all very confusing, deeply troubling, and it was definitely making it impossible to sleep. Honor moved uneasily, adjusting the covers with a futile gesture. She wished she wasn't so pulsatingly aware of Constantine Landry's presence in the next room. It was as though his own turbulent emotions were reaching out to tangle with hers. Lying there alone she couldn't be certain how much of the tightly-wound sensation she was feeling was due to her own jumbled thoughts or to her awareness of his. The sensation of commingling was strange, adding to her restlessness.

Surmounting all the questions, anger, doubts and fears, however, was a gradually strengthening desire to ease the pain she had seen in his eyes. The tension that had been flowing back and forth between herself and Conn all evening had taken its toll on him as well as on her. She wanted to ease the fierce intensity she sensed in him and in so doing, ease the uncertainty within herself.

But she would be a total idiot to go out into the other room and make any such efforts. There was enough of the predator in Landry to make such a move dangerous in the extreme. True, he had himself under control now, but if she wandered out there dressed in her nightgown, her hair tumbling around her shoulders, her feet bare, he was liable to read an open invitation in her actions. And who could blame him?

Still, she wasn't going to get to sleep tonight at this rate, and the turbulent state of her emotions demanded some positive action. The knowledge that Conn was experiencing his own heightened tension was enough to push Honor into doing something decisive, even if it was reckless.

With a surge of determination she pushed aside the covers and reached for her robe. When she stepped off the small rug beside the bed, her toes curled in response to the cold hardwood floor. But Honor ignored the chilly sensation and walked to her bedroom door. She opened it slowly, softly, and found the living room illuminated only with the faintly smoldering ruins of the fire.

Standing there in the doorway, her fingers clutching the lapels of the robe, Honor swept the shadows with her gaze. She was seeking the man whose unsettled state seemed to have been tangling with her own. When her eyes found his lean form still sprawled in the overstuffed chair in front of the hearth, some of her initial determination faltered. She stood very still in the doorway, not certain what to say now that the moment was upon her.

"Conn?"

"Go back to bed, Honor." The words were spoken in a flat, inflexible tone of warning. Conn didn't move.

Honor took a step forward, the robe flaring gently around her ankles. "I want to talk to you," she said.

"I don't think that's such a good idea right now." He kept his brooding gaze on the fire.

Honor took another step and then a third. She kept going until she was standing beside his chair. "I can't sleep, and it doesn't look as though you've been doing much sleeping, either. We need to talk, Conn."

"About what?" he asked roughly. The pale flicker of the remnants of the fire highlighted the harsh lines of his face as he continued to gaze down into the embers. "We've had trouble talking all evening, in case you haven't noticed. Why should we try it again now? I think it would be much more intelligent on your part if you went back into that bedroom and closed the door."

Honor caught her breath and sank down onto her knees beside the chair so that she could meet his eyes. Her movement finally forced him to look at her, and when he did, she saw the turmoil of frustration and pain and hunger in his gaze.

"Maybe you're right," she said softly. "Maybe now isn't the time to talk."

"Get out of here, Honor. Believe me, it would be best if you went back to your room. I'm not—" He broke off, searching for words and then continued evenly, "I'm not sure of myself right now. I'm not sure that I'm in complete control."

He sounded vaguely dazed by the admission and the words released much of the restraint Honor had tried to put on her own emotions. She reached out and touched his fingers as they lay curling tightly into the arm of the chair. "It's all right, Conn. I'm not in complete control, either. But, then, I never am around you." She risked a tentative smile.

He stared at her. "Woman, do you know what you're doing?"

"Yes. No. Not completely. I only know I can't go back into that bedroom alone. There is too much going on between us. Too much that is unsettled."

The hand she had been lightly touching moved, shifting abruptly to catch her questing fingers in a grip of iron. "Unsettled questions are dangerous, Honor. Don't you know that?"

"I'm learning."

He drew in a deep breath and she could see the decision in his burning eyes. "Why are you so willing to take risks tonight?" he demanded softly.

"I don't seem to have any choice."

Conn gave her a strange look. "You may be right." For a moment longer he simply gripped her hand, not moving as he continued to search her face. "No more choice than I've got in the matter. We're trapped in this web together, you and I. It's been like that from the beginning. I should have realized how it would be. But how could I have guessed?"

"Conn? I don't understand—"

But he didn't allow her to finish the question. Instead, he uncoiled to his feet, retaining his hold on her and drawing her up to stand in front of him. Honor felt the fine trembling in his touch as he pulled her slowly, inevitably, against the length of his body. The heat in him seemed to reach out, engulfing her, and she responded with a soft cry. Her arms went around his waist and she let her head sink down on his shoulder.

"Neither of us can find the words right now," he grated hoarsely. "There's no point trying. You've come to me when you could have stayed safely in your room."

"Yes."

"Then there's nothing else to talk about." He lifted her face with the edge of his palm. For a few intense, vital seconds he stared down into her soft eyes and then he muttered something incomprehensible. Whatever it was got swallowed up in the kiss that followed.

Honor gave herself over to the drugging emotion of the embrace. It seemed to her now that only the flaring passion that ignited so quickly between them could bridge the chasm that stretched between herself and Conn. A part of her would pay any price to cross that abyss tonight. Even if the bridge was made of rainbows and fire and would disintegrate before morning, she would build it because the need to reach him was so overwhelming.

Conn's mouth was a furnace of damp heat that communicated his passion without any restraint. His hands slid down her back to her hips, moving possessively on her. The fierce urgency in him sought to overtake her and bring her to the ground. The predatory quality in Conn that Honor had sensed from the beginning was fully alive tonight, but she understood it because there was an echo of it in herself. Her own need to communicate, even though the communication was on the sensual level, approached the violent in its intensity.

"Honor, I have to have you now. I couldn't stop even if I wanted to try. Woman, you don't know how it is with me tonight, what I feel like inside. I'm burning." Conn's mouth moved heavily on hers, staking a claim before moving to the curve of her shoulder.

Honor gasped as she felt the light touch of his teeth on her bare skin. Then her robe was being loosened, pulled free of her body and discarded at her feet. She shivered as his hands shaped the curves of her breast, the heat of his palms sinking into her through the soft nightgown. And then the interior of the cottage spun around her as Conn abruptly swept her up into his arms.

She closed her eyes and drew her fingers lightly along the nape of his neck as he carried her into the bedroom. The strength in him made her feel secure, even though a small voice whispered that perhaps she should fear it.

Conn settled her into the depths of the tousled bed and stood for a moment looking down at her. His eyes never left hers as he unbuttoned his shirt and unfastened his belt. When at last he stood naked, his maleness an aggressive force dominating the room, Honor moved. She put out a hand to draw him down to her.

"Honor, honey. Oh, *Honor!*"

He came to her, stripping off her nightgown in a swift, impatient movement that left the material crumpled in a heap at the foot of the bed. Then Conn moved across her body with the power of a wave breaking on a reef. Honor felt herself responding vibrantly, her body achingly alive and aware. The emotional tension that had been tightening within her all day was transmuted into a physical tension. It sang through her nerve endings and throbbed deep in her lower body.

She traced the outline of Conn's hard, muscled frame with soft fingers that held a woman's demands. He groaned in response to her touch, pushing himself into her palm when she drew her hand down his thighs.

"Conn," she whispered as the driving power in him throbbed under her touch.

"I want you, Honor. I can't stop wanting you," he rasped. His lips roved from one nipple to the other, exciting and challenging. When Honor lifted her hips instinctively, moving against him with unconscious need, he traced a sensuous path down her body to the apex of her legs. "Open for me, sweetheart. Let me feel the passion in you."

She writhed beneath him, obeying the command. His husky words of encouragement and demand were dark and heavy in her ears. Then she felt his fingers working exotic magic amid the secrets of her body and she cried out again.

"You want me," he growled, pushing his strong legs between her soft thighs. "Say it. Say you want me!"

"Yes, darling. I want you. With everything that's in me. I've never needed anyone the way I need you."

Her words seemed to thrust him over the edge. Conn muttered her name between clenched teeth, and then he was forging into her warmth, claiming her fire for his own with relentless force.

"Hold me," he ordered with an aching harshness. "Hold me, Honor. Wrap yourself around me and don't let go!"

Honor had the fleeting but vivid impression that Conn wasn't even aware of his own rough command but she reacted to it with everything that was in her. With all her strength she clung to him, riding the whirlwind. The final burst of unraveling excitement sent shivers through her that generated a powerful reaction in Conn. His fingers sank into the skin of her shoulders and he arched heavily into her softness. There was a thick muffled, wholly male cry of release and satisfaction from far back in his throat and then he was collapsing damply along her body.

For a long while Honor lay quietly beneath Conn's muscled weight, recovering her energy and her senses.

She was beginning to think he might have gone to sleep when he finally stirred and opened his eyes to look down at her flushed face.

"I wonder," Conn murmured at last, "if you have any idea of what you've done."

"They say that in reality it doesn't work," she whispered soberly.

"What doesn't work?"

"Going to bed with a man in order to achieve some sense of communication. The conventional wisdom has it that in the end all you get is a few moments of illusion. In the morning everything's the same."

His lashes lowered until she couldn't read the expression in the gray eyes. "Is that what you were doing? Trying to communicate?"

"I suppose, I couldn't stand the distance between us any longer. I guess a part of me thought that if we...if I...."

"A part of you thought that if you seduced me the distance between us would disappear?" He toyed with a tendril of her hair as it lay along her bare shoulder. "You took a big risk."

"Did I?"

He paused a few beats as if thinking it over. "Yes. I could use you now. Let you think that you were achieving your mystical, nonverbal communication for a few days."

"While you worked me out of your system?" she dared.

"Ummm. And when I've had enough I could simply walk out the door." He twisted the tendril of hair between his fingers and tugged slightly, his mouth tightening.

"Yes," she agreed. "You could do that."

"There's just one problem," Conn continued thoughtfully.

"What's that?"

"I don't think I could ever get enough of you to work you out of my system. I'd be deluding myself if I decided to try that route."

Honor closed her eyes briefly, aware of the precarious balance between them. "I was deluding myself when I decided to try going to bed with you in order to communicate more effectively."

He went still. "Were you?"

"I went to bed with you because I love you," she admitted softly. "I suppose communication is a part of love, but the truth is that I would have walked out into that living room tonight even if I knew that I'd never see you again afterward."

"Honor," he breathed, lowering his head to brush his mouth against hers, "I'm glad."

"You probably are," she agreed wistfully. "The way it stands now, I get to take all the risks, don't I?"

"Loving me is a risk?" He frowned.

"A big one. I never dreamed I'd fall in love with a man who couldn't give me his trust. But, then, I never thought I'd be foolish enough to fall in love with a man I couldn't trust, either."

Conn's frown metamorphosed into cold anger, but he didn't move. "You're saying you love me but you don't trust me? I don't believe you, Honor. I've never given you any reason not to trust me."

"You didn't tell me you were Richard Stoner's son," she reminded him.

"That's different," he flared, visibly offended by her interpretation of his silence on that score. "I never lied to you about it. I simply decided not to mention it until ... until I got to know you better.''

''Until you'd decided how you'd take your revenge?''

He shook his head once with savage impatience. ''No. I knew it would introduce a problem into our relationship and I didn't want to do that. Not when everything between us was so new and fragile. I wanted to move cautiously until I knew you understood how things were between us.''

She stared up at him. ''And how are things between us?'' Honor whispered.

Conn's head lifted with faint masculine challenge. ''I want you and you love me. That pretty well sums it all up, don't you think?''

''I think I'm getting the short end of the deal,'' she tossed back. ''Other than that—''

''No,'' Conn interrupted grittily. ''You're not getting the short end of the deal. You're getting everything I have to give.''

Dumbfounded, Honor looked up at him. ''All you have to give? I don't understand.''

His hands framed her face, holding her still. ''I want you,'' he said evenly, ''more than I've ever wanted any woman in my life. It goes beyond wanting in a physical sense. I could handle that if it only involved a desire to take you to bed. But it's more than that. I need you in some way I can't explain. And because I have to have you in order to stay sane I'm prepared to take a risk. More of a risk than I have ever taken with another human being. I've been thinking about it all afternoon. It's what was going through my head out there in front of the fire. It's been eating at me since I got here this morning. I have to trust you. I don't seem to have any choice. Tell me again that you didn't try to poison Legacy."

"I didn't try to hurt Legacy in any way," she answered in a low but very steady voice.

He sighed and she felt something in him relax. "I've met a lot of people who can lie while they smile and look you straight in the eye. Enough of them to know you're probably not one of them. It's taken me a few hours to work it out because everything hit me like a ton of bricks this morning."

"And you instinctively expected the worst from me because I'm Nick Mayfield's daughter, right?" she asked with resigned bitterness.

"I'm accustomed to expecting the worst from people in general," he admitted calmly. "Life is safer and simpler that way. That philosophy has been responsible for keeping me alive on occasion."

"I can imagine." But she knew he missed the note of irony. Conn was too busy finishing what he had to say.

"But there's a softness in you that wouldn't mesh very well with a woman who would try to get revenge on a man by poisoning a horse. You give yourself too completely when you give yourself to me. You don't hold back. Even tonight when you thought you were only seducing me in order to reestablish communication you weren't careful or cautious. There is no restraint in you when you take me in your arms. You wrap yourself around me and make it very clear that you want me and need me. You're *vulnerable* to me, aren't you?"

"Not by choice."

A cool, laconic smile flickered briefly at the edge of his mouth. "No, not by choice. In spite of yourself. You know you should be wary of me. You're smart enough to realize I could be dangerous. From the very beginning you've tried to be careful around me, put some distance between us. But it didn't work, did it?"

"No."

He nodded in deep satisfaction. "When you opened the door and walked out into the living room tonight, I knew for certain."

Honor moved her head uneasily on the pillow. His palms slid down to her throat. "Knew what for certain?"

"That you couldn't stand the space between us. The knowledge that what we had together was teetering on the brink was eating at you, wasn't it? You couldn't bear to let it all fall apart. When you came out into that room to find me, I realized you couldn't let me go any more than I could allow you to walk away from me."

"You make it sound as though we're trapped together."

"We are. Caught up in a web from which neither of us can escape. We need each other. You label your emotion love and I call mine wanting, but it amounts to the same thing."

Desperately Honor tried to think it all through. "You believe I didn't try to get at you through Legacy?"

"I believe you didn't try to poison the colt," Conn stated quietly.

The breath Honor had been holding escaped in a long sigh. "Thank you, Conn."

His thumb moved slowly along the base of her throat. "It's your turn. Do you believe I didn't deliberately seduce you in order to get revenge for what happened between our parents?"

"I think," Honor said very honestly, "that you would use some other method if you were really out to punish me for what you think happened fifteen years ago. As I said earlier, if you ever went for my throat, you'd be quick and brutal about it. You wouldn't make love to me the way you do."

The smile reappeared fleetingly. "And just how do I make love to you?"

"Completely. Overwhelmingly. I can't believe that you're playing bedroom games with me. There's too much of...of *you* in the way you make love." It was the truth, Honor realized. There was a quality of blatant, fundamental honesty in the way Conn staked his claim of passion and possession. No games, no fancy techniques such as another man might employ to achieve a woman's surrender. Just rock-solid desire that carried its own kind of reassurance and established its own integrity. She, too, had had a chance to do some thinking this afternoon and evening, Honor decided with sudden insight.

"I think we both needed the breathing space we got this afternoon," Conn said, his eyes intent.

"Did you mean what you said a minute ago? That your idea of wanting and my notion of love amount to the same thing?" She wasn't certain why she risked the question. There was too much riding on it, too much hope. It was reckless to ask questions like that, but she needed to know exactly how he felt about her. If he chose to label his love for her "wanting" and "needing," she could live with that. So long as underneath she knew that what he really felt was equivalent to what she felt.

The gray eyes softened indulgently. "Why do women always want to dress it up by calling it love?"

"It's not a matter of dressing it up. Love is what it is. Why not call it by its proper name?" It was Honor's turn to be indulgent. "I think you're the one who's searching for labels. Do you love me, Conn? Are you playing it safe again by hiding behind more acceptable macho words like *want* and *need*?"

His eyes narrowed faintly. "I'm not trying to play it safe. I'm trying to be honest with you. I want nothing but honesty between us from here on in, Honor. We have to establish that if we're to have a basis for a future."

"I agree," she whispered tremulously. "We need honesty. But if we're to have a future, we also need love. I thought—that is, I was beginning to think—that maybe you were falling in love with me and that you just weren't sure of the words yet. But that's not the case, is it?"

"I know the words don't mean much. Do you want me to say them even though I don't believe in them?" he challenged roughly.

"No." She shook her head quickly. "No, I don't want you to lie to me. Not ever."

"I won't, honey," he soothed, stroking her cheek with infinite care. "You can believe anything I tell you."

"What about the things you don't tell me?"

He shrugged, his sleek shoulders moving easily in the shadows. "The things I don't tell you aren't important for you to know. They don't impact us."

She swallowed, a little stunned. "You're so incredibly arrogant at times. And the most arrogant thing of all is that I don't think you even realize it. You just take your own assurance for granted. Will you take me for granted, I wonder?"

He moved his head in a gesture of absolute denial. "Never. I'll take care of you, Honor. I'll protect you.

I'll take you to bed as often as possible and I'll always tell you the truth. But I swear I'll never take you for granted. How could I? I've been around long enough to realize that some things are unique in the universe."

"But you don't love me," she concluded sadly.

Anger flashed quickly across his face. "What I feel for you hasn't got anything to do with something as rosy and soft and ephemeral as love. It's a hell of a lot more certain and more real. I'm making a commitment to you, lady. And I'm asking for a commitment in return. Something we can both count on, something solid and sure. If I'm going to get tangled up in this web with you, I'm going to pull all the strands as tight as possible."

"Because you always tie up loose ends," she finished for him.

"Always." He relaxed again. "Why do you keep pushing, sweetheart? You know it's settled now, don't you?"

"I think it is. For you."

"It works both ways. Whatever chance you had of freeing yourself from the trap in which we're caught disappeared when you came out into the living room to find me tonight." He lowered his head to seal the words against her mouth. "I don't want to talk anymore for a while, Honor." His palm slid meaningfully down her arm until his fingers twined with hers. Then he raised her hand to a level with her ear and turned it so that he could kiss the vulnerable inside of her wrist.

Honor hesitated for a moment, trying to hold back long enough to force him to continue the dialogue that had just been established. Then she gave up the effort. What was the point? She'd accomplished so much. She would make herself be content with what she had achieved tonight. After all, she had known from the beginning that Conn Landry did not understand love. She could hardly expect the revelation to hit him on top of everything else that had happened today. At the moment she would be grateful that the relationship between herself and the man she loved had not fallen over the brink on which it had been so precariously balanced. Together she and Conn had rescued it.

Love would come eventually, Honor reassured herself as she surrendered to the insistence of Conn's touch. For him the trust was the hard part and she hoped that tonight his belief in her integrity had been established. There was time to work on building the rest.

Honor awoke a long time later, vaguely aware that she was lying alone in bed. It took a moment to reorient herself, and when she did, she sat up with a sudden, panicked jerk.

"Conn?"

"I'm in the kitchen. Be back in a minute. I just wanted a glass of water."

"Oh." In relief Honor glanced at the clock beside the bed. It was two-thirty in the morning. Now that she was awake, she felt a little thirsty herself. Sleepily she pushed aside the quilt and padded barefoot into the kitchen. Conn was standing near the sink, drinking his glass of water while he studied yet another shot of Stylish Legacy.

"Hey, it's cold out here," he murmured as Honor reached into the cupboard to get a glass for herself. "You should have put on your robe."

"You're a fine one to talk," she grumbled, eyeing his attire, which consisted solely of a pair of white briefs. "You've got on a lot less than I have." She yawned as she filled the glass.

"I was planning on using you to warm myself up as soon as I got back into bed," Conn informed her absently as he bent a little closer to Stylish Legacy's photo. "You know, I think Legacy inherited his sire's basic conformation, especially the strong hindquarters."

Honor gave him a small, amused smile. "You've got it bad, Conn."

"What?" He turned his head to glance at her in surprise.

"Racing. I can see it's really getting a hold on you. My father was that way about it. He tried to keep Stylish Legacy just a business deal, a tax shelter. But the truth was that he was hooked on the whole racing scene."

Conn watched her drink her water. "So was my father. Just look at the two of them in this photo. You'd think they'd won the Kentucky Derby instead of just another stakes race."

Automatically Honor's gaze followed his. She rarely looked at the photos closely. Whenever she saw the pictures of her father and his partner, the old, unsettled sensation swept over her. As a result she had gotten into the habit of never really studying the photos.

But for some reason Conn's deep interest in the pictures of Stylish Legacy intrigued her. For the first time in years she found herself looking at the jumble of people around the winning horse. Conn was right. Regardless of what had happened between them later, at the time this picture was taken Richard Stoner and Nick Mayfield were two very happy, very satisfied racehorse owners.

"They do look quite pleased with themselves," she acknowledged softly.

"So does everyone else in the photo. How do all those strangers always manage to crowd into the picture?"

"I expect it's kind of a game. Like getting yourself on TV when a television film crew shows up." Honor realized that she wasn't feeling the usual uncomfortable sadness she remembered experiencing in the past whenever she'd looked at these pictures. Out of curiosity she moved across the kitchen to glance at another. Her trained eye began to pick out details, automatically recording the color of the riding silks the jockey wore, the fifteen-year-old suit her father had on and the cowboy hat on the head of the man standing directly behind Richard Stoner.

Honor blinked and leaned closer.

"What is it?" Conn asked, moving across to stand beside her.

"I think this guy in the hat behind your stepfather is also in that other photo."

"The trainer, probably."

"No, I don't think so. There's something familiar about that hat, Conn." Thoughtfully Honor went back to stare at the other picture. "Same hat. I can't really see his face, but I'd swear there was something about him...." Honor moved to yet another picture, and in this one the face beneath the brim of the cowboy hat was much clearer. "Conn! It's Ethan Bailey. A lot slimmer than he is now and fifteen years younger, but I'd swear it's Ethan."

Conn leaned over her shoulder to stare at the man in the hat. "You're right. But Ethan barely knew either of our fathers. Why would he show up in three winner's circle photos with Dad and Mayfield?"

"At three different tracks, too. He's hardly the type

to run down into the circle to get into the picture just for kicks. That sort of activity is for kids and pranksters.''

Conn straightened, shaking his head. ''We'll have to ask him about it sometime.'' He reached for Honor's hand. ''Come on, honey, let's go back to bed. My feet are getting cold. Along with a few other parts of my anatomy.''

''You expect me to warm all of those parts?''

''It would be a nice, considerate gesture.''

A wifely gesture, Honor thought wistfully. But she kept the comment to herself.

''You know,'' Conn observed lazily as he snuggled Honor down into the covers a moment later, ''I feel as though I'm finally able to think normally again. I spent most of the day feeling bruised, battered, hung over and furious. Now at last everything's begun to settle down.''

''That must be a relief,'' Honor murmured, running her fingers through his hair. ''I have a hunch you're not used to being shaken up and confused, are you?''

''No,'' he growled. ''I'm not.'' He curled Honor closer into his body, luxuriating in the warmth of her.

''Well, if it's any consolation, neither am I,'' she told him gently.

It was then that Conn's new clearheadedness reminded him of the question he had intended to ask Honor. He paused, his mouth hovering just over hers.

''How did you find out I was Richard Stoner's son?''

Honor was quiet for a moment and then she said calmly, ''Ethan Bailey told me.''

Landry swore very softly and sat up in bed. ''Why is it that every time I turn around lately, Ethan Bailey seems to be nearby?''

Chapter Nine

"Didn't you realize that Ethan Bailey knew who you were?" Honor asked. She lay propped up on the pillows, watching Conn as he swung his feet over the edge of the bed and turned on the lamp.

"The subject never came up with Ethan."

"You've said yourself that racetrack rumors are prevalent. And Ethan's been around racetracks for years. Other than using your own name instead of Stoner, did you ever make any effort to hide your connection with Stylish Legacy and his original owners?"

"No." The answer was clipped, impatient, as if Conn's mind was busy tracing a pattern and didn't want to be bothered with side issues. Conn stared unseeingly at the wall for several tense minutes, his face set in familiar, harsh lines.

Uneasily Honor leaned forward to touch his shoulder. "Conn?"

"Ethan was the one who found the apples in Legacy's feed this morning. The one who told me you'd been seen around the barns very early today."

"Oh." She didn't quite know what to say in response. Her hand dropped from his shoulder.

Conn twisted around to meet her eyes, his gaze cold and intent. "When did he tell you who I was?"

"Yesterday. He came downtown to my office and said he felt obliged to warn me that you might not be telling me the whole truth about yourself," Honor said in a low voice. Conn's mouth became even grimmer. "It wasn't the first time he'd tried to warn me about you."

Conn caught her chin on the edge of his hand and held her still. The gunmetal-gray of his eyes was almost lethal in the soft light. "What else did he tell you about me?"

Honor licked her suddenly dry lower lip. From out of nowhere the fear of Constantine Landry resurfaced. A knot of tension began tightening in her stomach as she felt the power in his hand. He wasn't hurting her, merely anchoring her in place for the moment, but the leashed savagery in his eyes was more than enough to trigger elemental alarms all over again. Forcibly she fought down the doubts and uncertainties. Conn's violence was not aimed at her.

"He implied at one point that you might be mixed up in gambling up at Tahoe. I wondered if that was why you knew how to bring pressure to bear on Granger," she admitted unsteadily.

"That bastard," Conn said far too calmly. He didn't release her.

Honor wasn't certain if he was referring to Ethan Bailey or Granger. Taking a grip on her nerves she continued more firmly. "He told me that I wasn't your usual type."

"As if he'd know."

"Yes. Well, then yesterday he said he'd realized who both of us were and he wanted to warn me that you'd once sworn revenge on my family. He implied you were playing some kind of cat-and-mouse game with me." With a touch of anger Honor wrenched herself free of Conn's grasp and drew her knees up under the sheet. She balanced an elbow on each knee, folded her arms and rested her chin on them. "Which you were, in a way."

Conn exhaled slowly. "Which I was, in a way," he agreed coolly.

He made no immediate move to touch her, but Honor could feel the implacable intensity of his eyes. "For the record," she asked softly, "just how do you make a living that allows you to buy expensive racehorses and gives you the free time to hang around Pasadena looking up old family acquaintances?"

There was a measure of silence before Conn retorted, "Does it matter?"

She slid him a sidelong glance and then returned to her contemplation of the foot of the bed. *Did it matter?* She could practically feel the challenge in him. He was deliberately pushing her, she thought, and wondered why. There were two possible causes: arrogance and insecurity.

The idea of Conn Landry feeling insecure and needing reassurance was laughable. But even Landry's arrogance had its limits. She took another risk.

"Do you mean, does it matter in terms of how it affects our relationship? No, it doesn't. But I guess I'd like to know whether or not I'm going to be expected to entertain business acquaintances like Mr. Granger on a frequent basis."

"Relax, Honor," he murmured, his voice softening with a combination of amusement and satisfaction, "I don't make my living by investing in Granger's kind of business. The investments I've made are mostly in real estate. I was paid far too much for the kind of work I did overseas, and since I had no one to spend it on and was too busy to use it myself, I just kept funneling it into stateside property. By the time I came back to the States, there was a nice nest egg waiting for me.''

The way he said it was just a little too smooth, Honor decided, not without a trace of amusement. She lifted her chin off her arms and looked at him. ''How is it you were able to deal so effectively with Granger? Or was he just intimidated by your, uh, forceful personality?''

Honor could have sworn that a red stain appeared momentarily along Conn's cheekbones. She found it almost endearing.

''I occasionally do some consulting work,'' Landry admitted with great care. ''You get to know people that way. Make certain contacts.''

''Consulting work for whom?'' she pressed more out of curiosity now than uneasiness.

''Businesses,'' he said very easily. ''It was my field of expertise, you know. People hired me to analyze security procedures and come up with ways to minimize risks overseas. The same needs exist here in the States.''

''Go on,'' she encouraged, intrigued now.

''Well,'' Conn continued cautiously, ''one of my first jobs when I got back to the States was to analyze the security arrangements around a certain, er, businessman who deals heavily with some of the rougher elements of society.''

''You did consulting work for a gangster.'' Honor nodded in sudden comprehension.

Conn's expression turned distant and forbidding. ''He was a friend of mine. Someone I met a long time ago. He and I had a lot in common at one time but he chose to take a slightly different route to success. When

I got back to the States he got in touch. Said I was the only man he could trust to set up a security system for him. I owed him, Honor. He saved my life once when we worked together briefly several years ago. I always pay my debts. At any rate I used my connection with my former, uh, client, when I confronted Granger. Clout, you might say."

"It's all right, Conn. I trust you," Honor said with a smile. "No more questions about how you managed to intimidate Granger."

He frowned. "Are you sure?"

"I'm sure."

"That still leaves us with the current problem," he remarked, clearly relieved to be able to put the other aside.

"Ethan Bailey."

Conn nodded, saying nothing.

"Ethan did more than tell me you were looking for revenge," Honor offered offhandedly. "He also told me you lied about Granger."

"Lied about Granger! What did he say?" Conn demanded.

"That Granger had never been picked up that day at the track. That he hadn't walked into any trap."

"The implication being, of course, that I hadn't saved you from getting mixed up in the mess. That the whole story had been a fabrication designed to establish a link between you and me. A link I could use." Conn sounded coldly bitter.

"You've implied more than once that I was under some sort of obligation to you," she reminded him gently.

"Damn right," he shot back. "You were. But it was a legitimate obligation. I didn't fake it."

Honor shook her head, another flash of amusement lighting her eyes. "So arrogant."

Conn's mouth curved wryly. "I must seem that way to you at times."

"So Granger really did walk into a trap set by the authorities that day?" she queried.

"Oh, yes. And he was released on bail shortly thereafter."

"What would you have done if I hadn't conveniently needed rescuing?" Honor asked, accepting his version of the truth.

"Found another way to approach you. When I realized you were following Granger, I decided to wait and see what was happening. It raised a lot of questions. Brought up the possibility that you were in trouble."

"So you decided to take advantage of the situation."

Conn shrugged. "That's the way I am, Honor. I take advantage of my opportunities. I wanted a solid approach to take with you, and that business with Granger gave it to me. I would have been a fool to let it slide."

"I can see why you've been financially successful," she said dryly. The predator in him would never be far below the surface.

"I suggest we get back to Ethan Bailey," Conn said harshly. "It seems very clear that he's the reason we're both here instead of having dinner in Pasadena. He warned you off of me."

"Perhaps out of genuine concern," Honor pointed out.

Conn brushed that aside. "He did more than warn you; he lied to you about Granger. Implied I had lied to you."

Honor heard the emphasis on his last words. "That

really bothers you, doesn't it? That he made it sound as though you'd been less than truthful with me."

"I told you earlier tonight that I've never lied to you," he said grittily.

Honor nodded quickly, aware of the simmering fury in him. "All right. We've got a situation in which Ethan Bailey keeps cropping up, apparently with the goal of making each of us distrust the other."

"He sure as hell implied that it had to be you who tried to give the poison to Legacy," Conn said. "But why? It makes no sense."

"I know. No sense at all. Why should Ethan care about you and me getting together?"

"There's another name that keeps recurring, too—Granger." Conn became thoughtful for a long moment. "It seems to me we've found ourselves talking about him almost as often as we've talked about Bailey."

Honor put her chin back down on her arms. "Remember the evening that guy in the pickup truck hassled me?"

"Yes." He looked at her sharply.

"Well, I could have sworn a similar sort of pickup followed me when I left Pasadena yesterday evening."

Conn was suddenly tense. He leaned forward and caught her shoulder, pulling her around to face him. "You're sure?"

"No. No, I'm not sure," she said honestly. "Traffic was heavy and I could have been mistaken. There are a million pickups on the road these days. You know that. I didn't notice it after a while. Just for a time there, after I got on the freeway. It made me nervous. Then it disappeared. It was probably just my imagination."

"Right now I'm not willing to write anything off to

imagination," Conn said bluntly. "This is getting screwy."

"We've got so little to go on. Ethan in those photos with Dad and your stepfather. The guy in the pickup truck. Granger."

"The guy in the pickup truck could be associated with Granger," Conn said slowly. "But I don't know why. Granger and I did business together. When it was concluded I thought each side was reasonably satisfied with the results."

"Maybe he didn't like the way you got involved in the affair," Honor suggested. "After all, it was between him and Adena."

Conn shook his head. "I guess he might have decided to teach me a lesson." He sounded as though he thought it was highly unlikely.

"If he did would he have been capable of hurting Legacy in order to punish you?"

Conn gave her a pitying glance. "Granger has been successfully collecting money from his loan shark operations for years. Believe me, he's resorted to more exotic techniques than poisoning a horse."

"So I'm a little naive," she mumbled. "I just can't see someone deliberately poisoning a beautiful animal like Legacy."

"You're right. You're a little naive." There was affection in his tone as Conn threaded his fingers through her tangled hair.

"You know, we're forgetting something here," she went on musingly. "Legacy never was actually poisoned. You said Ethan showed you the evidence?"

"That's right. Claimed he got it out of Legacy's stall."

"And then he told you I'd been seen around the barns."

"Yes." The affection disappeared from Conn's voice.

Honor shook her head. "You must have hated me for a while."

He hesitated. "I felt betrayed," he finally acknowledged.

"Like father, like daughter?"

He winced. "I'll admit the thought went through my head. But you must have felt the same way after Ethan told you his tales."

"I did. Betrayed."

There was another moment of silence before Conn said softly, "Ironic, isn't it?"

"Because of the betrayal that occurred between your father and mine? Maybe it was inevitable once you and I made contact."

"No, it was not inevitable," Conn muttered tightly. "The sense of betrayal you and I experienced was deliberately fostered by a third party."

"Ethan Bailey. But he had the material with which to work, didn't he? And he was right, in a way," Honor added.

"Right about what?"

"I'm probably not your usual type," she explained lightly.

"Am I yours?" he retorted.

"Well, no, you're not. Adena was right about that fact, I'm afraid."

"Lady, are you teasing me?" Conn moved abruptly, pushing her back against the pillows and pinning her there. He searched her face, daring her to admit it.

"Maybe. A little."

Conn groaned and then gave her a quick, hard kiss before sitting upright again. "If it matters, I don't think I have a usual type. There haven't been a lot of women in my life, Honor." He looked down at his hands.

"I'm not surprised," she said calmly.

He slid her a startled glance. "Why do you say that? Am I that poor a catch?"

"You wouldn't make a poor catch, just an extremely difficult one to land," she drawled thoughtfully. "A woman would need a very carefully built net."

His eyes narrowed. "It's academic now, isn't it? You and I wound up in the net together. We're both caught."

No, Honor thought, *not quite. I don't have you, not completely. But you do have me. A little unfair, but that's the way the world works, I guess.* Aloud she said, "As you say, it's academic. Especially tonight."

"Especially tonight. Tonight we've got to think a little more about Ethan Bailey."

"And Granger," she added.

Conn suddenly surged to his feet, reaching out for his jeans and pulling them on quickly. "Maybe I can get a few answers about Granger at least."

"Right now?" Honor asked. "In the middle of the night?"

"Some of the people who would know about Granger tend to work the night shift," Conn informed her, buttoning his shirt. "In my line of work I tend to make just as many contacts on the right side of the fence as I do on the wrong side."

"What are you going to do?" Honor slid out of bed and tugged on her robe.

"Make a few phone calls." He started out into the living room with a purposeful stride. "Good thing you keep a phone here."

"Have to. The people I rent to usually can't afford to be without access to a telephone, even when they're on vacation. They're always wheeling and dealing or pretending that they are. Part of the L.A. image." Honor followed him, stepping into her slippers en route. She reached the bedroom doorway just as Conn reached for the phone.

She saw the sudden hardening of his expression even before he started to dial.

"Damn," he muttered, tossing the receiver back into its cradle.

"What's wrong?"

"Phone's out of order." He stood staring at her, gaze unreadable.

"Are you sure? There hasn't been a storm or anything recently."

"No, there hasn't, has there? Get dressed, Honor."

"Dressed! But it's three o'clock in the morning."

"I'm aware of that. It's three o'clock in the morning, the phone's out of order, and we're miles from town. Add to that a short list of rather pithy questions that remain unanswered and the fact that I'm finally starting to think clearly again—and you've got a very messy situation. I want us both out of here. Now. Go get dressed and don't waste any time on the job." He started toward her.

"All right, all right, I'm going," she said quickly. Honor spun around and headed back into the bedroom, spurred on by the cool command in his words. "Are you always like this when you're working?"

He was busy stuffing a few of her things into her suitcase. "Like what?"

"Overbearing and intimidating. You sound like you've had a lot of experience giving orders." She yanked on the jeans and a vividly striped cotton sweater.

"Maybe. Frankly, I've never thought about it." He snapped the case shut. "Ready?"

"No."

"Too bad. Let's get going." He took her arm and towed her toward the door.

"Do you think it's possible you're overreacting to a dead telephone?" Honor inquired dryly.

"Possible. Even probable."

"But that's not going to slow us down, is it?"

"Not a bit." He opened the front door, slamming it behind them and fishing the Porsche keys out of his pocket in one movement. "Get into the car, Honor."

She was beginning to absorb some of his strange sense of urgency, Honor realized, as she hurried around the front of the Porsche and opened the passenger door. He was inside, twisting the key in the ignition even as she dropped into the seat beside him. The normally responsive engine came alive briefly, shuddered and died.

Conn swore and tried again. This time there was even less reaction. He didn't bother to try a third time. Instead he drummed his fingers lightly on the steering wheel and stared out into the darkness.

"We," he announced mildly, "have very big trouble."

"We could try my car," she volunteered tentatively, sensing his deadly serious concern.

"We could, but I have a strange hunch it wouldn't do any good." He shoved open the car door. "Come on, Honor, let's go."

"Where are we going this time? And what do you mean about my car being dead, too?" Anxiously she leaped out of the Porsche, wresting her own keys out of her purse.

Conn glanced around, sweeping the night-dark scene around the cottage. He seemed to make a decision. "Okay, let me have the keys. We'll give it a try."

When her car didn't start on the first attempt, Conn didn't bother with a second. He was out of the seat, grabbing Honor's wrist and yanking her along behind him before the car door had swung shut.

"You think someone sabotaged the cars?" she gasped in amazement, stumbling a little as he pulled her back toward the cottage.

It wasn't Conn who answered her. Another voice responded to the question. "If he does think that, he'd be right," drawled the man who had last been seen driving a black pickup truck. He stepped around the corner of the cottage, allowing the weak moonlight to illuminate the gun he held.

Honor was so startled that she stumbled heavily against Conn. He automatically reached out to steady her but somehow managed to pull her even more thoroughly off balance. In the next instant they both tumbled to the ground with Honor landing in an undignified sprawl across Conn's body.

"Golly, lady. You got a problem or something?" demanded the man with the gun. "Get up. Both of you. Mr. Granger don't want no delays."

"Granger!" The astonishment as well as the anger in Conn's tone was real. Slowly he got to his feet, using his left hand to steady Honor. She was trembling, he realized, but there was little he could do at the moment to reassure her. "Granger sent you?"

"I guess you must have made Mr. Granger mad, moving in on his turf and all." The young punk motioned with the nose of the Saturday night special. "Let's go. Don't got all night."

Conn kept his hold on Honor's arm, pulling her with him as he slowly obeyed the gunman's orders.

"Conn?" Honor spoke his name softly, questioningly, but she followed the urging of his grip as they set out toward the beach.

"Do as he says, honey. He's wired," Conn said in a low voice. The sound of the surf covered his last words but they were dangerously true. The guy with the gun was probably only eighteen or nineteen, street-tough, but riding some kind of high. Perhaps it was just the tense excitement of holding a gun on two people or the rush of power that undoubtedly was coursing through him. Perhaps he'd indulged in a few chemicals to work up his nerve for the task. Whatever it was, the man was lethally high-strung and therefore very unpredictable. Conn had seen the syndrome before. The only way to deal with it at this point was to keep him talking. Conn needed an opening.

"I thought Granger and I had a deal," Conn said, projecting his voice over the increasing noise of the surf. "I was under the impression Mr. Granger stuck by his deals." The gunman was herding his captives out onto the beach where there was virtually no cover behind which a desperate man could dodge. The sand became a further barrier to quick movement, dragging at Conn's shoes and causing Honor to stumble occasionally.

"Mr. Granger don't like the way you conduct business, slick. He said to tell you that you won't be getting in his way again after tonight. It's me that's got a deal with Granger," the punk added with pride.

Conn seized on the hint of arrogance. "Granger trusts you to take care of us?"

Beside him Honor gasped as her foot collided with a

stray piece of driftwood. Other than that she hadn't said a word, Conn realized grimly. She was scared to death, but she wasn't panicking. He felt a possessive admiration for her self-control. The last thing he needed right now was a hysterical woman. The next few minutes were going to be extremely precarious.

"Granger's sent word that he's giving me my chance to prove I can handle jobs for him," the gunman explained. "And you can bet I ain't gonna let him down. Getting in with Granger's a quick way to the big time and I ain't gonna do nothing to blow my chances."

Honor spoke for the first time, glancing over her shoulder to search the man's face in the watery moonlight. It was cold and there was a stiff breeze snapping the air from off the waves. She shivered again under Conn's hand. "You're the man in the black pickup truck who followed me home the other night, aren't you?"

"You got it, lady."

"And you also followed her out of Pasadena?" Conn put in coolly.

"Had to see where you were heading. We knew that wherever the broad went, you'd be sure to follow."

Conn thought about that for a few seconds. "Is that right?"

"You should of stayed in your own league, Landry. Shouldn't have tried to mess around with Granger. He's big-time."

"I didn't realize he was extending his scope of activities to include this kind of thing," Conn admitted dryly. "But I guess it's safe enough for him. After all, you're the one taking all the chances."

The gunman's eyes narrowed in the moonlight. Conn saw the hot, tense anger in the man's face and the uneasy way he lifted the weapon. "I ain't taking no chances, Landry. I told you, Granger's big. He's got this all planned out. All I got to do is carry out instructions and everything's going to be just fine. No sweat."

"The only reason Granger got to be big-time is because he pays people like you to take the risks for him," Conn pointed out calmly.

"Shut up, unless you want it here and now," the punk rasped.

"I take it here and now isn't the way Granger wants it done?" Conn retorted. He felt the fury in himself and wondered at it. It wasn't just that he knew he'd been stupid for having allowed this situation to occur. It went beyond that, centering around his self-disgust at having failed to properly protect Honor. She was his woman, he thought tautly. It was his responsibility to protect her. Yet he'd allowed the reckless passion and the conflicting feelings of betrayal and inexplicable trust to swamp his normally cold-blooded, clear thinking to the point where he'd put Honor in jeopardy. It was traumatic to realize just how deeply involved he was with Honor Mayfield.

"Granger was real particular about how he'd like this done, but if you get tricky, I'm supposed to go ahead and finish things any way I can."

"Where are we going?" Honor asked softly.

"What's that?" the punk demanded suspiciously.

"I asked where we're going," she repeated obediently.

"Down to the far end of the beach. The water's supposed to be dangerous down by the point. Couple of bodies might not resurface for days, if ever."

"I see," Honor muttered.

Conn felt her drawing in deep, even breaths, trying

to control her fear. The knowledge that she was so frightened enraged him further. Savagely he clamped a lid on his emotional reaction. It wouldn't help matters if he allowed his own control to disintegrate. He was unaware of how roughly he had begun to grip Honor's arm until she looked up at him questioningly. He relaxed his hold but he didn't release her. It was cold out here, he thought vaguely. The water would be unbearable.

"You seem to know a lot about the ocean currents around here," Conn managed to observe as they reached the water's edge and turned toward the rocky point at the far end of the beach. There wasn't much more time. The point was only about fifty yards away, looming dark and forbidding in the shadows. Around its base white water foamed evilly.

"I got all the instructions," the gunman informed him sullenly. "I told you everything was planned."

"Were you the one who moved the screen in my bedroom?" Honor asked tightly.

"I don't know what the hell you're talking about, lady. I ain't never been in your bedroom."

Conn slanted a quick, curious glance down at Honor but she was concentrating on her footing. It seemed to him that she was having more than the normal amount of trouble walking in the sand. After all, yesterday morning she'd been running on the beach without this degree of awkwardness. Her present lack of coordination suited him perfectly, however. So perfectly that he wondered whether she was stumbling on purpose. There was no doubt that the gunman wasn't paying much attention to her troubles as long as she stayed on her feet and kept moving. But he must be accustomed to her awkward progress by now. If she were to suddenly stumble to her knees, he probably wouldn't panic and pull the trigger.

Tentatively, uncertain how to get the message across to Honor, Conn tugged at her arm. Was it his imagination or did she actually incline her head slightly? His right hand tightened around the object he had palmed back at the cottage when he'd tugged Honor off balance the first time. He was only going to get one chance, so it would have to count and count heavily. Beside him he felt Honor's new level of tension as she seemed to pull herself physically together.

She was going to do it, Conn realized. She knew what he wanted. He felt another overwhelming rush of pride in her perception. Honor Mayfield was quite a woman to have beside you in a crisis, he decided.

"Let's move it, you two. Hurry up, lady. What's the matter with you? Can't you walk straight?"

"I'm a little scared," Honor retorted flatly.

"Tough. That's your problem, ain't it?" The gunman sounded pleased with the power he was wielding. "If it makes you feel any better, Granger wants this to look real romantic."

"Romantic!" Honor repeated, sounding horrified.

"Yeah. You know. A lovers' quarrel. What the cops like to call a *domestic*."

"My heavens," Honor breathed. And then she stumbled to her knees.

Conn released her at once, making no attempt to break her fall. Instead he swung around in a smooth rush, hurling the metal star-shaped object that had been nestled in his palm.

"Damn you—" the gunman began to yell at Honor, outraged at her clumsiness. But he never finished the sentence.

The razor-sharp blades that formed the points on the star sliced into his shoulder, cutting through the denim shirt he wore as though the material were delicate silk.

The punk screamed in fear and rage. His arm jerked spasmodically and the gun went flying. It landed on the wet sand at the water's edge and an instant later was lost below a breaking wave.

Conn didn't waste any time looking for the weapon. He was on top of the other man in an instant, his body uncoiling with controlled violence.

"Conn!" Honor shot to her feet, her eyes going from the sight of the two men locked together on the beach to the gun that appeared briefly, half covered with wet sand. She started to reach for it but stopped when Conn's gritted words halted her. Even as he spoke another wave covered the weapon.

"Forget the gun. It's useless now. And our pal here isn't going anywhere."

Honor swung back to see Conn releasing his captive. The man on the sand was whimpering softly, clutching at his bleeding shoulder. Conn was wiping the star-shaped weapon against his jeans. Honor realized it was blood that was leaving the damp streaks on the denim fabric. Then he dropped the lethal object into his shirt pocket. There was a respectful casualness about the way he handled the object that spoke volumes.

"On your feet." Conn nudged his victim with the toe of his shoe. "I'm afraid that your fast-track route up Granger's corporate ladder just met with a delay. Probably a permanent one. Young, ambitious executive types like you don't usually get second chances from people like Granger."

The man glowered in mute rage but stumbled to his

feet. He didn't let go of the bleeding wound in his shoulder. "I got to have a doctor," he muttered.

"I don't think they make house calls anymore," Conn said easily. "And since both our cars are out of commission..."

"My truck," the man gasped, shambling ahead as Conn pushed him forward. "I got my truck parked down the road a ways."

"Good. We can use it to drive you into town and turn you over to the cops."

"Granger will take care of me," the punk declared. His own uncertainty about that fact was quite clear in his voice. "The guy who hired me said Granger always takes care of his people."

"Which brings us to an interesting question," Conn murmured, glancing back at Honor who was moving beside him without her former clumsiness. "Just who did hire you? Not Granger himself, apparently."

"I ain't talking," the man informed him haughtily.

Conn didn't bother to persuade him to make the effort. He turned his attention to Honor.

"Are you all right, honey?" he asked as they neared the cottage.

"I'm okay." But she couldn't disguise the stark, too-flat tone of her voice. Nor could she understand why she was still trembling. Reaction, she decided. It must be reaction.

"You handled yourself well back there," Conn went on, his voice husky with approval and pride.

"Gee, thanks. Maybe I've missed my calling somewhere along the line." The flippancy didn't feel any more natural than the tremor in her limbs, but Conn seemed to understand.

"It's all right, Honor," he soothed as he waited for

her to open the door of the cottage. "You'll be fine in a little while."

He stayed back for a moment, watching the wounded man carefully as he followed Honor through the door.

It was Honor, therefore, who first realized there was another visitor to the cottage that night. She stopped short at the sight of a familiar face studying a photo of Stylish Legacy.

"Ethan!" she whispered.

Ethan Bailey glanced up and then swung around to cover the trio in the doorway with the gun in his hand.

"So things didn't go quite perfectly, I see," he noted in pained resignation.

"They rarely do," Conn said, sighing.

Chapter Ten

"It wasn't my fault, Mr. Bailey! I swear it wasn't. You got to explain that to Mr. Granger. I did exactly like I was told. I put the cars out of commission. I took the two assignments out to the point where the water's rough. I did my part exactly right. But you never told me about that knife thing he carries. He cut me bad. Real bad. I got to have a doctor."

"Knife thing?" Ethan favored Conn with a mildly questioning eyebrow. "Oh, yes, that fancy letter opener you said was a souvenir. Let's have it, Landry." He didn't point the gun at Conn but at Honor instead.

Honor stood very still, alert to the fact that without the element of surprise Conn would not be able to use his weapon before Ethan could shoot her. Wordlessly Conn removed the star blade from his pocket and dropped it down on the floor.

"Much better," Ethan approved. Then he turned his attention to the wounded man. "You'd better go find yourself a doctor. Although it's going to be tricky explaining that wound to an emergency room medic, isn't it?" He shook his head. "I should have realized you wouldn't be able to handle this by yourself."

"But you said Mr. Granger had everything planned

out, right to the last detail. You said nothing could go wrong," the man whined.

"Well, son, I was wrong. It happens occasionally. The older you get, the more you realize that." Ethan waved the gun encouragingly. "On your way."

"I don't know if I can drive like this. I'm bleeding pretty bad."

"Try," Bailey suggested coolly. "Try real hard. Mr. Granger doesn't like screwups. If I were you, I think I'd get out of his vicinity. Find some new territory, Tony. I think it would be healthier for you if you did."

The man called Tony stared at Ethan's mildly implacable face and then he turned and walked out of the cottage without another word. The door closed behind him.

Honor stood staring at Ethan Bailey as a strange silence descended on the small room. She felt the renewed tension humming through her, mingling with the reaction from the first incident out on the beach. All of her nerves felt as though someone had scared them with a flame. Over and above her own shaky, unnatural sensation of fear and anger, Honor could have sworn she felt Conn's fierce reaction. But he seemed under control, as always. The knowledge steadied her on the one hand and raised grim questions about his past on the other. Conn's self-control was unnerving. What had he done to learn it?

"I take it," Conn said finally, "that poor Tony is under a slight misconception?"

"About the identity of his real employer?" Ethan nodded blandly. "I'm afraid so. Seemed simpler to have the boy think he was working for Granger. Kid was so anxious to make it big in a hurry. I couldn't resist taking advantage of all that drive and ambition.

There he was, hanging around the fringes of Granger's crowd whenever Granger appeared at the track. I heard through the rumor mill that the boy was looking for work, Granger's kind of work. I decided that since I needed some temporary help, I might as well use him. He seeemed happy enough with the job until a few minutes ago.''

"I don't understand," Honor said in a whisper. "Isn't Granger involved at all?"

It was Conn who answered. "No. He was just a very convenient red herring, wasn't he, Ethan?"

"Yup. Would have been even more convenient if old Tony hadn't made a mess of things. But I learned a long time ago that a man has to be flexible, has to take advantage of his opportunities and be prepared with a backup plan when things go wrong. Didn't get where I am today without practicing what I preach.''

"You want us dead," Honor said in a remote tone that didn't sound at all like herself, not even to her own ears.

"It would have been mighty convenient if you two had played your parts out correctly," Ethan explained. He stood easily, the gun in his hand held at a relaxed but alert level.

"You mean if I'd really believed she was the one who tried to poison Legacy?" Conn put in casually. He moved slightly, taking a few steps away from Honor.

"Stay where you are, boy. That's far enough." Ethan's gun hand tightened fractionally. Conn stopped.

Honor hastily interrupted, trying to divert Ethan's attention to herself. "You wanted Conn and me to distrust each other, didn't you? You wanted us to quarrel."

"It set the scene nicely. Everyone at the track saw

Conn leave this morning and knew he was in a rage. Couple of owners had even seen him drinking purty heavy the night before. They knew the two of you had ties that went back a long, long way.''

Conn's eyes slitted. "They know it because you made certain they found out, right?"

Ethan shrugged. "You know what racetrack gossip's like, son. Especially when it concerns a stallion like Stylish Legacy and the men who owned him. Bound to be some talk when one owner's son shows up with a colt sired by the famous horse. When you started dating Honor, here, why folks were just downright fascinated. Leastways, they became fascinated after I reminded them of the old story."

"Do you mind explaining just why you're going to all this trouble, Ethan?" Conn asked coolly.

"I'm afraid it's a long tale. And I'm not sure we have time to go into it tonight. I looked up the tides before I set this whole plan in motion. The high tide will be peaking right soon. I want you and the little lady here following it out to sea."

"Assisted by a couple of bullet holes?" Conn tossed back.

"Something like that. Might as well head back down to the point. Looks like I'll have to take care of the little job I hired Tony to do. Hard to find good help these days."

Honor felt Conn tense. He would make a suicidal effort, she knew. He would do anything he could to protect her. That knowledge was as sure and solid in her mind and heart as the knowledge of his passion. She had to act first or risk having him throw himself straight into Ethan's gun.

"You can take care of us, but it's going to be tough

to stop the gossip that will be hitting the track when this is all over," Honor told Ethan with sudden conviction.

Ethan frowned. "You don't have to worry about the gossip. You won't be around."

"I'm not talking about what people will say of Conn and me. It's what they'll be speculating about you that should interest you. My sister, Adena, knows everything I know. I called her this afternoon and left the information on her telephone-answering machine."

Conn shot her a startled glance, fully aware that she hadn't used the telephone. His attention went back to Ethan almost immediately.

"Now just what the devil are you talking about, little lady?" Ethan demanded impatiently.

"I'm talking about the fact that Adena won't keep her mouth shut. When I don't return from this little jaunt she's liable to go straight to the police."

"With what?" Ethan snapped, more of his patience disintegrating. On the opposite side of the room, Conn stood balanced and poised. Ethan was focusing entirely on Honor.

Honor drew a deep breath and played her one and only card. "With the information that there was another owner of Stylish Legacy fifteen years ago. A silent partner named Ethan Bailey."

The effect on Bailey was electric. The easy, good-old-boy image disappeared in a flash, leaving the face of a raw, embittered and infuriated man.

"You're lying, bitch," he breathed tightly. "You don't know what the hell you're talking about!"

"Don't I? It's all there," Honor said, gesturing calmly toward the wood-and-iron locker that sat in the corner, draped with the folded horse blanket. "All the proof anyone would ever need."

"What proof?" Bailey hissed, his gaze momentarily riveted on the locker. But he seemed to sense that Conn was waiting for an opening. Ethan kept the nose of the gun firmly pointed at Honor. It would still be a simple matter for him to pull the trigger before Conn was halfway across the room. *"What proof?"*

Honor sucked in her breath and tried to think logically. She had to make this sound good. She badly wished the fear-inspired adrenaline racing through her system would calm down. As it was she could see the tips of her fingers trembling as she bent down toward the locker. Awkwardly she patted the black-and-white blanket lying on top.

"Dad was a businessman. First, last and always. As excited as he used to get about Stylish Legacy's wins, he always claimed the horse was really nothing more than an elaborate tax shelter. Nothing more than a business matter. And because it was a business matter, he kept very good records."

"I don't believe you," Bailey snarled. "If you knew anything you would have put it all together a long time ago."

Honor shook her head. "I didn't put it together all these years because I never wanted to go through all the records and souvenirs my father had left to me. It was too painful. Every time I looked at this trunk I was forced to remember what had happened to Dad. On the other hand, I couldn't bear to throw it all away, either. So I told myself I was putting the various mementos to good design use by decorating the cottage with them." She gestured at the photos and racing paraphernalia on the walls. "Creates just the right ambience, don't you think? Casual but chic, rustic but elegant. It's made the cottage very popular, you know. I rarely have any trouble keeping it rented." Her voice broke a little on the last word and Honor quickly stopped talking while she regained her control.

"If you haven't investigated the contents of that trunk in all these years, why would you have done it on this visit to the cabin?" Ethan challenged.

"If I hadn't met you at the track, I would never have recognized the third man who always seemed to show up in Stylish Legacy's winning photos," Honor told him simply. "I've rarely studied the pictures, anyway, but after Conn arrived yesterday and became so interested in Legacy's sire, I started looking at the photos a little more closely. And when I look at things closely, Ethan, I tend to see things. I've been trained to see details," she added with a wry touch of apology. "It's something designers get very good at, I'm afraid. The smallest details make all the difference in a well-designed room."

"You little bitch," Ethan breathed.

Honor plowed on determinedly. Ethan was still holding the gun with far too much concentration. She turned back to the trunk. "Once I realized you were in so many of those winner's circle shots and once I saw the expression on your face—"

"The expression on my face!"

Honor inclined her head ruefully. "It's always the same, the expression on the face of the owners and trainers. That look of satisfaction and victory and excitement. It's really unique. Look around, Ethan. That expression is on my father's face in all the photos. It's on Richard Stoner's face, too. I saw it on Conn's face the other afternoon when Legacy won. And it's on your face in all the photographs of Stylish Legacy in the winners' circles. No matter how hard people try to keep it on a business level, racing seems to get into the blood. It's always more than a business."

"That proves nothing! Absolutely nothing!"

"True, but it was enough to make me curious. I opened the trunk, Ethan. I started looking through some of Dad's records and papers. As I said, he was a businessman. In his own fashion, he paid as much attention to detail as I do. It's all here, Ethan," she concluded, hoping she wouldn't have to fake it any further. It was very difficult being creative on your feet when someone was holding a gun on you. Out of the corner of her eye she saw Conn advance on catlike feet, making no sound as he approached Ethan. The older man's attention was still zeroed in on Honor.

"You're lying," Ethan muttered, his eyes moving uneasily now from Honor to the trunk. "There's nothing in that trunk."

"Want to see the records?" Honor taunted, her hand hovering just above the horse blanket.

"You're damn right, I want to see them! Show me your fancy proof, little lady," Bailey growled furiously.

Honor bent down and lifted the heavy wool horse blanket.

"Bailey!" Conn snapped loudly.

Instinctively Ethan swiveled around at the clipped command. He panicked as he realized that Conn was much too close to him. But Honor already had the blanket in motion, whipping it toward Bailey.

"Damn you!" Bailey shouted, pulling the trigger reflexively. But the blanket was floating over him, settling around his head and shoulders, and the shot went wild.

In the same instant Conn was on him, propelling the older man to the floor and wrenching the gun free. It was all over in a moment. Conn was far younger and stronger than Bailey and the struggle was fated to end in only one way. Ethan lay still, sagging with the knowledge that he had lost. Slowly Conn rose to one knee and picked up the weapon. He stared down at the fallen man and then he flicked a quick, assessing glance at Honor.

"Are you all right, honey?"

"Peachy keen," Honor mumbled, sinking down onto the top of the trunk. "Just peachy keen. Except for my knees. They don't seem to be functioning properly." She took several deep breaths, willing herself to calm down. "I don't think I can take too much more of this tonight, though, Conn. A little seems to go a long way."

He was on his feet now, squeezing her shoulder tightly. "I know what you mean. Why do you think I gave up those cushy security jobs overseas in favor of a little consulting work and real estate investment? This sort of thing gets to you after a while. I've never been so scared in my life as I was this evening. Twice someone held a gun on you and I was terrified I wasn't going to be able to protect you."

She glanced up at his ravaged features and her love for him shone softly in her eyes. "That's funny. I never had any doubts at all. I just don't tolerate the tension well."

Conn looked at her, his gaze unreadable. "No doubts?"

"I knew you'd do whatever you thought had to be done," she said quietly. It was the truth. Conn would have given his life for her tonight and she was fully aware of that. She had been equally determined that he wouldn't make the sacrifice.

"Thank you, Honor," he said softly.

"For what?"

He shrugged. "For having faith in me."

Honor touched his hand but she couldn't find any words. Her eyes met his in a silent communication that was shattered by Ethan Bailey's groan. She turned to look at the man as he sat up slowly. There was something different about Ethan now. He looked like a broken man. Or one who has come to the end of a long road. It was Conn who spoke first.

"I think," he said, "that it's time we had some answers." He sat down on the trunk beside Honor, the gun held almost casually in his right hand. There was a grimness to him that was frightening. "Were you really a silent partner in Stylish Legacy?" he asked, staring at Ethan.

"Ask her, she seems to know all about it," Bailey muttered, massaging the back of his head.

"It was an educated guess," Honor confessed. "I've never looked inside the trunk. I made a stab in the dark, based on your appearance in all those photographs. No one can resist getting into the photo when the horse wins, least of all the owners."

"You might as well tell us everything," Conn suggested, watching Bailey with a brooding expression. "Now that the connection has been made, it shouldn't be too difficult to dig into the past and find out the whole truth. It just hinged on knowing there was an association between you and our parents. I have a hunch that association involved more than a racehorse. There was something more, wasn't there, Ethan? Something you had to cover up, even if it meant killing the son and daughter of Stylish Legacy's original owners."

Bailey glowered at him and then went limp. "If you

really start digging you'll probably find it," he admitted. "For fifteen years I've been afraid of what would happen if someone went looking for answers. I thought I was safe because no one seemed inclined to probe too deeply. The most dangerous time was right after the *incident.*"

"Incident?" Honor demanded. "You mean after Stoner and my father died?"

Bailey nodded. "I thought that if I got through that part okay, I'd be home free. I had to let you sell Stylish Legacy, of course. I didn't dare come forth with a claim on the horse. That would have been too risky, because I'd taken such pains to make sure no one knew I was involved financially."

Conn thought about that for a moment. "You didn't want anyone to know you had a financial interest in the horse," he finally repeated carefully. "Because if someone knew that he might suspect that you were involved with our parents in other ways?"

Honor shot him a swift, questioning glance. What was Conn after?

Bailey nodded with a dismal air. "Couldn't take any chances. It hurt to lose Stylish Legacy. Best colt on the West Coast in those days. Could have made a fortune off of him. I didn't even dare to buy one of his offspring. I didn't want to risk it. But I kept track of how the runners he sired were doing. Couldn't help myself. When I learned one of his colts got picked up by Richard Stoner's son, I had a feeling..." His voice trailed off sadly.

"A premonition that something was going to go wrong?" Honor suggested.

Bailey nodded. "It seemed dangerous. As if fate had stepped in and forced me to get involved with everything I'd closed the door on fifteen years ago. I thought I'd just make contact with you, Landry. Easiest way to do that was transfer a couple of my horses over to Humphrey's stable. It was simple to introduce myself to you as a fellow owner using the same trainer. I could keep tabs on you that way. Make sure you never got too curious. Or at least have some warning if you did."

"And then I got in touch with Nick Mayfield's daughter," Conn murmured. "You must have really gotten nervous then."

"It all seemed to be getting too dangerous, too close. Fate."

Honor frowned. "You tried to plant a few seeds of doubt at first, hoping I'd back away from any relationship with Conn, didn't you?"

"If you'd backed away from him everything might have gone back to being safe." Ethan sighed. "But you didn't. I could see the two of you getting more and more involved with each other. I knew that once you knew who he was, you'd probably get angry," Bailey explained. "And I thought that if Landry realized you had betrayed him by trying to poison Legacy, he'd be furious."

"So you set up the situation and then you hired good old Tony to pull the trigger, right?" Conn growled. "Okay, I can figure that much out for myself. But why don't you save us all some time and explain why you didn't want your association with my stepfather and Mayfield to come to light? Seems to me, there could only be one reason for that."

Honor held her breath as her mind leaped to the same intuitive explanation. "You killed them?" she whispered tightly, staring at Ethan. "You killed my father and Stoner?"

A forbidding silence settled on the room and then Bailey nodded once. "Had to, don't you see? They found out I'd been running guns, using their connections and facilities in the Middle East. The night they got wise, I had to act. There wasn't time to think," he went on, his eyes becoming remote as he looked back fifteen years. "It all happened so quickly. I didn't know they'd been suspicious. I thought they believed I was just curious about the operations. After all, they'd let me put a lot of money into their business."

"Once again as a silent partner?" Conn asked with ice in his voice.

"Had to insist on that. I didn't want anyone connecting me with the guns if they were ever discovered. I'd been small-time until then. Don't get me wrong, I'd made money selling weapons to anyone who'd buy them and I'd made a fair amount of money, but I wanted to expand. I needed a safe cover for really big shipments. There was so much more money to be made in that line. Somewhere in the world there's always someone wanting to go to war, you know. Big wars, little wars, guerrilla wars, revolutionary wars. Bandits with political motivations and just plain outlaws. A never-ending market. A businessman's dream. But you got to take precautions."

"You needed a legitimate cover and you needed reliable transportation facilities." Conn nodded with a degree of understanding that rather shocked Honor. "You needed an established business that had contacts in places like the Middle East."

"I met your father and Mayfield when they first got interested in buying a racehorse together. I used to own a couple of horses back then, although none of them were in Stylish Legacy's league. But I've always been involved with the track. And I kept up with track rumors. I knew your fathers were international businessmen and I made friends with them. I'm the one who put them on to Stylish Legacy. I'd planned to buy him myself, but when I suggested we all go in as partners, they were happy enough to agree.''

"One kind of partnership led to another, I suppose?'' Conn said.

"That was right about the time when Mayfield and Stoner were thinking of leaving the big corporation they'd been working for. They planned to set up their own business. I offered to pour some money into it. Any new business needs capital, and they agreed to let me invest. Things worked real well for a while after they'd established their new business operation. I greased a few palms, used a few contacts, and the first thing I knew, I had shipments of rifles riding right alongside the steel piping and oil field equipment your fathers were shipping overseas. No one looked too closely at the other end because Mayfield and Stoner were trusted. They knew folks. The right folks.''

"And if anyone had looked too closely, you'd have been in the clear because you were just a silent partner,'' Conn finished. "No one knew you were involved.''

"I made sure my name was left off all the paperwork. Just a private gentlemen's agreement.''

"Then one night Stoner and Mayfield became suspicious.'' Conn's thumb moved with a hint of restlessness on the grip of the gun.

"They set up a trap,'' Ethan snarled with a trace of returning belligerence. "One of the men I'd bribed talked, and they found out when I had another shipment due to arrive overseas. They knew I had to be there in order to conclude the deal. They got there ahead of me. What they didn't realize was that the man who'd sold them information also sold me information. He was playing both sides of the fence, and I got lucky."

"You were able to set up your own trap," Honor hazarded bleakly. "You made it look as though my father and Richard Stoner had been smuggling the guns and had quarreled over a shipment. You killed them both."

"After that I got nervous," Bailey admitted. "I figured my luck was running out. Decided to get out of the gunrunning business altogether. After all, I'd made a pile. Time to invest it in more legitimate things. Investments people wouldn't be inclined to question."

Conn and Honor looked at him for a long time. Bailey seemed unaware of any of their emotions. He was lost in his own world, examining where it had all gone wrong.

"You bastard," Conn finally said but there was no heat in the words. Only a weary acceptance that the past could not be changed.

"I knew," Honor said softly. "I knew there was something wrong with the notion that Stoner and Mayfield had betrayed each other. It never felt right."

Conn nodded. "I know. Too many loose ends. Too many unanswered questions. That's one of the reasons I came looking for you, Honor. I can't deny it. And I don't regret it, because otherwise we would never have met."

"The questions needed to be answered," she agreed quietly.

He looked at her. "That was pretty slick, the way you pulled the basic connection out of thin air. If you hadn't realized that Bailey's association with Stylish Legacy was a solid one, the rest of it wouldn't have fallen into place so neatly. You're fast on your feet, lady. You've got guts."

Honor smiled shakily. "Coming from you, I'll assume that's a compliment."

Conn blinked in surprise. "Of course it is."

"You moved fairly rapidly yourself when the occasion warranted," she returned dryly.

He lifted one shoulder in a gesture of dismissal. "I spent a lot of years learning to do it. It was just part of the job."

"Some job!" Honor broke off thoughtfully, glancing back at Ethan. "What do we do now?"

"We've got all the evidence we need to get Bailey here out of our lives," Conn began slowly. "But I'm not sure we'll ever be able to pin the past on him. Unless there really are some incriminating records in this old trunk."

"I doubt it," Honor said. "I did glance briefly through the stuff when I moved it here to the cottage. I don't recall anything that might be useful in connecting Bailey with what happened fifteen years ago. But who knows? I didn't realize the significance of Ethan being in all those photographs until yesterday. Maybe there is something buried in this trunk." She paused. "It was all a long time ago, wasn't it? It's over now."

Conn glanced at her. "We know the answers. There aren't any more loose ends." He sounded strangely satisfied.

Honor understood the feeling. There was a deep sadness underlying the sensation, but also a sense of peace. No more loose ends.

Well, maybe one. Honor remembered the question

that still hovered at the back of her mind. She turned to Ethan. "Was it you who moved the screen in my bedroom?"

He came out of his gloomy reverie long enough to appear vaguely startled. "How did you know I searched your room? I hardly touched a thing!"

Honor's mouth twisted wryly. "One thing slightly off is all it takes, I'm afraid. I'm beginning to think my eye for detail is going to be the bane of my existence."

Bailey slipped back into his memories. "I just wanted to see if you had any stuff on Stylish Legacy lying around. I needed to know how much you knew about the horse and who had owned it. Didn't realize you had all the answers here at the beach house."

"Neither did I," Honor said.

It was MIDMORNING by the time Ethan Bailey had been taken into custody and the necessary paperwork completed. The authorities notified the hospital emergency rooms in the area to be on the alert for a man of Tony's description seeking care for an odd knife wound.

Honor and Conn returned to Pasadena late that afternoon.

They talked quietly over dinner at Honor's apartment, both of them coming to grips with the results of the traumatic events. Gradually they both began to relax and accept what had happened. There was a feeling of companionship, of being bonded together, Honor thought at one point. She and Conn now shared a past and the secrets that had been buried there. It deepened the sense of commitment she felt about the future, but something was missing. Something wasn't right about the way they were preparing to face that future.

It wasn't until later that evening that Honor realized

that soon she would have to deal with the problem that had precipitated the entire matter: her relationship with Constantine Landry. If she didn't confront it directly it would haunt her, leaving an element of uncertainty deep in her mind. And it was a cinch that Conn himself would never of his own accord resolve the gray area because he simply didn't admit it existed. But by the time the thought flitted through her mind, Honor was slipping rapidly into sleep. Her body curled deep into the comforting warmth of Conn's as they lay together in her bed.

Tomorrow, Honor promised herself just before she closed her eyes. Tomorrow she would find a way to make Conn understand that what he felt for her was love. He needed to acknowledge that fact for both their sakes. He had to know that what they shared was something that went beyond an amalgam of want and need and desire.

Unless he took that final step, Honor realized, Conn would never be able to give himself as completely to her as she was willing to give herself to him. There would always be a part of him that was remote and untouchable.

Was it selfish, she wondered, this need she had to make him understand that he was vulnerable to her? Possibly. No, *probably*. Perhaps it wasn't right to expect him to lower his guard as far as she had lowered hers. He had been alone a long time in a harsh world, and the barriers he had built around himself made sense on many levels. She had seen the fierceness in him at the beach house, had come to know the relentless, utterly determined side of his nature. The predatory part of him had helped save their lives; she could hardly quarrel with its existence.

But the hunter in him made it difficult for Conn to admit to love. He could commit himself; she didn't doubt that. He could also give passion and protection. In turn he demanded a great deal. Loyalty, respect, commitment, passion—all of those and more he wanted from Honor. She had given him more. She had given him her love. But so far he hadn't shown any willingness to take the dangerous step himself. He wasn't able yet to admit that he was vulnerable and that what he felt for her was love.

Until Conn could do that there would always be loose ends in their relationship.

Chapter Eleven

Honor awoke with the conviction that there were still matters remaining to be settled between herself and Conn, but she hadn't even begun to formulate a plan for resolving the uncertainties when he unwittingly pushed her into a corner.

Honor opened her eyes to find Conn sitting up against the headboard, the sheet carelessly bunched at his waist. He wasn't wearing anything that she could see but he'd obviously arisen earlier because he had a mug of coffee in his hand.

"You're certainly bright-eyed and chipper this morning," she complained, stretching languidly. "Isn't it a little early to be looking so alert? After all we've been through during the past couple of days, I think we deserve some extra sleep."

"I've been thinking," he told her very seriously. He didn't respond to her light greeting.

A small warning bell went off somewhere, but Honor couldn't imagine why. "Oh?" She eyed the coffee with increasing interest.

"We can fly to Vegas this afternoon, spend the night in one of the big hotels and be back here in time to see Legacy run tomorrow afternoon."

Honor tried to assimilate all that. "I suppose we could. Any reason why we should? And did you make me a cup of coffee while you were at it?"

Conn frowned and reached around to lift another mug off the end table. "Here. And the reason we should go to Vegas is because it would be the quickest and easiest way to get married."

"Married!" Honor nearly spilled the hot coffee on the sheets as she accepted the mug and struggled to a sitting position. As it was, a few drops struck the bodice of the black-and-white-striped nightgown. She dabbed at them furiously while she tried to think. "Married?"

Conn reached out to hold the mug while she finished attending to the small drops. "I suppose we could go ahead and apply for a license here in California, but there's the waiting period, and I'd just as soon take care of things as quickly and neatly as possible."

Honor finally ceased her efforts at cleaning the nightgown and went still. She seemed to be having a problem focusing on the main issue. Her mind was skittering around in circles, looking for an escape. In that moment Honor didn't bother to question why she wanted the escape.

"Are you quite certain you want marriage, Conn?" she asked slowly.

His expression grew even more implacable. "It's the only logical conclusion. We could simply live together but somehow that doesn't seem *formal* enough for what we have. You belong to me now. We belong together. There's a commitment between us. Obligations, duties, responsibilities. All those things go with marriage, not a casual affair. And I think you know it." He took a sip of his coffee and added blandly, "After all, aren't you the one who keeps saying you love me?"

Honor paled beneath the well-aimed thrust. The man was, indeed, a hunter. He knew exactly where to strike. Frantically she rallied her forces.

"Yes, I'm the one," Honor agreed bleakly. "I'll take my coffee back now."

He handed it to her, faint wariness flickering in his eyes. "Honor? What's the matter?"

She took a long swallow of hot coffee. "Nothing, Conn. But I need time. We both need time." Her mind seized on the only escape it could find. "There's so much to work out, so many plans to make. Where are we going to live, for example? I have a business established here in Pasadena. I can't just pick it up and move it elsewhere. And I imagine you have your business headquarters well established up in the San Francisco area."

"My business is movable," he interrupted flatly. "I can shift my operations to Pasadena without too much difficulty."

Honor blinked uneasily, sensing he had deliberately acted to forestall her protest before she could even get it properly outlined. She rushed to find another excuse. "There's Adena to consider."

"Believe me, from what I've seen of Adena, she wouldn't care at all if you got married. I think she approves of me."

"Well, it wasn't exactly her approval I was worrying about. I just thought it might be nice if she were invited to the wedding!" Honor flared.

"You can invite her if you wish. I don't mind picking up an extra airline ticket for her," Conn said.

"The police may have more questions for us to answer during the next few days," Honor fretted.

"They know where to find us."

"I have clients to see," Honor went on doggedly. "I really shouldn't take any more time off just now."

"We can plan a honeymoon for some other time. You won't be away from Pasadena except overnight. Not unless you want to take some time off again to go away for a few days."

"My mother—"

"We'll notify her," Conn said promptly. "Later, when we take the honeymoon we can visit her, if you like."

Honor groped for other excuses and found she had exhausted the lot. Except for the truth. "It's just too soon, Conn. I need time."

He drained his coffee and set down the mug with an air of finality. "You're stalling."

"Well, maybe I am!" she blurted, feeling cornered.

"Why should you want to stall?" he challenged softly. "You love me, remember? I can make you come alive with passion. I've saved your neck. We share a bond that goes back fifteen years. We're committed to each other. Are you going to deny it?"

"No, I'm not denying it but I'll be darned if I'll let you push me into marriage when you don't know how you feel toward me!"

He stared at her in astonishment. "What the devil do you think you're saying? I know how I feel toward you. You're mine. I'll take care of you, protect you, make love to you. What more to do you want from me?"

"Love! I want you to understand that what you feel for me is love!" She could no longer control her tongue. Her emotions overwhelmed her, causing her to say things she was very much afraid she would regret later. Already she could see the anger beginning to burn in Conn's eyes. It frightened her, but she couldn't stop.

He reached out and caught her wrist, removing the coffee mug from her fingers and dragging her across his chest. Beneath dark lashes he gazed grimly down at her. "I asked you once if you wanted me to lie to you. You said no. Have you changed your mind?"

"No, of course not," she gasped.

"Then are you trying to blackmail me into saying the words you want to hear? Are you setting a trap of your own, Honor? Trying to push me into a corner by saying I can't have you unless I do things your way?"

"Typical of you to decide that I'm trying to trap you. You're the one who's so skilled at weaving webs, remember? I fell into all the nets you strung, all down the line, but it stops here. You want everything from me but you're not willing to give everything of yourself. I want a man who is as vulnerable to me as I am to him. I don't want a one-sided relationship, Conn."

"Vulnerable?" he grated. "I doubt you even know the meaning of the word. Vulnerable people don't survive long in this world unless they've got someone else to take care of them."

"I'll take care of you," she promised rashly. "I won't betray you or hurt you. I love you."

"If you meant that you wouldn't be playing word games with me."

"You don't understand," she cried.

"You're trying to force me into conforming to your mental image of a husband and a lover. You want to know you have power over me. That's what you really mean by *vulnerable*, isn't it? You want to know I'm weak when it comes to you."

"You seem to enjoy your power over me," she flung back furiously.

"So you're trying to even the score?"

"Maybe I don't happen to like unbalanced accounts, either! You're not the only one with a monopoly on keeping the score even." By now she was no longer making any attempt to keep her words rational and calm. Honor's emotions had taken over completely as she sensed herself being pushed into yet another of Constantine Landry's intricate webs.

"You don't have any choice in this case," he told her savagely. "You belong to me."

"It works both ways."

"All right, so I belong to you. That's grounds for marriage, lady."

"It's grounds for an affair," she retorted. "Not marriage."

"You're going to split hairs over a four-letter word?" he demanded.

"Love is more than a four-letter word. If that's all it was, you wouldn't have so much trouble dealing with it!"

"I'm beginning to realize exactly what it does mean," he said grittily. "In your mind, at least. It means vulnerability and weakness and a knowledge of your own power over me. Admit it, Honor. That's what you're looking for."

She stared up at him helplessly. "If that's what you think it means, then there's not much point in continuing this discussion, is there?"

His jaw tightened as he sensed her weary withdrawal from the argument. "Oh, no, you don't, Honor. You're not backing out of this that easily. You're going to marry me. I'll make you a good husband. There will always be honesty between us. Honesty and commitment. And passion. Nothing else matters."

She fought for composure. "You mean it wouldn't

bother you at all if I stopped loving you? As long as I continued to supply my share of the honesty and commitment? Oh, and the passion, naturally.''

He looked slightly startled. The expression was immediately replaced with a taut frown. ''What you call your love for me is really your sense of being vulnerable to me. And you can't change that, honey. By marrying me you'll be admitting that you trust me with that kind of power. I won't abuse that trust.''

''You're the one who's playing word games.'' Freeing her wrist, Honor slipped away from him. He let her go, watching through narrowed eyes as she tugged a robe out of the closet and tied the sash. When she dared meet his gaze again she realized that all the soft, gentle comfort she had known from him during the night had vanished. The predatory challenge was radiating from Conn in a way that effectively destroyed her last hopes.

''You're throwing a tantrum because you can't find a way to reassure yourself that you have as much control over me as I do over you. That's all this is about, isn't it?'' he asked icily.

''From the beginning you seem to have been manipulating me,'' she said, sighing. ''You've woven so many webs around me that I haven't always been able to think straight. I suppose that's why you now assume I'm trying to reverse the process. I'm not, Conn, but I've got to draw the line somewhere.''

''So you can keep the books balanced?''

''You taught me the importance of that.'' She turned and walked into the bathroom, not trusting herself to stay in the same room with him any longer. Mingled despair and anger were causing her to be almost as unsteady as fear had the previous night. Honor deci she was sick and tired of being at the mercy of such strong emotions. They took too much out of a person, sending her to euphoric highs one moment and despairing lows the next.

As she switched on the shower, she lectured herself on control. The kind of self-control Conn seemed able to exert much of the time was suddenly an enviable attribute. She'd work on it, Honor vowed as she stepped under the spray. She'd work very hard to develop it. No more would she allow herself to be swept up in her responses to Conn. Never again would she allow him to manipulate her or weave nets around her. She was a strong-minded woman, or at least she always had been. You didn't make a success out of yourself in Southern California without a fair degree of fortitude and determination. She could handle Conn Landry on her terms. She would force him to acknowledge his true feelings, force him to become really emotionally committed to her. She didn't want a man whose sense of commitment seemed to stem almost entirely from the harsher sides of his masculine nature. Possessiveness, sexual satisfaction, a feeling of protectiveness were strong factors, important factors. But they fell short of love.

Honor was still telling herself that fifteen minutes later when she stepped out of the bathrom and discovered Conn had left the apartment.

TWENTY MINUTES after he'd stormed out of Honor's apartment, Conn walked into the barn where Humphrey stabled the thoroughbreds in his care. Two grooms with whom he was on friendly terms took one look at the expression on his face and discreetly disappeared. A goat that had free run of the stables because it had a calming effect on the high-strung horses, showed the intelligence goats are noted for and ambled off out of range.

Conn found Legacy's stall and came to a halt. The colt turned inquiringly and didn't seem particularly put off by the dark tension in the man. He shuffled to the door and thrust his nose into Conn's hand.

"Sorry, fella. Absolutely nothing special for you today. You have to run tomorrow. Can't take any risks," Conn murmured, stroking the sleek neck. The horse's ears pricked at the approach of another man.

"Hello, Landry," the trainer said easily as he came to stand in front of Legacy's stall. "Come to check up on your horse?" Humphrey peered perceptively at his client. "He's looking very good. Very good indeed. No reason he shouldn't do as well for you tomorrow as he did in his last race. I've scheduled Eddie Campbell to ride him. Told him to hold him back a bit at the start and then just let him have his head."

Conn nodded, only half listening to the familiar trainer patter. If Legacy lost tomorrow there would be an equally reassuring patter listing all the reasons why: The track was muddy, the horse was too nervous, the jockey didn't handle him right on the course and so on. It was all part of the horse-racing scene. Just like the rumor mill. Conn wondered if any rumors about Ethan Bailey had filtered into the network yet. Apparently not, because Humphrey didn't mention them. The trainer came to the end of his analysis of the horse and then arched an eyebrow inquiringly at his client.

"Did you have a question?"

"No." Conn shook his head, unable to come up with any form of idle conversation. What he really wanted right now was to be alone. He probably shouldn't h come to the track. But the thought of going back to his hotel room was depressing. "Just wanted to take another look at Legacy. Do you think he has the potential of his sire?"

"Stylish Legacy? I believe he does." Humphrey nodded toward the colt. "Legacy got the best of Stylish Legacy's genes, if you ask me. Good shoulders, strong hindquarters. Smart. Fast. Likes to run. Can't ask for more from a horse."

How much could you ask of a woman, Conn wondered silently. How much could a woman ask of a man? Legacy was a friendly animal, willing to give his all on the racetrack. He'd respond with everything that was in him when called upon. But that didn't mean he was emotionally involved with human beings.

Damn it, Conn thought violently, *I'm going crazy. How dumb can you get, Landry? You can't draw parallels between animals and humans. Not when it comes to relationships.*

"Well, I'll be around if you need me," Humphrey announced with a nod of farewell. "Want to use the box today?"

"No thanks. I'm not going to watch the races."

Humphrey nodded again and departed, leaving Conn alone with his horse. Absently he continued to stroke Legacy's nose.

Honor wouldn't be able to maintain the distance she had put between them this morning, Conn told himself. He had been saying the words in various formats since he'd left the apartment. In her own words, she was vulnerable to him. She wanted him, needed him. Hell, she loved him! And she knew he was committed to her. She *knew* it! She had to know it in the depths of soul. He'd never felt like this about any other woman. The impact she had made on him had thrown his whole life off balance.

He knew his impact on her had been equally strong. He was sure of it in his bones. She couldn't hide the completeness with which she surrendered in his arms. Yet she had balked at taking the final step of marriage. Conn racked his brain trying to understand why. He had accused her of wanting power over him, but now he wasn't so certain. Another infinitely more devastating possibility flashed through his thoughts.

What if she was nervous about formalizing their relationship for the simple reason that she still didn't trust him?

Conn's hand stopped moving on Legacy's nose as the knowledge exploded within him. Of course she trusted him. She had to trust him. She'd said she'd trusted him, damn it!

But something was holding her back from making the final commitment. She claimed she wanted love, and Conn had told her that she was using the word to mean power. But perhaps he had been wrong. Perhaps what the word really meant was trust.

Legacy nuzzled Conn's shoulder in a puzzled fashion, seeking more attention. When Conn didn't oblige, but simply stood staring unseeingly into the stall, the colt moved philosophically back to his feed.

It was intolerable to think that she might not trust him after all they had been through, Conn thought, dazed. Absolutely intolerable. The realization that she might lack faith in him was shattering in its intensity. Didn't she understand that he would do virtually anything for her? Protect her with his life?

Conn turned away from the stall and walked as if i<nowiki> </nowiki>dream to the far end of the long barn. There he fou bench. No one was around. Slowly he sank down onto the hard wood surface and tried to understand what was happening to him.

He trusted her, he thought. Completely. At least he assumed he did. But perhaps he hadn't actually trusted her to know her own mind. She'd said she was in love with him. And he hadn't really trusted her to know what she meant.

She must think him incredibly arrogant. And he was, Conn realized. Unbelievably arrogant. How could she trust him totally if she knew deep in her heart that he didn't even trust her to know her own mind? When you gave something, you wanted something equally valuable in return. He hadn't given her what she needed.

INSTINCT GUIDED Honor as she drove out of the underground garage and headed toward the freeway. Conn would head for the track. She knew it intuitively. It was where she would go if she were he. He wasn't the type to sit and sulk in his hotel room.

What a fool she had been this morning. She'd risked so much for so little. Conn was right. She'd been playing word games, searching for reassurance when all along she'd known intellectually that he was giving her everything he had to give a woman. She would find him and tell him that it was enough, more than enough. She loved him and what he felt for her had to be very close to that emotion. What did it matter if he couldn't or wouldn't verbalize it?

If only she'd kept her head this morning and not allowed emotions to rule her tongue. Bitterly Honor ⁔stigated herself for the way she'd handled Conn's ⁔posal of marriage.

Except that it hadn't actually been a proposal, she reminded herself with a rueful sigh. Perhaps if he'd actually asked her properly instead of arrogantly assuming she would want to marry him as quickly as possible she wouldn't have lost her temper and her head.

Life with Conn was not going to be entirely uncomplicated. The man was made of iron, and he surrounded himself with almost invincible emotional barriers.

But they weren't totally invincible and that was what she had to keep in mind. It would take work getting him to trust her to the point where he could lower them, perhaps years of work. Honor told herself she was more than willing to make the effort to gain his complete, unqualified trust. She had no choice because she loved him.

She parked the car in the lot and made her way to the barns, flashing the visitor's badge Conn had provided for her. Then Honor turned toward Legacy's stable. Blinking a little as she walked from brilliant sunlight into cool shade, she glanced around and saw the horse looking out of his stall. There was no sign of Conn. Slowly she walked toward Legacy, wondering if she'd been wrong in her guess as to where Conn had gone.

"Hello, Legacy," she murmured soothingly. "Have you seen him?"

The horse went into his attention-getting routine, nuzzling her shoulder. Honor obliged for a few moments, her gaze searching the shaded interior of the long barn. It took a while before she realized Conn was watching her from a bench at the far end of the building.

He didn't move as she turned to look at him, but hi eyes absorbed the sight of her standing there in t' jeans and bright-coral sweater in which she had hastily dressed. Honor had been so certain of what she wanted to say when she left the apartment, but now she couldn't seem to get the words straight in her head. Slowly she lowered her hand from Legacy's muzzle. Then she started toward Conn.

He stood up as she approached, the lean, tough quality of his body outlined beneath snug jeans and a white long-sleeved shirt. He let her come to him, not moving as she walked forward. There was a moment when Honor feared she had made the wrong decision, taken too big a risk. It seemed to her in those few seconds that the predatory side of him was the ruling side and that she stood no chance of suppressing it. Then she was close enough to read his eyes and at that point nothing could have kept her from going into his arms. She ran the last few steps, coming into his waiting embrace with a small rush. His arms tightened around her with reassuring urgency.

"I'm sorry, Conn," she whispered breathlessly. "I never meant to push you this morning. Of course I'll marry you, if you'll still have me. We belong to each other. I don't know why I doubted it. I know you'll give me everything you can of yourself. I realize you wouldn't talk of commitment unless you meant it. What more could I ask for?"

His hands moved roughly on her back. "How about a little trust?" His voice was hoarse with barely controlled emotion.

She lifted her head from his shoulder, her eyes widening in shock. "You trust me, don't you?"

"I thought I did, Honor," he groaned, pulling her head back down against his shirt. His fingers tangled in er hair. "I sure as hell trusted you more than I've trusted anyone else for longer than I care to remember. But in the final analysis, I guess I didn't trust you completely."

Panic surged through her. "But why? What have I done to make you think I'd betray you? I thought everything was resolved between us. I love you, Conn."

"That's the part I wasn't willing to believe. I didn't give you credit for knowing your own mind because you were talking about an emotion I've never really believed existed. I stormed out of the apartment this morning thinking that you were simply trying to push me into saying the words you wanted to hear, that you wanted to hear them because they would give you some assurance of your own power over me."

"No—" she began desperately but he silenced her gently with his hand.

"Even though I was furious, I had to admit that you had the right to know that I wasn't going to dominate the relationship completely. It must seem to you that I've been running things between us from the beginning. I tracked you down, engineered our first meeting, kept tightening the strands of the web until there was nowhere for you to turn except into my arms. I thought that by demanding some wild declaration of love from me, you were really just trying to reassert yourself in the relationship."

"I was, but not because I wanted to control you," she explained in despair.

"I realize that," he admitted thickly, lacing his fingers at the nape of her neck and bending his forehead down until it touched hers. "Now I realize it. I didn't trust you enough to give your feelings and emotions full credit. I kept trying to assume that what I felt had to be what you felt. You were either mislabeling dramatizing or looking for a wedge. I didn't trust you to simply have fallen in love with me."

Honor heard the aching unhappiness in him and her arms went around his waist. "And now?" she whispered tremulously, her eyes bright with unshed tears.

"I trust you, sweetheart. Really trust you." He caught her chin under his thumbs and lifted her mouth for a quick, hard kiss that conveyed the full scope of his feelings. When he freed her mouth he went on huskily, "I want everything you can give me, including this thing you call love. I'm not altogether sure just what you mean by it but I want it."

"It's yours, Conn. It will always be yours."

He shook his head once. "I'll give you everything I can in return, honey."

"I know."

"I'm not sure yet just what that includes. Will that hurt you? I can't bear to hurt you."

"No," she denied. "You won't hurt me if you give yourself as completely as possible. And I know you will. With you, there is no other way."

He exhaled slowly, as if a great weight had been lifted from him. Then Conn folded her close, holding her in silence for a long moment before he spoke again.

"Vegas?"

She nodded her head against his chest. "Yes."

"I'll get the tickets this afternoon. Do you want Adena to go with us?"

"It's not necessary. She'll understand. I was just using her as an excuse this morning."

"You were looking for a way out," he growled.

"I guess I wasn't able to trust you completely at that point, either."

"And now?"

"Now I do," she told him simply.

"I thought we'd settled all that at the beach cottage." He sighed, easing her against his side so that he could start them back down the length of the barn.

"We talked about trust and we promised it to each other, but we didn't think about all that it meant. We assumed it was only a matter of telling the truth about facts. We didn't realize it also meant trusting each other's emotions and feelings," Honor said with a small smile. "But I expect we can make a few excuses for ourselves. After all, everything has been happening so quickly. It's no wonder we were still feeling our way with each other this morning."

Conn nodded wryly. "I was sitting there on that bench a little while ago, trying to think of how to approach you. I've finally realized just how arrogant I must seem to you."

"Terribly arrogant at times," she agreed cheerfully.

He winced. "I'm going to try very hard to control that part of me."

"Uh-huh."

He slid her a sidelong glance. "You sound skeptical."

"Oh, I believe you'll try," she told him with a tiny grin.

"But not that I'll succeed?"

"I think it's a very basic part of you. And I think it's been well tempered over the years."

"You don't seem worried about it any longer," he noted with interest. His gunmetal eyes softened, and Honor could have sworn there was both relief and amusement in his gaze.

"I imagine I'll be obliged to point out the error of your ways occasionally to you in the future. Part of my wifely duties."

"You can yell at me until doomsday as long as you marry me," he assured her emphatically. Then he brought them to a short stop in front of Legacy's stall. The colt thrust his head out again and eyed the two humans curiously.

"You're going to win tomorrow, aren't you?" Honor asked the animal.

"He'll run his heart out," Conn said quietly. "He'll give it all he's got out there on the course."

Honor glanced at Conn as she patted the horse. His face had reset into harsh, all too familiar lines. "Legacy's a fine horse," she observed tentatively.

"But he'll run because he was born and trained to do exactly that. And there's an instinct in him that makes him want to lead the pack. That makes him a winner. But he doesn't run and win to please me or Humphrey or the guy on his back. He doesn't do it for any of us. He does it because that's just the way he is."

Honor hesitated, trying to read between the lines. "Are you trying to tell me something, Conn?"

Conn swung his gaze from the colt to Honor's face. "Legacy's not emotionally involved with humans except on a very superficial level. He enjoys our company but he could get along fine without any of us as long as he had access to food and other horses."

Honor felt as though she were missing something important, but she couldn't put her finger on it. "Well, he is an animal, after all."

"Just an animal," Conn repeated in a low voice.

"And he operates on his own kind of logic. I understand." She smiled. "Still, if he does win tomorrow I'd like to think he's doing it as a wedding present for us."

Conn relaxed and took her arm again. "Speaking of a wedding, I have to go get one arranged. Why don't you go on back to the apartment? I'll meet you there as soon as I've made the reservations."

"All right."

But Honor still had the feeling she had missed a crucial piece of communication from Conn. He walked her out to the parking lot in silence. She nodded in the direction of her car and he turned to guide her toward it. She was struggling to find a way to ask him if there wasn't something more he wanted to say on the subject of Legacy when two men dressed in a style that was strongly reminiscent of Granger walked out from between a row of parked cars.

"Damn." Conn stopped abruptly, yanking Honor to a halt beside him. "Why is it that just when I think everything's finally settled with all the loose ends tied up, something like this happens?"

It was clearly a rhetorical question and neither of the two men seemed inclined to respond to it directly. Large diamond rings flashed in the sunlight as one of the men made an apologetic gesture.

"We're here on behalf of Mr. Granger," the first man began.

"I was afraid of that," Conn groaned.

Honor felt the tension in him, but it wasn't the coiled, lethal kind of tension she had sensed when they had faced first Tony and then Ethan Bailey. This time Conn seemed wary but not unduly alarmed. Honor wished she could be that much at ease around two men who had openly stated they worked for a loan shark but it was impossible. Living in Southern Califor might give one a certain amount of panache, but there were limits.

"Mr. Granger would like you to know that he's real sorry about the inconvenience you've recently experienced at the hands of a certain person named Tony," the second man said very civilly. "Mr. Granger don't do hits. And he don't like people saying they're on his payroll when they ain't. He told us to keep an eye out for the aforementioned person here at the track. Just in case. We been watching most carefully. Me, I said old Tony would be heading for the border, but Joe here figured he might just try to sneak back. Looks as if I lose another one to Joe."

The man called Joe grunted but said nothing.

"Mr. Landry?" the first man said with an air of grave politeness. "Mr. Granger says to tell you he's real sorry about all this. He'll take responsibility for cleaning up the mess. Says you and him had a deal and he don't want you to think he reneged."

Conn kept his fingers wrapped around Honor's arm. "Tell Mr. Granger I appreciate his integrity. Tough to find businessmen with integrity these days."

"Mr. Granger looks after his reputation," Joe remarked with a certain air of pride. He obviously appreciated the fact that he worked for a man with a good business reputation.

"I'm aware that Mr. Granger's word can be relied upon," Conn said coolly.

"Good." The other man nodded. "He'll be pleased to hear that. Well, no sense holding you folks up any longer. Just wanted you to know Mr. Granger has taken care of things."

"Do I assume, then, that you've picked up Tony?" Conn asked quietly.

"Got him trying to sneak into the barns," Joe said with obvious satisfaction. "Mr. Granger was real pleased. Picked him up an hour ago."

"You picked him up?" Honor broke in, startled. "You've got Tony?"

"Yes, ma'am. No need for further worry."

"But what are you going to do with him?" she gasped, ignoring Conn's suddenly tightening grip.

"Why, ma'am, we intend to make certain Tony don't go around misrepresenting himself in the future," she was told very gently.

"If . . . if I might suggest," Honor began carefully.

"Honor, shut up," Conn hissed under his breath.

She licked her lips as the first man and Joe turned polite, inquiring gazes on her. "Just . . . just a thought," she managed weakly.

"What's that, ma'am?"

Behind her Conn groaned and his fingers dug into her arm. She knew he was ready to yank her back against him and shut her mouth completely if she said anything dangerous.

"The police are already looking for Tony. They want him in connection with a certain, uh, incident over on the coast. You say your Mr. Granger doesn't do, er, hits?"

"We can handle Tony," Joe explained as though she weren't very bright.

"Honor, these gentlemen know what they're doing," Conn began firmly.

"I was only going to suggest that they turn him over to the cops. Then Mr. Granger wouldn't have to worry about him and neither would we. It would certainly keep things cleaner for your boss," she added helpfully to the one called Joe. "He wouldn't have to get hands dirty protecting his reputation. He could let the police do it for him. Don't you think he'd appreciate that?''

To everyone's apparent astonishment, Joe seemed to find the suggestion mildly interesting. "I'll pass your notion along to the boss," he finally said with a nod. "He might like it. Might at that. Appeal to his sense of humor. Come on, Carl. Let's go see Mr. Granger."

The two men disappeared down the row of parked cars.

Honor was left shivering in Conn's grasp. She turned stricken eyes up to meet his wry expression. "Do you think they'll kill him?" she asked uneasily.

"Honor, you're a babe in the woods." He sighed. "Too naive for your own good."

"I am not naive! I'm from Southern California. No one is naive out here!" she exploded.

"It's all right, honey," he soothed. "I'll take care of you."

"Well, if your lack of naiveté is due to the fact that you've been dealing with people like Granger and Joe and Carl and Bailey and Tony all your life, then you're the one who needs protection. I'm the one who's going to have to take care of you. I'll keep you from getting mixed up with bad company."

He glanced down at her in surprise as he opened the door of her car for her. "I never thought of it like that. You may have a point."

He bent down to kiss her possessively and then slammed the door shut.

Chapter Twelve

Legacy won by a full three lengths the following afternoon. No sooner had the results flashed on the board
than Conn was dragging his new bride at a dead run
toward the winner's circle. Adena, who had attended
the races with Conn and Honor, grinned delightedly as
she hastened along beside her sister.

Laughing with excitement, Honor allowed herself to
be swept up in Conn's wake, her new gold band spar-
kling in the sunlight. Breathlessly she stood beside Legacy's proud owner as the photograph was taken. The
usual assortment of gawkers, pranksters and miscella-
neous folk crowded into the shot but no one minded.
Least of all the colt who tossed his head with spirited
arrogance.

"Are you quite sure he isn't emotionally involved in
all this?" Honor murmured to Conn as she watched
the groom and trainer lead the horse back toward the
barns.

Conn's mouth curved briefly. "I'll admit that at the
moment it's tough to tell just what that horse is thinking."

"He gave you both a great wedding gift," Adena observed. "When are you leaving for the beach house?

"Just as soon as I can get Honor back to the parking lot and into the car," Conn vowed determinedly.

"Don't you just love a forceful man?" Adena cooed mockingly to her sister.

"Just this particular forceful man," Honor replied so softly that no one heard her.

"How long are you going to be gone?" Adena went on interestedly.

"Just a couple of days." Conn was striding briskly through the crowd, towing the two women behind him. "Honor has to get back to work. She's finishing some projects and can't afford to be away too long."

"That was great news about the police locating that awful Tony person, wasn't it?" Adena commented. "Imagine finding him locked inside a tack room. Makes you wonder how he got inside in the first place, doesn't it?"

"It certainly does," Conn said with great feeling. "Racing gear is expensive, though. They have to keep it locked up. I suppose Tony went into one of those rooms and someone came along behind him and shut and locked the door, not realizing he was inside."

"Sure." Honor grinned. "And then a casually patrolling guard just happened to check the tack room and find him. Recognized him instantly and turned him over to the cops. Very neat."

Conn slanted her a look. "Very." He paused. "You're looking a trifle smug, darling."

"Am I?" Honor feigned surprise.

"Listen," Adena broke in, waving energetically at a young man dressed in leather and silk, "I see someone I know. He'll give me a ride home. Have a good time at the beach and I'll see you when you get back. We'll throw a real bash. 'Bye!"

Conn swung an assessing glance at the young man in the exotic clothes. "You know him?"

"Oh, yes. That's Jason. He's very sweet, really. Works in the men's department of a local high-style boutique. Adena's dated him on and off for ages. Quite safe, Conn. You don't have to play big brother."

He shrugged and turned back to the task of getting her out to the waiting Porsche. "I only do it for your sake," he explained almost apologetically.

"What? Play big brother?" Honor smiled. "I know. You're trying to assume the responsibility so that I won't have to watch out for her. But I've been keeping tabs on Adena for years. And she's really getting to be quite grown-up. Soon she won't need anyone watching over her."

"As long as you worry about her, I'll worry about her, I suppose." Conn reached the Porsche and opened the passenger door.

"I know." But she wound up saying the words to herself because he'd already closed the door. He would worry about Adena because he was in love with Honor and what affected Honor, affected Conn. It was an intricate, tightly woven web, one neither of them could escape. And one day, Honor promised herself, Conn would know that the kind of emotional involvement he was feeling was called love.

Conn slid into the driver's seat and thrust the key into the ignition. There was a strange mixture of satisfaction and hunger in his expression. The combination had been there since last evening when he'd slipped the ring on Honor's finger and repeated his vows. She still shivered when she remembered the passionate, possessive way he had made love to her later in the elegant hotel room.

The drive back up the coast to the beach cottage was a pleasant one. The sun was shining but the clouds were gathering far out at sea. There would be a storm later, Honor knew. The thought of a pleasant fire in the fireplace and a glass of warm brandy made her smile. By the time she and Conn unlocked the front door of the cottage she was feeling surprisingly content with life.

The first thing she noticed as she walked back into the cottage was that she no longer experienced that vague air of depression she had always sensed in the past. The beach house felt right, now. No lingering questions or disquieting memories. It felt good.

Conn took her for a long walk on the beach before they sat down to a home-cooked meal of paella and wine. Honor teased her new mate about his ability in the kitchen and he assured her she had gotten a real bargain of a husband.

It wasn't until they were sitting together on the sofa in front of the fire, sipping brandy, that Honor's gaze fell on the old iron-and-wood trunk. She stared at it thoughtfully for a long moment.

"What are you thinking, honey?" Conn asked softly.

"I was just wondering what, exactly, might be hidden in that old trunk. I never really did go through Dad's stuff properly. It was just too painful a process. Maybe it's time I took a look."

Conn watched her for a moment or two and then without a word he got to his feet and went across the room to unlatch the iron lock. The top groaned as he pushed it open. Honor stood up and went across the room to join him, looking down into the trunk.

"Just more photos and form books and copies of the

racing trade journals," she observed. Kneeling, she began to lift out some of the yellowed papers. Conn dropped down onto one knee beside her.

They spent nearly two hours going through the contents of the trunk. Much of the time was taken up by Conn who paused to read everything he found on Stylish Legacy.

"Humphrey says Legacy might do just as well as his sire in another year or so," he told Honor proudly. "Then we'll retire him to stud."

"Legacy will probably enjoy that." Honor grinned, reaching for yet another folded copy of the *Daily Racing Form.* "Being a male, he probably does a lot of thinking and fantasizing about that sort of thing."

"There you go again," Conn complained. He stopped as a small, leather-bound book fell from the folded newspaper. "What's that?"

"Looks like a diary or a notebook," Honor said, turning the volume over and over in her hands. She opened it cautiously and stared at the bold scrawl on the pages inside. "My father's. I'm sure of it. It looks like some sort of financial record."

"Here, let me see." Conn reached over to take the book from her hand. "You're right. It's a running account of a debt. Want to take a guess who was being systematically paid every three months?"

"Ethan Bailey?" Honor leaned over his shoulder to peer down at the page in front of him.

Conn nodded. "There had to be some record. You just don't borrow a huge sum of money from a man like Ethan Bailey and not keep track of the payback. It's all here. A good accountant could probably trace the whole history of the transaction, given this book."

"And prove that Bailey was involved with Dad and

Stoner," Honor concluded. "I don't know how far that would get us, though. It's been so long."

Conn kept turning the pages, working his way toward the back of the volume. The precise account of the debt continued to be recorded, but now there were remarks at the bottom of the page. Conn paused so that he and Honor could read them.

"'Dick says he's getting uneasy feelings about Bailey. Says there's something about the man he just doesn't trust,'" Conn read.

"Dick was your stepfather?" Honor asked curiously. "Short for Richard?"

"Right. Listen to this." Conn picked another passage and read it aloud.

I have to agree with Dick. This business with Bailey needs to be checked out. I'm going to start leaving more complete notations in this account book. It will serve as a record in the event that what Dick and I fear is taking place is actually happening. If we're wrong, Ethan will never need to know we distrusted him. If we're right, the new firm of Stoner & Mayfield is in big trouble. A scandal of this size will be difficult to smash.

From there on, the details of suspected weapons smuggling were given along with the name of the man who was selling information. There was a brief description of the trap that had been set and then there were no further entries in the leather volume.

Honor sighed a long time later as Conn closed the book and set it back inside the trunk. "It's all there."

"Do you want to make it public? I still don't think

we could make it stick. It's an old tale and it happened in a foreign country a long time ago.''

"I wonder what story Bailey is giving the police?"

Conn shook his head. "I doubt he'll open up that weapons-smuggling scandal. He's too smart to raise more questions about his past than necessary."

"But what if he does, Conn? He could drag our fathers' names through the mud again."

"This time around we'll have the book." He indicated the leather volume.

"That might not stop him," Honor fretted. "Bailey might decide he's got nothing to lose. We never really thought about that aspect of it. If he talks, really talks, it will open the whole mess up again."

"I think we could both survive another round of scandal, don't you?" Conn asked softly.

She smiled gently. "I think we could survive just about anything together."

He reached out to close the trunk. "This is such old news now that very few people would be interested, anyway. Except, naturally, for the folks who hang around racetracks. It would probably just focus a lot of attention on Legacy. Make a mystery horse out of him or something. Might be just the touch of magic he needs to make his name in racing circles. Great horses always have stories and myths told about them."

Honor couldn't help it; she broke out laughing. "You're one very determined owner, Conn Landry. You've got the fever."

He straightened and reached down to pull her into his arms, his gunmetal eyes suddenly intent. "Not nearly as bad as the fever I've got for you, Honor May-field Landry. And I think I've finally got a word to describe it. It's been burning in my mind ever since I made you my wife."

She went still in his arms. "Has it, Conn?"

"I love you, Honor." The words came from him in a thick, husky voice that shook her to the core. "I don't know why it took me so long to realize it. But I know. I'm sure now. So very sure."

"I'm glad, Conn," she whispered, touching the side of his face with gentle fingertips. "I love you so much."

"I'm sorry it took me all this time to get the words straight. I was worrying about other things, like trust and honesty. I didn't stop to realize until tonight that I wouldn't have been so concerned about those other things if I wasn't already in love with you. It's all so simple once you look at it from the right direction. Heaven only knows why I was so blind."

"As you said, you had other things on your mind." She smiled invitingly. "But I was sure that you weren't a racehorse."

"What?" He looked blank.

"That's what you meant earlier, wasn't it? When you talked about the reasons Legacy runs and wins? You told me he wasn't emotionally involved with humans. He gives them his best when they ask it of him, but he does it because that's just the way he is. But you're involved with me, Conn. You don't protect me and care for me and occasionally yell at me just because I ask it of you. I never did actually ask it of you, as I recall," she added thoughtfully. "I knew you did all that because you were involved on some deeper level than even you realized. At least, that's what I kept telling myself."

"Completely involved. I've never been so involved

with another human being before in my life! I know it sounds ridiculous but I knew I didn't want it any other way with you. I didn't want to be separated from you in some manner. I didn't want to be like Legacy. I'm a human being, not some thoroughbred who doesn't really need people." He seized her abruptly, lifting her high into his arms with a fierce joy. "I knew I needed you, honey, but I thought most of that need was tied in with the way I wanted you physically. But it's so much more. I never understood. I just never understood."

His surging wonder was contagious. Honor's own happiness was shining in her eyes as Conn carried her into the bedroom.

The storm that had been building out at sea broke just as Conn came down onto the bed alongside Honor. He gathered her into his arms, all the words that had once been so alien to his tongue tumbling forth in a glorious litany of love.

"Hold me," he breathed as he flowed over her body and let himself sink into her welcoming warmth. "Hold me, Honor. I love you so much."

Honor held him, giving herself up to the passion that was binding them together as Conn proved beyond a doubt that he was, indeed, emotionally involved with her.

Conn Landry knew how to love.

Take these 4 best-selling novels FREE

...our sophisticated, ...porary love stories by...world-famous authors of romance FREE, as your introduction to the Harlequin Presents subscription plan. Thrill to **Anne Mather**'s passionate story BORN OUT OF LOVE, set in the Caribbean.... Travel to darkest Africa in **Violet Winspear**'s TIME OF THE TEMPTRESS....Let **Charlotte Lamb** take you to the fascinating world of London's Fleet Street in MAN'S WORLD ....Discover beautiful Greece in **Sally Wentworth**'s moving romance SAY HELLO TO YESTERDAY.

Harlequin Presents...

The very finest in romance fiction

Join the millions of avid Harlequin readers all over the world who delight in the magic of a really exciting novel. EIGHT great NEW titles published EACH MONTH! Each month you will get to know exciting, interesting, true-to-life people .... You'll be swept to distant lands you've dreamed of visiting .... Intrigue, adventure, romance, and the destiny of many lives will thrill you through each Harlequin Presents novel.

Get all the latest books before they're sold out!

As a Harlequin subscriber you actually receive your personal copies of the latest Presents novels immediately after they come off the press, so you're sure of getting all 8 each month.

Cancel your subscription whenever you wish!

You don't have to buy any minimum number of books. Whenever you decide to stop your subscription just let us know and we'll cancel all further shipments.